Night Cat
Night Trap

ROLAND MCLEAN

**SAMS and
Night Carrier Landings**

Copyright © 2024 by Roland McLean.

All rights reserved.

No part of this publication may be reproduced, distributed, or transmitted in any form or by any means, including photocopying, recording, or other electronic or mechanical methods, without the prior written permission of the publisher, except as permitted by U.S. copyright law. For permission requests, contact [include publisher/author contact info].

The story, all names, characters, and incidents portrayed in this production are fictitious. No identification with actual persons (living or deceased), places, buildings, and products is intended or should be inferred.

ISBN: 9798301427220

DEDICATION

I wrote this novel to show the heroics of those who went before me in the F8 community as well as the A4, F4, A6, A7 and A3 communities of Naval Aviators in Vietnam. The F8 pilots were my instructors in the F8 Replacement Air Group. Their squadrons suffered tremendous losses during the 1966, 1967 and 1968 cruises which somehow has become a forgotten detail of the Vietnam War. They never got the honor they deserved.

I also dedicate this to our squadron mates FC Green and Harvey Kessler. They are missed.

PROLOGUE

On Yankee Station, some 110 miles east of Dong Hoi, North Vietnam
Latitude 17 30 North, 108 30 East
3 March, 1967

Somewhere below, in the darkness, the giant old warship thundered along, firing into the dark night its lethal payload of fighters and dive-bombers. In calm seas, it churned at more than thirty knots, making its own wind to help the flight of the planes off the twin catapults mounted on the bow. Phosphorescence glowed white in its wake. Old boilers were pushed to the maximum to drive four massive propellers.

The ship was filled with noise and vibration. Although early in the cruise, the men had grown accustomed to the groans and rattles of the old lady. Steam hissed through innumerable pipes coated in asbestos. Hatches clanged, alarms sounded, and the incessant Bosun pipes sounded announcing: "Now, sweepers man your brooms. Let's have a clean sweep down fore and aft."

"The smoking lamp is lit from frames 112 to 156 on the main deck and below."

"Flight Quarters. Flight Quarters."

"Now reveille, reveille. All hands heave out and trice up"

"Now hear this, the smoking lamp is out while venting avgas."

"Set the special sea and anchor detail for underway replenishment."

As the catapults were fired, the whole ship shook. With a tremendous hissing of steam like a dragon's roar, the shuttle flew down the slotted metal that formed the catapult track for a hundred yards or so to the very end of the bow, towing and hurling a screaming jet off the front toward the waves of a black, but glittering sea and a terrifying night of absolute darkness. A huge boom that shook the entire ship always followed the rush and scream of metal on metal as the shuttle reached speeds of almost two hundred knots. Day and night the shuttle crashed into its mechanical stop at the end of its stroke.

Among all the sounds of mechanical chaos, the sea was heard swooshing against and crashing, splashing away from the hull. A reminder that the massive ship was, despite its size, only a temporary man-made intrusion on the sea.

From the keel up to the main deck, she was a normal ship. With a traditional pointed bow, a slender keel, and square stern she could have been a very large battleship. Steam engines, boilers, evaporators, enlisted quarters with hammock style bunks hung six high, various workshops, and the mess decks where chow was served were all about the same as other naval warships, only larger. She smelled like a combination of machine oil and steel. There was always a hint of some chemical or jet fuel in the air and a slight odor of gunpowder. Every effort was made to keep her clean, but since fresh water was scarce, there was always a slight human stench underlying the scent of soaps and cleansers.

From the main deck up was the transformation. Below she could have been a very large battleship, but above she was nothing but an aircraft carrier. The flight deck was stuck on her relatively thin, speedy hull, making her look top heavy and clumsy. Lethal, but clumsy. Between the main deck and flight deck was the hangar deck with its shops of the airwing squadrons and the aircraft being prepared for flight operations. Above the hangar decks were the squadron line shacks, aircraft stores, other shops, the squadron Ready Rooms, and most of the officer quarters for both ship's company and the airwing.

With a wartime complement, the ship was crowded. In Officers' Country, every bunk was taken and in the air-conditioned spaces hot racking, or two men on different shifts sharing the same bunk, was common.

The first-class mess, normally set aside for the first-class petty officers, was converted into the bomb assembly space. These men were forced back into the enlisted mess, which often had a two-hour waiting line due to the crowding. Flight deck crews and the squadron flight deck personnel often missed meals since they had no time to wait during flight operations.

A late World War Two carrier, she had suffered a kamikaze attack on her bridge at Okinawa. After the war, she had been mothballed, only to be called up for duty in Korea. Later, she had been framed and rebuilt into an angle deck carrier to allow the new jets the luxury of going around, and boltering, if they didn't catch a wire. Her hydraulic cats had been stripped out, replaced with the newer, more powerful steam catapults. The British-developed mirror landing system, which consisted of a series of datum lights, was mounted on the port stern of the ship, giving the pilots a reference ball that moved on the mirror to precisely indicate whether the aircraft was high or low, replacing the manual paddles of the old landing signal officers.

She had been upgraded with several of her peers to a 27 Charlie class aircraft carrier. A huge warship, she was a small carrier compared to the new nuclear and conventional ships. Still she, along with Bonnie Dick, Hancock, Oriskany, and Ticonderoga, were constantly on the job in Vietnam, sharing the same duties with the big decks. Her airwing of F8s, A4s, KA3s, A1s, E 1s, and helos was at least as capable as any other carrier.

As soon as a launch was over, preparation was quickly made for recovery of aircraft. In the one and one half-hour cyclic operations, basically one-half hour was given to launch, one half hour to recovery, and one-half hour to refuel, rearm, repair, and re-spot the aircraft that had been recovered. Flying midnight to noon or noon to midnight, the flight deck crews worked fourteen-to-sixteen-hour days in extremely hazardous conditions. They spent their days and nights dodging white-hot jet blasts and the giant vacuum cleaner of intakes. They felt pieces of the wooden flight deck, torn up by the winds, hitting their faces where they were exposed under the protective goggles. When the wind stopped between recovery and launch, the South China Sea heat was oppressive, and their heavy flight deck clothing was drenched in sweat.

There was little or no time to eat during flight ops since almost every division was working at maximum speed and could not afford to let men go. While division officers and chiefs looked the other way, most units set up surreptitious sandwich messes with food stolen during underway replenishment. Otherwise, the men might only eat one time per day. Living conditions for the more than three thousand men aboard were difficult. The enlisted men were jammed into massive berthing areas with frame hammocks six high. Water for bathing and laundry was rationed and often not available as the old evaporators struggled to keep up with the fresh water demands of the boilers and steam catapults. Sometimes precious drinking water was not available as strict water hours were enforced. Officers fared a little better. Air conditioning was rare and inefficient in the tropical heat. Sleep was fitful with all the noise, sweat, heat, and watches throughout the nights. Conditions in most prisons were less crowded and better.

Still, morale among the men was generally high. They worked long and hard hours, often in dangerous conditions, but they were proud of their ability to overcome the difficult conditions; scornful of those stationed on the new ships with their air-conditioning, televisions, and plentiful messes. They were aware that, as difficult as their conditions were, they were better off than the marines in the jungle.

Work never stopped while at sea. As soon as flight quarters ended, the Bosun Mates went to work on underway replenishment, loading food and bombs. Both the ship fuel oil tanks and aircraft JP4 tanks were constantly refueled. Anything the ship needed from spare parts to a Catholic navy chaplain was high lined from the supply vessels. At times, massive twin-engine helicopters from the fast supply ships ferried bombs to redshirted ordnance men on the flight deck. Simultaneously, the cable high line system was used to transfer mundane supplies between the vessels while they maintained course and speed. The ships could not stop or maneuver during replenishment and occasionally a small Vietnamese fishing junk was sucked into the vortex between the ships and shot out behind at high speeds.

Below decks, machinist mates worked frantically in hellish heat to keep worn out boilers and steam turbines running while pushed to the maximum by the demand of making a constant thirty knots of speed for flight operations. The ship's laundry struggled to keep clothes for over three thousand men clean without adequate water. Cooks and bakers kept the mess going throughout all the watches.

The ship was always moving. Like a raging bull in a tight pen, it steamed from one edge of the Tonkin Gulf to the other, fighting to maintain enough precious sea space to keep flight ops going. Her escorts scurried to keep up through all the maneuvers. Escort destroyers and cruisers were constantly turning, trying to keep up with the speedy old carrier while staying out of the way. Not an easy task.

All this was done to keep the aircrafts flying, day and night. Without the planes, the old warship had no weapons. Without the planes of the airwing she was just a fast, very large, self-propelled barge hurtling through the night.

Chapter One

DAY CAT NIGHT TRAP 1
5 March 1967 Yankee Station

As he approached the ship, he slowly eased the throttle back, making the transition from the high-speed dash as smooth as possible for his wingman. Slowing through 350 knots he looked to the right, moved his left hand to the stick, and signaled with the thumb down on his right hand for the hook. As he watched, he moved his hand to the handle at the right edge of his cockpit and lowered his own tailhook.

In his mirrors he saw his wingman automatically slide into close form and then cross under him to inspect his plane. *Rhodes is going to be a good stick*, he thought. *He maintained perfect formation throughout the flight.* He expected any pilot in the squadron to fly formation well, but Rhodes had flown close and smooth. Three days into his first cruise and he had the makings of a good fighter pilot, if he could handle the night trap.

In the waning light of a setting sun, he again signaled to Rhodes with his right hand, first pointing to himself and then to the wingman to indicate the lead change. After the acknowledgement of the change, he effortlessly eased back and under the other plane checking for any leaks or problems. Sliding back into position, he gave Rhodes a thumbs-up and signaled to take the lead back.

"Sand Box, Heater Zero Seven to enter Marshall holding hands with Heater Zero Four."

"Roger Heater Zero Seven. Your angels two zero, Zero Four take two one. Inbound bearing One niner two. Your times three seven and three eight. Current weather is twelve hundred scattered, three thousand overcast, visibility one and one half miles in haze."

"Roger. Understand two zero and two one. Times three seven and three eight." The weather sounded pretty bad. It was going to be dark down the chute. He then held his right thumb to his mouth, flying with his left. The response was immediate from Reid. First three fingers up and then two. A fuel state of thirty-two hundred pounds. He looked at his own gauge and noted thirty-four hundred. Both of them should be in good shape in the groove, light enough to trap aboard yet enough fuel to go around in case of bolter or foul deck wave off.

He gradually pulled back on the stick, climbing to 21,000 feet to put Heater Zero Four in position for the carrier approach at Marshall. A good leader, all his movements also were smooth. He wanted his wingman to be as comfortable as possible for the descent from the gradually darkening sky of twilight into the black hole that was the carrier at night.

If it was tough on experienced pilots, he thought, *what was it like for a nugget?* He remembered back to his first night traps in the F9 and shuddered. In peacetime then, it wasn't a regularly scheduled event. Just every now and then they flew at night to prove they could do it. "Practicing bleeding," they called it. Fear and excitement were the prevalent emotions. In the Ready Room before the flight and now, as they got ready to go down. Fear at the vertigo-inducing descent. Fear at the black hole that was the back of the ship. Fear of the bolter that would make you start it all again. But there was also excitement at seeing your name on that night schedule. Excitement while you tried to sleep before manning. Excited to prove that you were one of the best.

In those days, they did cancel night ops when there was no horizon. Now it was supposed to be routine. Everyone had to fly at night all the time. The All-Weather fighters had to be up to protect the three carriers and support fleet on Yankee Station at all times. Every carrier fighter squadron shared the duties of Barcap with each other. He supposed the new guys were at least adjusted to the certainty of night flying although you never got over the dread. It had to be easier for the Phantom pilots flying off the big decks.

What a shame. The Crusader was really made to fly off the new carriers.

When he first started flying F8s he had been on the new Kitty Hawk and it had been great. However, Congress had not approved building as many of the new carriers as the navy needed to handle Vietnam and its continual countering of the Russian fleet in the Mediterranean. They were stuck flying off these old, small deck, World War Two refitted carriers. The F4 Phantoms were too heavy for the arresting gear of the old carriers. Ironic that the hardest to land aircraft in the navy had to fly off the smallest ships. Still, it was a challenge they lived for.

As he approached thirty-five miles on the ship's Tacan, he called: "Heater Zero Seven entering Marshall."

He flicked his lights once to let Reid know to break away, watched him separate as he began a gradual descent to twenty thousand feet. As he leveled at twenty, he began to calculate the racetrack pattern that would allow him to descend precisely on time. If he descended early, he would get a foul deck wave off and screw up the pattern. If he descended late, then he would cause a foul deck wave off for the next pilot.

He looked to the west and saw the remaining light of the sun. As the light dimmed, he turned up the rheostat on his instrument lights and the cockpit was now immersed in a red glow. Looking down to where he knew the USS *Adams* had to be he saw only black. One of his senior lieutenants, John Phillips had once described the descent into the black as like diving off a cliff and hoping that water was actually down there. A complete act of faith.

"On my mark at ten, nine, eight . . . three, two, one, mark time two eight," the time check by approach jarred him back to reality. At the mark he started the cockpit stopwatch, quickly calculating the nine minutes of holding until his descent. "Shit! I can't even maintain altitude. Got to get the scan going." As he drifted two hundred feet high.

He tried to shake off his fatigue. He had slept little the first two nights on the line, planning the flak suppression for the airwing's first "Mini" Alpha Strike and worrying about his boys—the pilots he was leading to war. He wondered how many he would lose this cruise. How many letters to families he would have to write. The last cruise was bad. He hoped this would be better.

Concentrate, he tried to tell himself. *You are starting the descent for the most difficult evolution an F8 pilot can make.* He had to force himself to think of nothing but flying for the next fifteen or twenty minutes of the approach. He knew, even with his experience, that he needed total concentration to make it aboard.

Turning the final leg to the inbound heading of 192, he saw that he was going to be a little late, maybe as much as ten seconds. He pushed the throttle up and called "Heater Zero Seven descending," even though it would be at least seven seconds before he started down. No sense letting everyone in the airwing know he had screwed up. He would make up the time in the descent.

When he reached thirty miles, he thumbed the speed brake switch and felt himself forced forward in the straps as the boards came out. Pointing the nose down about fifteen degrees on his attitude gyro, he descended at 270 knots to get himself back on time—twenty knots faster than the descent prescribed by NATOPS, the regulation for all flight operations.

The descent was as black as he had ever seen. He peered over the nose and gunsight into the darkness, quickly realizing that he had better stay on instruments. On a night this dark there would be absolutely no horizon. No visual references to ease the way. A hazy layer kept him from seeing the dim lights of the ship or the stars. Fighting vertigo the whole time, he forced himself to believe the instruments.

God it was shitty to launch in daylight and recover at night. The whole flight in light did not allow the eyes and senses enough time to adjust. Did not prepare the brain for the sheer terror of the dark descent. Did not prepare the mind for the quick and efficient instrument scan that was necessary in a night carrier approach.

Pilots who had never made a night descent over the open ocean had no concept of how dark, dark could be. A darkness that gave no sign of up or down, right or left. A darkness that made one wonder if he had flown off the end of the world and there was nothing below but more black emptiness. A darkness as black as the deepest cave.

He felt beads of sweat form on his forehead under the helmet and run into his eyes. He reached for his visor with the left hand and pulled it up, wiping his eyes with the flight suit sleeve, feeling the roughness of the nomex, feeling pure oxygen coolly burning as it leaked from his mask into his eyes. Fatigue was gone now, replaced by an increasing fear. *I'm getting too old for this shit.*

At sixteen miles he pulled the nose up and fought to smoothly slow the beast, calling, "Heater Zero Seven Approaching Gate."

"Roger Zero Seven. Now contact CCA on 233.8."

"Roger. Two thirty-three point eight." As he bent his head down to the right to change the radio, he felt the vertigo increase. He fought to believe the instruments and not let his senses convince him he was in a steep diving turn to the right. Keying the mike he called, "Sandbox Heater Zero Seven at the gate."

"Roger. We have you in radar contact. Descend to one thousand feet and dirty up when comfortable."

"Shit!" There was no getting comfortable. His scan felt slow. As he slowed through 220 knots, unlocking the wing incidence handle and raising the wing, he felt himself balloon up to 1200 feet. With the variable incidence wing coming up and the slats coming out, he felt Zero Seven begin to wallow in the uncomfortable manner of a dirty F8.

Clean, she was the purest aircraft ever built: totally responsive, awesome roll rate, great climbing ability. Dirty, she was just too slow on the power response, too difficult to keep on speed.

As he dropped the gear handle, he pulled the throttle back a little and pushed the nose down to get on altitude, punching the Automatic Power Control (APC) button as the light that was the on-speed donut flashed to amber. Nothing happened and he had to quickly add power to prevent a stall. Again, he tried to engage the APC that would keep the plane on speed.

"Damn! As shitty a night as can be and I'm manual."

"Heater Zero Seven, you are at five miles approaching the glide path. Come right to heading One Niner Four." He didn't acknowledge the call, knowing CCA would see he got it by the movement of the plane. "Heater Zero Seven, you are slightly above glide path, begin your descent."

Struggling to keep the scan going, he pulled power a bit to begin a descent of 500 feet per minute to match the glidepath of the CCA. He was totally flying instruments, keeping the scan going between heading, attitude gyro, rate of descent, and the speed indicator lights.

"Heater Zero Seven, you are further above. Come left to One Niner Two."

He pulled power to increase the descent and get back on glide path. He didn't remember the last time he had struggled so much to stay on glidepath. He was a good stick. He was good around the boat. Still, this was one of those nights. The F8 was such a joy to fly clean but such an unstable, underpowered bitch to fly dirty around the boat. *That is why we are so cocky. Most of the other bastards couldn't handle this.*

"Heater Zero Seven, you are below glide path."

"Below glide path."

He added power and immediately knew it was too much as he heard, "Heater Zero Seven, you are now approaching glide path and going slightly above. Call the ball."

Looking out the left corner of his windscreen he saw the datum lights of the mirror landing system, with the ball showing high, about to go off the top of the mirror.

He called, "Heater Zero Seven, Crusader Ball, Two Eight, Manual."

"Roger Ball. Keep it coming, you are slightly high," the landing signal officer (LSO) acknowledged his call. Standing on the landing signal platform slightly above the flight deck on the port stern, the airwing LSO had scheduled himself for this recovery, knowing it would be a bad one.

He was holding the pickle switch in his right hand, which allowed him to instantly hit wave-off lights in case of a foul deck or a bad approach. In his left hand he had the telephone-like radio that allowed him to talk to the pilots while still listening to the engine.

He peered through the dark using the approach lights and wing lights to determine aircraft attitude, altitude, and heading. He used his ears to listen to the critical sound of engine speed. He only had microseconds to make the decision since the F8 Crusader typically only had twenty-two seconds in the "groove" that was the final approach to the ship.

From his peripheral vision he saw the lights on the arresting gear panel change to indicate that the previous aircraft was now out of the cables that made up the arresting gear and that the gear had been reset. He now had a clear deck and full control over the landing.

Knowing the pilot was on manual, the LSO calmly said, "Keep it coming," hoping to reassure Heater Zero Seven that no drastic changes were necessary. The F8 on automatic throttle was bad enough, but on manual throttle at night he was always concerned.

In the cockpit CDR Huggins heard the call but had already begun his correction for what he saw on the mirror landing system. Compensating for the high ball, he pulled a little power and tried to ease an increase in the rate of descent. Holding the nose slightly too high, the speed indicator went from amber to the red light of slow. He quickly added a little power, and gratefully saw the speed go back to amber as the ball settled momentarily in the middle. Then, the ball started to ease up as he began to see in his peripheral the lights of the deck of the ship.

Shit! I'm going to bolter. Quickly he pulled some power to get back down just as the descent of Heater Zero Seven began to increase in reaction to the downdraft created by the airflow over the deck of the massive carrier steaming at thirty-plus knots.

Seeing and hearing what was happening the LSO immediately pickled the wave-off lights and shouted "Power! Power! Wave off! Wave Off!" He knew it was too late. A cardinal rule had been broken: the pilot should never, ever, reduce power close to the back of the ship.

Waiting until the last second, he dove to his right into the safety net, taking the other LSOs on the platform with him. He had waved enough Crusaders. He feared what would happen. While still in the air in his leap, he called "Eject! Eject! Eject!" into the radio.

CDR Huggins had already added full power, but sensed it was too late. In a split second, pride prevented him from ejecting and he selected afterburner in an attempt to clear the ramp of the ship. As the throttle went to the outboard position, the nozzles on the tail cone opened for burner light with a commensurate loss of 28 percent of the power. As a result, when the burner did light, Heater Zero Seven was well below the flight deck and impacted in a massive burning crash with only the nose cone above the ramp.

The pilot was dead from the shock load of impact well before the burning explosion of jet fuel and missiles hurled the cockpit and what was left of Heater Zero Seven over the ramp and onto the flight deck of CVA 23, USS *Adams*.

Curled into a ball, the LSO first heard the huge roar of the explosion. Next, he felt the whoosh as fire swept across them. Finally, he felt the air being sucked from his lungs to feed that fire. Once it was over, he could hear activity on the flight deck as the sailors tried to clear what was left of Heater Zero Seven off the ship.

The safety net and Nomex flight suits had saved him from the fire. His eyebrows were singed, but he was alive. Incredibly his headset still worked, and he heard the air boss call: "Heater Zero Four, wave off. Foul deck."

"Roger. I see the fire. What's going on?"

"Heater Zero Four, your signal is bingo. Climb and maintain FL 180, Steer 232 for Channel 77. Contact Danang approach on 234.7."

"Roger approach. What happened?"

"Will advise. Contact Danang at this time. Sand Box out."

Chapter Two

2 Ready Two

A door painted black with gold ink outlining a multitude of black wasps indicated the entrance to Ready Two, the home of the VF 188 Black Wasps. Entering Ready Two from the main passageway, one passed through the small counter area and open office of maintenance control where pilots read the aircraft logs and signed out for the planes prior to flights. A black floor to ceiling curtain divided the back-office area of organized filing cabinets and office equipment from the main Ready Room. A neatly organized counter, prior to entering the main Ready Room, contained the officer's coffee mess with the standard, large aluminum pot and mugs bearing squadron insignia and each officer's name.

A mostly successful attempt had been made to cloak the Ready Room in the ambiance of a men's club. Dark brown cork covered the walls where possible. Black carpet squares with the golden wasp of the squadron emblem covered the floor. In neat rows were dark green recliner chairs, looking like first-class airline seats. On almost every chair was a black headrest marked with each officer's name and rank in gold lettering. The pilot chairs also bore the gold navy wings below the name. All the chairs were occupied but there was none of the normal conversation, none of the joking, teasing, and mutual harassment that were the standard tension relief for naval aviators. The atmosphere was one of somber introspection and there was a general feeling of concern bordering on fear.

"This was not at all what I had planned for a change of command," began the executive officer, Commander Dan Prescott, his face showing concern and passion. "This morning CAG officially handed over VF 188 to me and I am going to do my damnedest to ensure that we remain the best fighter squadron in the navy. No one is more shocked at what happened to the Skipper than I am. He was one of the best damn sticks to ever fly the F8 and the best Skipper we could ever hope for. I am sure that all of us will miss him dearly. My heart goes out to Pam and the kids." Looking directly into the eyes of each of the pilots he said, "I hope that each and every of you will write a little note to them describing what a great Skipper he was. I am sure the kids will really appreciate it someday." In unison, they nodded somberly. "That said, we still have a job to do. We are the best damn fighter squadron in the navy, which makes us the best damn fighter pilots in the world! Get your heads up and let's learn something from this. That is what the skipper would want."

Most of the nuggets, or first cruise pilots, looked around the room to see the reaction of the others. The second cruise pilots, John Phillips, Joe Ames, and Dave Casper were almost uniformly looking down at their hands, knowing Cdr. Huggins so well, they were almost overcome with sadness.

"Bill, will you please go over the accident so we can all learn what not to do?" With that Commander Prescott sat down in his chair at the front left of the Ready Room.

"Roger, XO (Executive Officer) er Skipper." Lieutenant Commander (LCDR) "Wild" Bill Robinson, the squadron safety officer, stood up and moved to the front of the room. "In going over the plat tapes, radar, and discussing the pass with Sam Franks who waved him, it seems that the Skipper made a series of mistakes that led up to the fatal one at the ramp. These mistakes were not serious by themselves, but in combination with the amount of fatigue he must have had, they added up to an ever-increasing ball of wax. It looks like he was late leaving Marshal and pushed his speed up to compensate. No big deal, we have all done it. However, when you do it on a totally Instrument Flight Rules (IFR) black ass night, you set yourself up for a tough transition. Next, he almost certainly had vertigo on the descent. A night as bad as that is almost a guarantee, right Ray?"

"Yes sir!" Lieutenant Junior Grade (LTJG)Ray Rhodes had returned from the diversion to Danang at dawn to make the first trap aboard. "The vertigo was as bad as I have ever had it. What got me was the change from daylight to all of a sudden going totally IFR. I was having a hard time getting my scan going and, except for the circumstances, was glad to get the bingo. You ought to know though that the Skipper was totally smooth with me. He left me set up perfectly. No offense to anyone else, but he was definitely the best leader I have ever flown with." As he said this, he shook his head and actually stared down at his feet, not wanting anyone to see his eyes tear up.

"We all feel that way, I think." Letting out a loud sigh revealed just how heavy the loss they had suffered.. "Anyway, at the gate it looks like the Skipper's scan was slow. On radar, he ballooned up to 1200 feet, starting CCA high. He was hardly on glide path during the entire approach and was undoubtedly handicapped by a failure of his APC. When he called the ball, he was high and started a porpoising approach. He was never able to get it under control. Then when he got in close, he went a little high, probably thought he was going to bolter and chopped the throttle right when he hit the burble."

"Why the fuck didn't that goddamn CAG LSO wave him off?" LT Joe Ames, on his second cruise, was a seasoned combat pilot. He was also the squadron landing signal officer and often had confrontations with LCDR Franks, the airwing LSO Since Franks was an A4 pilot,

Ames thought he had no business waving F8s. He had been the wingman for CDR Huggins on the previous cruise and credited him with saving his life more than once over the beach.

"Joe, don't blame Sam. He was doing the best he could. He did wave him off in close and also called for him to eject. He admits that he knew he was waving the Skipper and probably let him go further than he would let a nugget, but you can't blame him for that."

"At the very end, when Sam called for him to eject, it appears the Skipper went to burner to try to get it out of the hole, but he was just in too deep. He had no chance at that point."

"Bill, I assume what we are learning from this is setup, setup, setup!" Interrupted LCDR Dick Knowles, as he jumped up and stood next to Ferguson in the front of the room. "Any of you swinging dicks out there think you can just dance this bird down to the ball have another think coming. You damn well better work your ass off from the moment you leave Marshal." LCDR Knowles was the senior lieutenant commander and squadron operations officer. He was known as a great tactical pilot, fearless and crazy in combat. He was smooth and practically flawless around the ship at night. "Get your scan going early!"

"Another thing I want you all to work on is crew rest. Any chance you get, hit the rack!" added Bill Ferguson.

"I don't want to be disrespectful Bill, but how the fuck are we supposed to do that?" asked LTJG Mike Twain angrily. "I haven't gotten more than four hours in the rack at a time since we left port between standing the alert five and that stupid aircraft handling watch."

"You have a good point, Aggie." Interjected Knowles. "You junior officers are under enough of a load on your first cruise without being hammered by bullshit watches. We have gotten together with CDR Johnson of 123 to convince the ship and airwing that we don't have to stand the alert five in the ready bird on the cat. We want to convince them to let us stand it in the Ready Rooms. That should give you the chance to get some sleep here while you are standing by."

"If we get that done, everybody has to understand that the ready bird has to be manned and launched on time if you get the call or Cag will have all our asses back out there in the plane." CDR Prescott delivered his message from his front seat chair by simply turning his head around so he could see all eleven pilots.

The ship-maintained fighter aircraft in a ready status on the catapults as fleet protection when flight operations were secured. Each fighter squadron rotated a watch to launch within five minutes the alert fighter in the event radar picked up any incoming bogies. Normally the watch was stood strapped into the aircraft.

"No one should have a problem," continued Knowles. "If you hustle, that is. Stay in here sleeping with all your gear on except for the helmet. Run your butt out the hatch and up on the flight deck and run to the plane. Do your preflight when you first go on duty, so you don't have to do it when launched. Get in the plane, and if the huffers are ready, which I doubt, turn up before you strap in. I tried it and was ready to launch in less than three minutes. There is no way in hell the ship will have the cats ready faster than that."

"Regarding the bullshit aircraft handling watch, I am going to get the senior spy to release our spook to take some of those watches while we are in flight ops." said John Philipps, standing in the middle of the ready room, turning to look directly at the junior officers. As the senior lieutenant in the squadron, he served as the senior watch officer. (SWO). "Also, we are trying to get the scooters and other squadrons to take more of it since they don't have to stand alert, but if they start getting hammered like last cruise, they won't have the people to handle it."

"All right men. Let me wrap this up before we start sounding like a bunch of old crybabies." Commander Prescott stood and faced them, a serious tone in his voice. "I see concern. Some of you look downright scared. You should be scared. I'm a little scared. But there is no point in doing this shit if you don't get your pulse going a little." He had everyone's attention. "One thing I know, I am better than this fucking ship! I fly the best and fastest single seat, single engine plane ever made. I am one of the chosen few. No one is going to kill my ass. No Mig pilot, no SAM, no triple-A because I am damn good! No one will ever get a clean shot at me. And no one on this ship will ever stick me on the ramp! Every one of you better think the same. Be a little scared. It makes you sharp. There is no reason to panic. You are the best. You know that or you wouldn't have the joy of flying this awesome machine. The Skipper loved what he was doing and wouldn't have traded it for anything. Now this meeting is over. See you all at the Memorial Service."

"Attention on deck!" Knowles called, and they all quickly stood to attention as the new skipper walked out the back of the room. Most of the rest of the pilots followed the Skipper out through the back hatch. Dick Knowles stopped to talk to John Philipps. "John, what do you think? You know the JO's better than any of us."

"They'll be all right. That was just the kind of kick ass speech we needed. Everyone is naturally pretty down when someone as good as Skipper Huggins buys it on the ramp. I do think that we might get Casper to go easy on some of the nuggets on night hops and flak suppression. I don't mind loading up this line period and I am sure both Casper and Joe will agree. Let's get them some time on the line before they are put under too much pressure."

"I agree. That's a good idea, but let's do it without announcing it. Give them some pinkies or full moon nights so they keep their numbers up and throw in some Mig Caps and easy photo escorts, so they get some points."

Every squadron made an attempt to balance the day and night traps or landings of the pilots. Points that went toward combat air medals were obtained for flights over North Vietnam and every effort was made to keep all pilots even in points.

"I'll go to the Skipper with that right now," Knowles said as he picked up the schedule board and walked out.

The jarring ring of the black dial telephone stopped the discussion of the ramp strike the four roommates were having. Ski Kowalski, answering the phone in the four-man stateroom said, "Yessir. He's here. I'll send him up right away." Hanging up the phone by his bunk, he yelled to the bunk above him, "Ray, the XO, er Skipper wants to see you in his stateroom ASAP!"

Dressing quickly in his tropical khaki uniform, Ray Rhodes left as fast as he could and went directly up to the senior officer quarters two decks above their stateroom. Knocking on the stateroom door he said, "Skipper, LTJG Rhodes reporting as ordered."

"Come on in, Ray."

Rhodes opened the door and walked into the small stateroom with a single bunk bed and standard metal desk bolted to the bulkhead. The skipper was seated at the desk. He motioned to the bunk and said, "Sit down. I have been watching you and I want you to be my wingman now. You have all the makings of a good stick. Flying with me, I will make you one of the best."

"Thank you, sir. I appreciate it that you want me, but what about Troy Davis?"

"He will fly with LCDR Robinson from now on. Flying with me is some good news and some bad news. The good news is that I get first choice of missions. The bad news for you is that I think a Skipper should take the toughest hops if he is going to be any kind of a leader. That means you are going to be in some bad shit."

Rhodes moved forward on the bunk and leaned toward the skipper, actually excited about finally getting to fly into combat..

"Another thing. Dick Knowles just left here. We have decided to let most of the nuggets take it easy for this first line period. Easy, pinkie or good weather, moonlit night hops. Only Mig Caps or easy photo escorts over the beach. However, we need you to fly the tough hops. Please don't say a damn thing about this to the others. I don't want to affect their confidence."

"Yes sir. I feel confident that I am ready to handle it."

"Ray, you are definitely ready. It is not an accident that you are in VF188. Cdr. Huggins and I, with our contacts in the Rag, got the best pilots coming out. And you, were rated the best of the best. That is why Cdr. Huggins wanted you as a wingman and I want you. That is why VF 188 is and will be the best fighter squadron in the navy.

"Remember, when we go over the beach, fly combat spread as well as you can fly it, but never stop moving. If I zig, then you zag, but keep the bird moving at all times. Keep your speed and energy up. Keep your head on a swivel. If I call break left or right, I want you to break the direction of the call without hesitation. If you have enough altitude, do a high g barrel roll in the direction of the break, but do it immediately when I call. Then pick me up when you get out of the maneuver. When the SAMs come up, think of it as a bullfight and you are the matador. You want to let the bull get close before you make your move. If you move too soon, the bull will move with you and gore you. Too late, and you can't get out of the way." Ray concentrating fully on the Skipper nodded his head in understanding. "When you do decide to go, turn down and into the SAM. Pull hard and do a six or seven G barrel roll right around it like you were trying to get on its tail. Always look for me when you come out of any evasion but keep looking for SAMs and Migs all the time. You cannot fly over the beach with your head in the cockpit. Understood?"

"Yessir!" He said firmly, with his back straight and his head upright.

"It should be exciting. I am a little scared, but mostly excited. I admit, I do not like flying around the boat at night, but I love going downtown over the beach. That is what we do. That is what we are good at. We can make a difference for those poor scooter pilots when we do a good job at flak suppression. And if we get a chance at a Mig, that's just gravy. It is the highest of highs. The pure exhilaration is why I am a fighter pilot. I feel so alive when I'm doing this! There is no place I would rather be."

"Yes sir!" Ray was fully committed to being the best wingman CDR Prescott ever had. He was convinced that he had the best deal flying with the new skipper who, being a leader, would look out for him and teach him. "Would you mind telling me how you got your Mig?"

"It was really pretty easy. We were doing a Mig Cap over Kep. The A4s were running an Alpha Strike downtown and we were covering. We got a call from the Big Look aircraft that Migs were taxiing out at Kep. We dove down just as Two 21s lifted off and I went down to fall behind the first when the second just popped right up in front of me. I got a tone right away and popped an AIM 9 right up his tailpipe almost before he had his gear up. My wingman was John Phillips. He tried to get the first guy, but his shot did not track and the guy beat feet to China before we could catch him."

The skipper placed both elbows on his desk and leaned closer. "Another thing, talking about Mig engagements, I am the Skipper here, but in the air we still fly by the tactics manual. I am the lead, but whoever sees the Migs calls the fight. If you have the best shot, you are going to take it. Our job is to shoot down Migs, protect the scooters and photos, and provide flak suppression. Neither one of us will jeopardize our mission and the other pilots who are up by putting personal glory first. Understood?"

"Yes sir."

"Also, we cover each other's ass. Should you go down you have my word that I will be all over your position as Rescap. I will do anything possible to get you out and get the choppers in. I am confident you would do the same for me or any other pilot out here or I wouldn't have asked you to be my wingman. It is hard to tell if any of the targets the scooters hit up North really make a difference to the grunts down South. I do know doing a good job of flak suppression makes a big difference to the A4s, but the most important thing anyone can do out here is Rescap. Any time a pilot is down, everyone has to make a maximum effort to get them out. I don't care if you are on Mig Cap or

Barcap or the crapper, get your ass to wherever he is down and assist with the Rescap. Strafe the gooks, keep contact with the guy on the ground and do not ever give up until the chopper has him or it is absolutely certain he is dead or captured. Is that understood?"

"Yessir!" His expression serious and committed.

"I will back you up with any action you take to get one of our guys out. If you are Mig Cap and someone goes down, chase any Migs off, but if there are none around, your immediate job becomes Rescap! Every Crusader pilot wants a Mig, but that is not nearly as important as getting someone out."

Looking straight at the skipper, Rhodes didn't miss a beat. "I understand. I won't let you down. I really appreciate getting the chance to fly with you."

"You may not appreciate it so much if we get into some shit. Speaking of which, in two days the airwing will conduct a Mini Alpha strike. You and I will fly flak suppression for four scooters who are trying to take out some small bridges between Haiphong and Hanoi. Spend some time with the maps to familiarize yourself with the area. Also go over all the airwing Standard Operating Procedures and know them by heart since this will be your first time over the beach. Now beat it out of here. I need to knock a few things out before I catch a few 'z's."

"Yessir!"

"But before you go we need to come up with your call sign. If we don't do it, Ames or John Phillips will come up with something you won't like. You know every pilot has to have a call sign. If you should have to lead a flight, it can't be Ray Flight"

"You are from a ranch, right?" Cdr. Prescott asked.

"Yessir"

"How about Cowboy or Bronco?"

"Sir, I did ride the horses some, but how I really worked on the ranch in summers was flying our little Piper Cub to look for strays in the National Forest land. My dad taught me to fly when I was twelve and by the time I was fourteen I spent all summer tracking down strays with the plane."

"Wow". Cdr Prescott said, nodding his head, "I am impressed."

"With a last name of Rhodes, how about Dusty?"

Nodding in ascent, Ray answered, "Yessir. Sounds good.'

"Also, Ray you probably know from your ROTC training that while Marines and Air Force junior officers are called by their rank … Lt. This, Captain that … etc. Navy Junior Officers are called Mr. from Ensign to LCDR." "However, in the squadrons we use first names unless in front of the enlisted. If I should call you Mr. Rhodes it would not normally be a good thing, understand?"

"Yessir"

"Well, Mr. Rhodes, get out of here but this is the navy. Get a haircut and trim those sideburns"

"Aye Aye Sir." Ray said, standing up and unconsciously touching his right sideburn as he went out the door.

Chapter Three

The JOs

Two levels below the hangar deck, their stateroom was one of six located in a small compartment on the starboard hull of the ship. The area was designated Officers' Country. Their four-man stateroom was a slight improvement over the JO bunk room located in the bow of the ship. Slightly smaller than an average prison cell, two bunks were mounted on the interior bulkhead and two more were on the hull side of the room. Below the bunks each pilot had a large drawer to hold personal effects. Two pull down desks were crammed into the stern bulkhead along with four small lockers serving as closets. Hanging on the forward bulkhead, next to the door, was a small sink with a mirror for shaving. The head was located one deck up and served other staterooms on that level. Each pull down desk had two small safes. Each officer was assigned a safe in which classified and personal material could be stored. Two small desk chairs were the only furnishings of the small space.

The entire area of the compartment and each stateroom was painted a depressing navy battleship gray. Hooks were placed on any empty space on a bulkhead in the staterooms. The green flight suits hanging on them added some color to the drab spaces. In an attempt to personalize the stateroom, red carpet tiles had been added to the deck in complete disregard of fire rules. Though new at the start of the cruise, they were already stained black in many areas from the grease brought in on flight boots.

Next to each bunk was a small, shelf-like area on which each pilot had placed tape decks purchased during their port call in the Philippines prior to going on the line at Yankee Station. Using headphones, each could listen to their own music on the built in preamps without bothering any of their roommates. By necessity, the stateroom was neat. Only the bare minimum of uniform items, survival pistols, and personal effects were kept in the stateroom. Other items were stowed in nooks and crannies in squadron spaces on the ship. During flight ops it was rare for all four roommates to be in the stateroom at the same time. Operating either midnight to noon or noon to midnight, even in the off time the pilots had other duties to perform and watches to stand. The navy believed that pilots were first naval officers and then aviators. As a result, every pilot had responsibilities in either maintenance, administration, or operations divisions.

Ray was surprised to see all his roommates still in the stateroom when he returned from his conversation with CDR Prescott. Kowalski and Twain, still dressed in their tropical khaki uniforms, were sitting on the desk chairs. Twain was at his desk writing a letter. A tall, lanky dark-haired Texan, the F8 was one of the few navy jets that would accommodate his height due to the large cockpit. Ski sat backward on his chair, his big, hairy arms drooping almost to the deck. At 6'2" he had been small for a tight end at Michigan, but he was big for a naval aviator. He had not been a starter at Michigan but had played some. Once, in flight training, he lost most of his bulk and now was almost lean at just over two hundred pounds.

Troy Davis, in his underwear, was sprawled on his bunk. Sandy haired and bearing a small scar across his upper lip from a high school lacrosse game, he was of average height with regular features and hazel eyes. An athlete, he was lean and muscular. He had been a starter on the Naval Academy's National Championship Lacrosse Team in 1965.

From his experience at the Academy, he specialized in checking the room for light leaks, knowing in the navy it was important to sleep at every opportunity.

All the roommates were commissioned on the same day: June 6, 1965. Thus, all had the same Date of Rank, which determined seniority. Davis had used his "boat school" credentials to work his way into the squadron jobs that took the least amount of effort. While an excellent pilot, he did not exert himself needlessly in non-flying activities.

"What did the Skipper want?" Ski asked.

"He told me that I was to be his wingman from now on. Sorry Troy, but he said that you would fly with LCDR Ferguson."

"No problem. That's fine with me. I don't want to be under the microscope on every hop. What do you think happened with Skipper Huggins ramp strike?"

"I don't know. I was having a rough time on the descent. Went from bright sky in Marshal to total darkness at the ship. I was fighting vertigo all the way down. I was glad to bingo."

"But the Skipper was such a great stick! Why didn't he go around or at least eject?" Twain was upset. Pacing around the room he said, "How the fuck am I ever going to get aboard at night if he couldn't?" Then abruptly, he sat down backwards in a desk chair and seemed to examine his hands.

"Aggie, you are as good as anybody. You wouldn't have gotten F8s if you didn't have top grades. You just must really focus on being exactly on speed and altitude when you start your approach and work your ass off for twenty-two seconds in the groove."

"Easy for you to say, Ray. You are good. We all know it and so does the Skipper. That's why he wants you."

"We are all good. That's why we're here."

"Well, some are gooder than others." Ski chimed in, waving his arms, "I think I can kick anyone's ass in dog fighting. Bring on the Migs.

I can fly formation as well as anyone. But around the boat I have to admit that I am just average in this squadron."

"Forget about the Skipper and Dickie. We know they are great. Look at Phillips and Casper. All they have on the greenie board are OK passes. They never even get a two wire, much less bolter."

A large board with each pilot's name on it was mounted in the Ready Room. After each trap aboard a grade was assigned by the LSO. Green was for an OK pass, yellow for average, red for a cut or no grade pass. For a pilot to receive an OK from the LSO, the plane normally had to catch the third of the four arresting cables on the flight deck.

"Why the fuck do we have to fly off these shitty old twenty-seven charlies?" Davis lifted up on an elbow from his bunk. "We fly the hardest, fastest planes in the fleet to land and they put us on old, small boats."

"Remember the LCDR who went through the rag with us? He had done two tours as a JO in F8s in the early sixties. Went to Monterey to post-grad school and came back to get current before he joined a fleet squadron. I heard he bought it on night workups on the Hancock. He was a good stick."

"Hey, let's knock off this shit. We can hack it or we wouldn't be here. Ray is right. This Aggie's hungry and we need to be in the wardroom in ten. Put your uni on Troy and let's go." Twain stood up and pushed the chair back under the desk.

Together they climbed up the ladder from their compartment to the second deck and through the passageway to the wardroom.

Pilots, aircrews, the cat and arresting gear officers, and those on watch could eat in the "dirty" mess when in flight quarters. Service was cafeteria style with no assigned seating. Pilots would wear flight suits, others their working uniforms. However, at all other times officers were required to eat in the wardroom wearing the uniform of the day. Even on an old carrier, the wardroom was large. It accommodated all the ship's officers who were not on duty as well as the airwing's pilots and staff, some one hundred and fifty in all. On the Adams, long tables were set up to accommodate about forty officers each. Junior officers sat at the back of the room. airwing JOs sat with their squadron mates of equal rank and pilots from the other squadrons. Each officer was assigned a seat, and each seat had a silver place setting and a silver napkin ring with a white cloth napkin inside.

At the Airwing senior officers' table the seat next to CDR Prescott, CDR Huggins' seat, was empty. Officers stood behind their chairs until the presiding officer, normally the executive officer of the ship, started service of the meal by taking his seat.

At that time, Filipino stewards began serving. Meals in the wardroom were generally good. Officers paid for their meals though their mess bill. Every month they received a basic allowance for subsistence, which generally covered the mess bill. The junior supply officer on the ship was usually the mess officer in charge of purchasing the food for the mess and billing the officers accordingly. Additionally, the officers' mess fund was used to provide gifts to visiting dignitaries.

"Gentlemen," the ship's Executive Officer (X/O), Captain Ware said, "before we take our seats, I would like to say a few words about my friend and former squadron mate, CDR Bob Huggins. Bob came to VF 111 when I was on my second cruise. It was immediately obvious that he was a good stick and became a great officer and asset to the squadron. Following that cruise, we remained good friends, and I regret his passing greatly. Let's have a moment of silence to remember him."

Together, they bowed their heads in respect. Some remembering the man, others wondering if they might be next.

Chapter Four

4 Mini Alpha
8 March 1967 Yankee Station

Crammed into the briefing room in Air Intelligence, the pilots shuffled preprinted briefing cards nervously or chatted with their counterparts from the rest of the airwing. The space was a relatively small room near Air Ops on the O1 level of the carrier. The back walls of the room were covered by high resolution, color maps showing areas of North Vietnam. There were also black and white photos of various SAM and gun emplacements.

Sitting in straight-backed chairs facing the maps, the pilots studied the briefing cards on their kneeboards, like nervous students cramming for some exam. The room looked like a small, gray, geography classroom. Typically, senior officers sat toward the front and junior pilots at the back, although there was no set order.

Although the briefing was for a mini-Alpha strike, the room was still full: The F8 Barcap, Mig Cap and flak suppression flights, the A4 attack or bombing flights, the KA3 refueling, the A1 Rescap pilots, the E 1 controller crews, and assorted intelligence personnel.

The pre-briefing excited banter subsided when the commander, who was the Airwing senior intelligence officer began, "Gentlemen, your target for today is this series of small bridges between Hanoi and Haiphong." Commander Dawkins, the head spook, pointed to the large map on the back wall that indicated an area approximately

110 miles west of the ship's operating area in the Tonkin Gulf between Hanoi and Hainan Island. "These bridges are lightly defended by AAA in these areas." He indicated gun emplacements near the bridges on the map. "We do not anticipate SAM activity in this area, but they are known to deploy throughout the area. The tactical strike frequency will be 234.3. Base today is 12,000 ft." In an attempt to confuse any enemy listening to the attack frequency, altitude was given in the code base plus. Twenty thousand feet on this date would be base plus eight. "The escape and evasion code letter is R. Please review your personal history information."

In the unlikely event a pilot was down and evading capture in enemy territory without a radio, he could signal by laying out the letter of the day in clothing or stomping down plants. North Vietnamese troops used radios of captured pilots to lure rescue aircraft and helicopters into the range of the gunners. Pilots filled out personal data cards, which were used by helicopter crews to validate that they were truly speaking to the downed pilot. In the same manner, the code letter would hopefully prevent traps set by enemy gunners to lure Rescap aircraft into firing range by making visual SOS signals.

"I will now turn over the brief to Commander Jeffries, the strike leader."

Commander Robert Jeffries, CO of VA 18, stood up. A Naval Academy graduate, this was his second tour with VA 18. Flying the old A4B in the previous cruise, the "Busters" of VA 18 had taken serious losses, nine planes shot down and six pilots dead or captured. He himself had been hit by AAA near Haiphong but had been able to nurse his damaged Skyhawk "Feet Wet" for an ejection over the sea where the rescue helo picked him up. Between cruises, VA 18 had transitioned to the new A4E with a more powerful engine and enhanced electronics. CDR Jeffries was optimistic that combat experience, the new plane, and improved tactics would give his squadron a better survival rate for this cruise.

A big man for the A4 cockpit, barely able to fold himself into the seat, he had been injured in the previous ejection and still moved his head cautiously, as though his neck and back still bothered him.

He started his briefing. "No disrespect intended for the spooks, but I think we should view this quick and dirty intelligence briefing as overly optimistic. We should expect these bridges to be heavily defended. We should all be ready and expect SAMs in the air. As a result, with CAG's approval, I have added an Ironhand element to this mini-Alpha strike. LT Koontz of VA 59 who has experience from last cruise with SAMs will fly the Ironhand aircraft. Escort for the Ironhand element will be flown by a Crusader from VF 123. LT Koontz, what is your callsign for the Ironhand?"

"Sir, we will be Beatle Flight."

"Roger, Beatle flight. Is that the bug or those British singers?" Laughter erupted in the tight room as Koontz responded.

"That would be Paul, Ringo, George, and John."

"Roger that. Just don't break out into song while the SAMs are airborne."

"No sir. We'll be on them."

Returning to the business of the brief, Commander Jeffries said, while pointing to the map of the target area, "Our VA 18 element will consist of two sections. I will lead our section of Doorknobs One and Two, LCDR Lane will lead the second section of Doorknobs Three and Four. We will commence our run in from over this Karst ridge just Northeast of the first bridge. The run in heading for the first section will be Two Four Two. The first section will take the first bridge. The second Doorknob section will take this second bridge east of the first one. We will commence both roll ins simultaneously just as the flak suppressors clear.

"Commander Prescott, you will be leading the Heater section in Flak suppression. We need you to hit this gun emplacement that appears to be between the two bridges hard. As soon as you call in hot, we're going to start our run so please try to cause as much hate and discontent as you can with those gunners."

"Shit Bobby, you know you can count on us. I don't expect this thing to be a cakewalk, but it doesn't appear to be anything we can't handle. We are arming up with two, two thousand pounders each and Zunis. We'll plan on dropping the bombs on the first run and save the Zunis in case we need a second."

"Let's try to avoid any multiple runs. Get in, hit the target, and get out! If we happen to miss a bridge, we can get it another day." Commander Jeffries did not want to lose planes and pilots this early in cruise on what he viewed as a minor league target. "Unless you have to, to avoid a SAM, let's stick to a floor of 6,000 feet for this strike. That will keep us well out of range of the 37s and away from most of the 57s. When you pull off the target, come off to starboard and pull up in a climbing turn to get back to the Karst area where there shouldn't be any guns. You should come off and head about Zero Seven Zero, jinking the whole time. Should they be necessary, the Rescap A1s will be holding off Quang Zen and should be able to be in within five or ten minutes. The Mig Cap will orbit over the Karst area and intercept any Migs that come up, should they be so lucky." He added, knowing the Crusader pilots wanted nothing more than a Mig engagement. "Our launch order will first be the Heater's since they have to refuel off the Cat, next the Doorknobs, the British singers," more laughter in the briefing area— "and the Half Dollar Mig Cap. We'll rendezvous at angels eighteen on the Sandbox 320 radial at 20 miles. Heaters, you take up a port combat spread, Doorknobs and Beatle will go in together on my lead, Beatle to starboard, Doorknob three to port, in loose deuce. Half Dollars, escort us in at twenty. We'll coast in here,"—pointing again to the map— "just north of Quang Yen. We shouldn't pick up any opposition until we hit the flat delta on our run in toward the target. Get in there fast and get back out over the Karst. We don't need to be feet dry more than five minutes." He looked around the room. "Any questions?"

"Yeah Bob, what's the story on post-strike refueling?" Commander Prescott asked.

"Good question, Dan. I forgot. The Big Boy whale is supposed to cover the recovery after our launch and then will proceed out the 320 and orbit just off the coast. He will be monitoring the strike frequency. Any more questions?" He saw no one had anything to say. "We'll be manning in thirty, see you on the flight deck."

Ray and the skipper walked out together.

"Ray, this will probably be a piece of cake. But in our own brief I want to go over our procedures in a little more detail. Nothing to be worried about, remember, this is supposed to be routine," the skipper said, trying to reassure Ray. "But it is better to be thoroughly prepared for anything that might happen."

They walked back to Ready Room Two with LCDR Ferguson who was the spare for the flight. In the event the skipper's plane went down, he would lead the flight. Normally a junior pilot or nugget would spare, but the skipper did not want to take a chance of two inexperienced pilots being launched together on this type of hop.

They sat down in the front of the Ready Room, gathered around the skipper's chair for the detailed flight brief. After reviewing the normal frequency changes, rendezvous point off the catapult, refueling, and joining of the rest of the Alpha strike, the skipper got down to the details of the strike.

"Ray, once we coast in feet dry move up into a loose deuce. Hopefully the guns will be where they say they are but keep your eyes open. I'll be surprised if there isn't more than one emplacement. If everything is as briefed, follow my run in. When I drop, it should keep their heads down while you make your run. Plan on giving me about a ten second lead. I'll run in a little more from the South, while you take a roll in point here." He indicated a position on his folded, plastic combat map that he would use in the cockpit. It was clear to Ray that the skipper was taking a more exposed position further out over the Delta while leaving Ray a roll in point closer to the Karst ridge. "Don't bust six thousand feet. Pickle about eight thousand, use about 110 mils up on your gunsight for the lead on your bomb run. If you get these thousand pounders anywhere close it will keep their heads down while the Scooters do their job. Pull off hard and in burner. Use that burner to get back up to twelve thousand feet and plan on joining up with me here,"—indicating another spot on the map over the Karst ridges—"Try to keep me in sight at all times except when you are in your run. As we coast in begin jinking and do not stop until we are back feet wet. The secret to good jinking is to keep the plane moving without bleeding off all your airspeed. You know how easy this baby rolls. Just roll one way and then the other, smoothly, but changing your direction in a random motion that doesn't bleed off your energy. You shouldn't need burner until you pull off, unless a SAM comes up. If we do get SAM activity, remember to wait until the last second and then pull hard and down into it. Don't forget to keep jinking as soon as you get by the SAM since they will be trying to drive you down into the AAA."

"Yes sir," Ray said, not missing a beat.

"Keep your head up at all times. Things happen awfully fast your first few times, the ALQ squawking, maybe some beepers going, everyone calling AAA and SAMs. Just stick with me and keep your head up. You'll do fine. Also, don't try to be a hero. There will be plenty of chances for medals when you have more experience. Today you want to get your feet wet. Learn, listen. We'll get the job done and get the hell out of there. Understood?"

"Yessir." Nodding his head in agreement.

"Remember, this is what all the training and practice was all about. I don't know if this classifies as fun, but I can't think of anything I would rather do. This is what I do, this is what we are about. We are warriors at war! Nothing makes me feel more alive."

Together, the three of them moved to the equipment room off the front of the Ready Room to get into their G-suits and torso harnesses.

In a ritual like knights donning armor for battle, they put on their "armor" and strapped on the survival vest and pistols. As they dressed, Willie Nelson's "My Heroes Always Were Cowboys" blared over the Ready Room sound system.

"Goddammit Ray, shut off the shit kicker crap!" the skipper yelled in mock anger.

"Sorry Skipper, I think you have the wrong cowboy. I may be from the Wild West, but I prefer the Doors. I think we have Aggie to thank for this." Ray said as he pointed out Twain hunched over the tape player. As squadron duty officer of the day (SDO), he was responsible for everything in the Ready Room.

"Goddamit Twain! This is our fucking Alpha strike, so we ought to get to pick the music to go to battle with! What do you want Ray?"

"Sir, I would like the Doors, 'Light My Fire'!"

"All right Twain. Throw some Doors at us. Note that when I get back, tonight before the movie, we are going to settle this pre-battle music shit. I want everyone to bring a sample of what they would like, and I will democratically determine our launch music. Tell Phillips to bring something classy. We are a fucking classy squadron, after all."

Just as the first strains of "Light My Fire" were coming from the big Teac reel-to-reel tape player, the 1MC sounded with "Now Pilots Man your Planes! Pilots Man your Planes!" Following Skipper Prescott and Ferguson out the hatch, Ray climbed up the outside ladder to the flight deck to man his plane for his first Alpha Strike. Perhaps by luck, or maybe because, as the line officer of the Maintenance Department, Chief Frederick seemed to like him, he had been assigned Two One Two. His name was on the port side of Two One Two, with Twain, who was slightly junior to him, on the starboard. To him it was a good omen that he been assigned Heater One Two. He loved the way One Two flew. It seemed to fit him and was easier to trim than the other planes. Nothing ever seemed to go wrong with it, and it apparently hadn't been bent like many of the others, with repeated hard carrier landings and high G-dog fights.

It was almost quiet as the pilots all came out of their Ready Rooms and up topside to man aircraft. The normal near hurricane of wind across the deck was still as the great old ship lingered in nearly calm seas, preserving critical sea room for the launch and recovery that made up the hour and one half of cyclic ops. The plane captains and line crews waited quietly in their brown shirts for their respective pilots. The electrical power units and huffer air units were plugged in and ready to go, but their engines were silent.

The flight deck was a contrast of color. The gray and black of the ship served as a backdrop for the brown jerseys of the line crews, yellow of the aircraft handlers, purple of fuels, red of ordinance, green of the aircraft troubleshooters, blues and whites of cats and arresting gears. The warplanes were mainly gray, but the subtle chin straps or intake colors of the squadrons highlighted the most prominent features: intake and tail of the F8s, wings of the A4s. The pilots mixed with their dark green Nomex flight suits, turtlenecks in squadron colors, and colorful helmets not unlike racecar drivers. The menacing looking bombs and missiles, mainly grays or white, but with dramatic touches of red or yellow added to the mix of color on the planes.

The fighters were arranged in a neat row on the port stern with the smaller A4s behind the island on the starboard side. The cats were empty, awaiting the first aircraft. The cat crews and aircraft handlers who guided the warplanes onto the catapults also waited, taking advantage of a few idle minutes during the frantic fourteen hours that made up their workday during flight quarters. Soon the flight deck would turn into a deadly place, with intakes and jet blast to avoid, pieces of the old wooden flight deck flying up into the wind and striking the face and body, noise vibrating through the whole body, past the protective Mickey Mouse ears and helmets worn by all flight deck crew. The noise of thirty jet engines turning up all at the same time was compounded by the wind of the ship and the bang of the cats. Not a workplace for the weak.

As he walked across the flight deck to where Heater One Two was parked on the port side near the stern, Ray swung his helmet by the strap and threw it the last ten yards to his plane captain. It was his ritual. It made him feel more relaxed about manning. He was excited, but not really afraid. The skipper was definitely right: this was why he had become a fighter pilot. He carefully preflighted the aircraft, paying close attention to the huge, two thousand pound bombs hanging from the MERS on each wing. He also carefully checked the fuselage mounted Zuni Rockets, making sure no wires or plugs were left undone on installation. His beautiful plane looked like a big, deadly beast of burden with everything hanging on it.

Directly across the deck from him, behind the island, he noticed Koontz pre-flighting the Shrike missile package that made up the Ironhand. Koontz was carefully going over every bit of the system. Looking up, he saw Ray and flashed him a quick thumbs-up with a confident smile. Ray returned both the smile and the thumbs-up, *thinking better him than me*. To fly the Ironhand was to engage in a game of chicken with the SAMs. Flying into the heart of the SAM envelope, the pilot made himself the target and, when the SAM had locked on and fired, locked his own Shrike missile on the enemy radar and fired back, hoping his missile would ride the beam down and destroy the SAM before the SAM got him. Not a mission for those lacking in courage. Only the good ones were given the mission, since the security of the whole strike could depend on the Ironhand.

He continued his preflight, passing to the starboard side. On the aft side of the angle deck, 212 was shoved back with the tail cone hanging over the water. This was usually the case on the ship, so he tried to check the burner section out as carefully as he could from the side. Hopefully the line crew had done a thorough preflight prior to spotting it there.

Checking all the fittings and the air gauges, air pressure was used for emergency activation of the wing and gear in the event of hydraulic failure, he moved up to the nose and cockpit area where he saw LTJG Twain painted on the starboard side.

Returning to port side, he mounted the steps and crawled into the cockpit, pre-flighting the ejection seat prior to sitting down. His plane captain, Airman Mears helped him strap in. As he left, he told Ray, "Give them Hell, sir. And bring her back in one piece."

"No problem, Mears. She's ready and so am I."

As the electrical power unit was signaled on, all his gauges came up. He noted that the fuel gauge only read 4000 pounds, 5000 below the full load. Although the bombs and rack only weighed a little over four thousand pounds, the lighter fuel load put less strain on the cat shot and allowed an easier climb out to altitude. He and the skipper would refuel immediately after launch.

Over the flight deck loudspeaker, he heard the air boss order, "Now pilots start your engines."

He looked to the right and twirled his index finger in a clockwise motion, signaling the line crew to start the huffer air start unit connected to his plane. As he watched the RPMs move up past seventy percent, he moved the throttle around the stop, hitting the igniters with an outboard push as he moved the handle to idle. The engine started immediately, and he carefully monitored the RPM and Exhaust Gas Temperature (EGT), as the revolutions increased to seventy percent.

Seeing the gauges settle into the green, he moved his hands and eyes quickly around the cockpit, beginning in the back right, turning on and checking the radio, putting the radar in standby, transponder on and in standby, ready with the proper IFF squawk when airborne. Turning on the ALQ 100, he listened as it went through the series of *brrts, deedles,* and *deedle deedle* that identified enemy radars and SAM launches, hoping that the gear would work as well in the air. He checked to make sure all gauges were good and that the attitude gyro and navigation equipment were working properly. He then turned his attention to Mears, who had been waiting patiently at the front port side of the aircraft.

As Mears signaled, he began to rotate through the functions, lowering and raising the tail hook, checking the refueling probe, raising the wing, testing all the controls with a sweep of the stick. As he moved the controls, he also watched the surfaces move in his mirrors, making certain that the surfaces moved in the proper direction. In his headset he heard, "Heater One up." He quickly keyed the mike and reported, "Heater Two up. Heater three up." He heard as the spare checked in.

Other flights began to check in. From what he could hear, it sounded like everyone was up and ready. In a few moments, Mears came over and motioned for him to close his canopy. As he manually pulled the canopy down, he watched the skipper taxi out toward the cat. A yellow shirt aircraft handler came over and signaled to pull chocks by thrusting both thumbs outward. Mears pulled the chocks from beneath his wheels and the aircraft handler signaled to move forward. He added power and pulled out, following the handler up the deck. Once clear of the other parked aircraft, he was given the signal to spread his wings. He reached down to the handle just outboard of the throttle on the left side and pushed the handle down, locking it carefully in place once the wings were spread.

With the canopy down, the aircraft was stiflingly hot. The plexiglass of the canopy acted like a greenhouse, concentrating the heat inside the cockpit. He was soon covered with sweat but didn't dare turn the air-conditioning up. Ineffective at idle power, if the a/c was turned to full cold, the cockpit would quickly fog up when full power was added prior to the cat shot. Thus, the pilots all learned to live with the heat for the few minutes before the launch when the canopy was down. The spares were affected the worst, they had to sit with canopies down for the launch and wait to be taxied forward before the recovery. They suffered through the heat, but never got to fly.

Following the signals of the aircraft handler, Ray taxied up to the starboard catapult, noticing the skipper getting ready to launch off the port. The F8 pilots had to be very careful positioning on the cat, as it was easy to use too much power going over the wedge-shaped shuttle and go too far, forcing the cat crew into a difficult push back. As a result, when Ray felt his nose gear touch the shuttle, he eased the power, ready with the brakes, when the wheel barely went over. The handler quickly gave him the X signal with his wands, but Ray had already applied the brakes as he felt the wheel fall. He looked to his left at the weight sign, at 26,500 pounds, it was lower than normal, but correct for his fuel and bomb load. He gave a thumbs-up to the weight.

The catapult officer, watching the installation of the shuttle on the nose gear, began to signal to Ray to turn up his engine by twirling his right hand above his head. Ray pushed the throttle to full, pulled up the T handle in front of it that would allow him to hold the throttle at full against the G-force of the launch, checked his instruments, and saluted the cat officer with his right hand after first cycling the control surfaces to make certain his ailerons and elevators were moving properly. He could always reach the stick during the launch, but his left hand had to stay locked on the throttle. If the throttle moved back during the launch, there was no way Heater One Two would fly.

As soon as he saluted, he kept his head straight ahead, left arm fully extended with hand locked around the throttle handle. He lightly held the stick in his right hand, allowing it to move back during the launch. Somehow, no matter how fast the launch, the wait always seemed to be forever with the aircraft at full power, anticipating the jolt of the catapult. After a delay—which seemed forever but was not more than five seconds—he felt the satisfying jolt in his back as Two One Two was thrust down the cat track. The exhilaration of the catapult shot was second to none. Shoved straight back in the seat, he felt the thrill of accelerating from zero to one hundred and eighty knots in less than three hundred feet. The thrill of instantly flying.

The Crusader might be a bitch to bring aboard, he thought. *But no plane took a better cat shot.* Nothing else made by man accelerated that fast. As he reached the end of the bow, he was already flying, noting 185 knots on the airspeed indicator. He raised the gear handle then quickly reached the wing handle on the left side of the cockpit, lowering and locking the wing. Heater One Two smoothly accelerated, at full military power on the J57 Pratt and Whitney jet engine, to 350 knots, climbing out with the vertical speed indicator pegged at 12,000 feet per minute, even while carrying two, two-thousand-pound bombs. Climbing out, he checked the gauges and noted everything was in the green. He switched his radio to tactical and headed for five thousand feet on the outbound Tacan radial as briefed, to rendezvous with the skipper. He quickly spotted the other Heater aircraft in a lazy left turn. Cutting inside the turn, he rendezvoused easily on the port side, then slid under to take his position in a starboard echelon. As he moved under, he quickly checked out the skipper's plane and bombs to make certain no damage had occurred during launch. He also carefully looked at the bombs, making sure they were not accidentally armed. The small propellers on the bombs were pinned in place until dropped from the plane, keeping the bombs safe until released.

Using signals to make a quick lead change, the skipper moved back and looked over his plane. Giving Ray a thumbs-up, he resumed the lead. Silently, they climbed toward the tanker rendezvous. Unconsciously making hundreds of small movements with stick and throttle, Ray flew perfect formation. He tried to always concentrate in the aircraft, taking a great deal of pride in doing the little things well, which separated him from the other, good, nugget pilots. No one flew F8s who wasn't a good stick.

As they approached the KA3 tanker, the skipper signaled Ray out to a loose form position and proceeded to call, "Mother Cow, Mother Cow, Heater One with two to drink."

"Roger, Heater One. We have a sweet package. You are cleared to drink your fill." Ray recognized the voice of Frank Potter, the KA3 pilot known as Coal Miner. He had been in many classes in flight training with Frank, one of the few black pilots in the navy. They had thrown back a few brews during happy hours at advanced training in Beeville, Texas. Frank had asked for fighters as a first choice but had been assigned to the KA3. A good stick, he had done well in the replacement air group (RAG) landing the large and difficult whale on the small decks of the 27 Charlie carriers. Like Ray, he was now on his first cruise.

Plugging, or refueling, the F8 was not easy since the refueling probe, when extended from the port side of the aircraft, was not visible to the pilot flying formation on the tanker and tanker drogue. The technique was to place the aircraft with the cockpit approximately five feet to the right of the drogue or basket of the tanker and slightly accelerate, driving the probe into the basket, causing a connection that opened the ball valve on the end of the probe and likewise opened a female valve on the basket. Once plugged in, the pilot then pushed the hose connected to the basket back onto the hose reel in the tanker aircraft until a green light on the tanker signaled that the fuel transfer had begun. The fighters all refueled daily since they were required to maintain a combat package of fuel in case of Mig activity. Thus, refueling became routine and they seldom missed, although it was always more difficult at night or when low fuel was an emergency.

Tanking from the KA3 was the easiest for the Crusader pilots. A twin engine, navy version of the B66, converted to tanker duty, the drogue was well clear of the jet wash that was always a problem with A4 tankers. Also, the big jet seemed to fly smoother. With a crew of three and internal refueling tanks, there were few problems with the KA3s. On the other hand, the A4s carried external, buddy stores that often seemed to fail. The A4 pilots also dreaded tanking duty and were sometimes intentionally careless with their rudder trim just to make the cocky fighter pilots' lives a bit more difficult. Of course, the Crusader pilots retaliated by thumping the A4s: flying at high speeds under them and pulling up just in front of their cockpits, filling the front windscreen with a plan view of the F8 screaming straight up.

The skipper quickly and smoothly tanked, backing out when full and settling in a form position behind and to the port of the tanker. Ray moved in, selected the probe switch on the bulkhead near the throttle, quickly glanced to see it extend and efficiently plugged in, seeing the satisfying green light on the rear of the tanker. Not wanting to overfill the fuel bladder, he watched as his gauge approached nine thousand pounds, pulling out with two hundred pounds to go.

Moving back, he rejoined on the skipper's starboard wing, hearing him call, "Thank you Mother Cow. Heaters are clear."

Frank answered with two clicks of the mike key.

Ray flew close formation until the skipper joined on Doorknob lead. He then was moved out by hand signals into the loose deuce position. Not wanting to divulge anything more than necessary over the radio, the strike rendezvous was made silently. The sections formed on the lead as briefed, with the Half Dollar Mig Cap flying escort above the formation. Almost as soon as they left the rendezvous point, Ray heard the *brrp* in his headset of a North Vietnamese height finder radar as duplicated by his ALQ 100 electronic countermeasure gear. Obviously, they had picked up the formation with search radar and were now confirming altitude to feed to the triple-A batteries, SAM sites, and Migs. Cruising in unobserved did not appear to be an option.

Checking his map and Tacan position from the ship, he knew they were nearing the coast in point. He was excited. There was nothing boring about this flight. He constantly scanned to maintain his position while checking his gauges. With the adrenaline rush of his first combat mission, he wanted to hurry, to be over the North sooner.

"Doorknobs, Go Switches Hot!" He heard CDR Jeffries call. As the Airwing gained experience, they would dispense with radio calls, but on this first mission Jeffries wanted to make sure his first cruise pilots were ready. Ray turned his master arm switch on and selected the wing position, which would automatically cycle to the fuselage mounted Zunis once the bombs were released. He also armed the guns, hearing the satisfying clunk of the rounds being thrust into the chamber. He was now ready.

As they crossed the coast, nothing happened. He did not know what he expected, but, somehow, he thought it would be different. No Migs or SAMs. No barrage of triple-A. Nothing on the radio or ALQ100 except the occasional *brrp* of the height finder radar.

Smoothly rolling right and then back left in erratic intervals, the skipper began to jink. Watching and mimicking, Ray also started to jink while maintaining a loose formation. He noticed that all the other flights had also begun to move in a similar way. The military precision of the formation a few moments earlier was gone, replaced by ten aircraft moving in the same general direction in a wildly variable path. The countryside below the attack group, the lush green Karst ridges, was beautiful. It was a rugged landscape of spires of limestone surrounded by brush or trees. Ray watched, fascinated, while locating prominent features on his map, figuring their location. The sharp *deedle deedle* of a Fansong acquisition radar from a SAM battery was a harsh pronouncement that intelligence was once again wrong. The soft target was defended by at least one SAM battery.

The Ironhand flight of the A4E and F8 separated from the main attack group and began to search for the SAM. Koontz began to track the radar with his shrike missile while his escort, Lieutenant Franconi from VF 123, flew a jinking pattern above him, watching carefully for the liftoff of any SAM. Koontz, homing on the radar, began to fly directly at it, hoping to entice the site to lock on, thereby giving him a good target. At the same time, Heater lead began to push his speed up and descend to the roll in point at twelve thousand feet. The Doorknob A4s were now slightly behind the F8s and Beatle flight. Above, the Mig

Cap of VF 123 orbited ready to pounce on any Migs or assist in Rescap if needed.

"Heater Flight, check switches hot."

Ray did a quick check and was satisfied that all the switches were in the proper position. It wouldn't do to make a tough run and be unable to drop because the switches weren't on. As they got closer to the target he noticed flashes of light from the AAA below. Puffs of black flak made ugly, small clouds below them.

"Heater Two, there is a second large gun emplacement just southwest of the second bridge. I'll take it, but you will have to roll in on your own."

"Roger Heater lead. I have the target in sight." The major AAA emplacements were easy to spot as they poured flak into the air. White puffs of 85s began to mix with the black of 57s and 37s. The two-gun sites could pour a steady column of flak in a crossfire aimed at smashing anyone attacking the bridges. The smaller gun sites made no attempt to track the incoming attack aircraft. They simply aimed their guns at a predetermined point where they thought the planes must fly through to drop their bombs or to pull off. It was a very effective tactic.

"Heater One is in."

After a few seconds, Ray called: "Heater Two is in."

He rolled in from twelve thousand feet and quickly located the AAA emplacement in his gunsight. The F8, not designed for bombing, had no bombsight, but was so stable in a high-speed dive, that lead was predetermined in mils on the gunsight depending on the dive angle. Fairly accurate bombing was achieved without a gyro-stabilized sight in this manner.

"Heater Two, keep jinking!" He heard one of the Half Dollar Mig Caps call. Immediately he began rolling right and left of the target line, while in the dive, still keeping the target in the site.

"Heater One is off."

In his peripheral vision he thought he saw a bomb blast. Before he reached the pickle point, the flak began to increase. His natural reaction was to pickle and pull to avoid it, but, concentrating on the target, he waited a few seconds for his altimeter to unwind in the steep dive. Just slightly above eight thousand feet, unable to wait any longer, he hit the pickle on the stick and felt the aircraft immediately react to the loss of the two thousand pounds of deadweight.

Pulling back hard on the stick, he pushed the throttle outboard and lit the burner as his nose began to come up. Flak was all around him momentarily as he bottomed out through six thousand feet, and then he was up through the deadly clouds as the Crusader climbed out rapidly.

"Nice shooting Heaters!" someone called. He turned to look at the targets as he rejoined on the skipper and saw that the big guns were no longer firing. The two Doorknob sections were beginning their runs on the bridges, and he watched closely as the Scooters made their run. Just as the first A4 was reaching the release point, they all heard the high pitched *deedle deedle* indicating a SAM launch. The fansong radar had gone from search to lock on mode. Someone was the target for a SAM.

"Beatle One, SAM airborne, three o'clock at about four miles." Franconi called to Koontz.

"Roger Two. I've got him." Determined to get the SAM site, Koontz turned his A4 to put the launch position on his nose and began a slight dive, accelerating to put himself in a good position to launch. The Shrike had a relatively short range of only two- and one-half miles. It was critical to avoid the SAMs with their far greater range while pressing on to the radar site that provided SAM guidance.

"Beatle One, it's on your twelve about two miles."

"Roger, Two. Give me a heads up when it gets close." This was the cool reply. With his head in the scope to make sure he was in range and locked on, he needed to be able to instantly find the SAM when he looked up.

"Doorknobs are off target heading feet wet. Don't hang around too long Beatle."

Their ordnance expended, the A4s of the main strike group could do little to help the Ironhand. Jinking their way back to the coast at full military power, their goal was to get to the safety of the water as fast as possible.

Flying loose deuce on the skipper, Ray saw that he was putting them in an orbit over the Karst area at about 12,000 feet. They were not going back feet wet as briefed.

"Doorknob lead, Heater one. We will stay and support Beatle."

"Roger that."

"Beatle One, this is Two. Heads up and get ready to break port. It's at one o'clock, one mile!" came the call from Franconi.

Koontz looked up from the scope just as he saw the lock-on and in-range lights come on. Almost instantly he saw the SAM as it tracked on him. Pulling up hard, he forced the SAM to commit, and then, at exactly the last second, he broke hard left and down in a high G-barrel roll. Unable to react to the maneuver, the SAM shot by, detonating milliseconds after he was clear. Knowing he wasn't close enough to set off the proximity fuse, he assumed it had been manually detonated when the controllers saw it wouldn't track. The bastards were clever.

With a good lock on the SAM site, Koontz continued down inverted, pointing the nose again at the launch site, he pressed the pickle and watched the missile begin to track the Fansong radar back to the launch pad. Almost immediately, he heard the radar shut down as the site saw the missile separate from the aircraft. Hopefully the missile had enough data to carry its 350 pound warhead close enough to destroy the site.

Committed inverted with his nose below the horizon, Koontz decided the fastest way out was to dive down, pulling hard and through in a split-S or bottom half of a loop, thereby reversing course back to the water and safety.

"Beatle One, pull hard and break left! You've got a 37 emplacement on your nose!"

The call was too late. Pressing down to attack and avoid the SAM, Koontz bottomed out below one thousand feet above the ground, almost on top of the guns. As he broke away from them, they had an easy shot at the departing A4s belly.

"You're hit. Eject Bill!" Black smoke streamed from the still fast moving A4.

"Negative. I'm not getting out until she quits flying!"

Climbing out toward the Karst area, the black smoke became fire as the Scooter slowed down, losing airspeed in the climb. Soon the whole plane was covered in flames.

"Guess this is it. See you in the funnies!" Both the Heater flight and Beatle Two watched as Koontz ejected. The parachute billowed and drifted down toward the Karst area. Franconi immediately began circling the chute, determined to follow it down and give cover to his lead.

"Beatle Two, break off! You'll get hit and show them where he is!" The skipper called, knowing that the ground forces who would quickly mobilize to capture the downed pilot might not know Koontz had ejected or have the chute in sight. "Join on us and we'll all fly close air support. We're at your three o'clock, slightly high."

"Roger, Tally-ho." Franconi called and turned to join them.

"Quick Draw, Quick Draw, this is Heater One. We have a pilot down approximately on the Sandbox 336 at 68. Need support and pick up, over."

"Roger Heater. We are already inbound. Estimate five minutes to your position. Quick Draw flight, knockers up!" The lead A1 Rescap pilot called for his wingman to arm guns and rockets.

The WWII designed A1 propeller plane provided the best close-air support for rescue missions. Slow, it had fuel to linger over the rescue area and could stay with the rescue helicopters. It carried a considerable package of close air support weapons. Although it was relatively easy to hit, it was hard to bring down. Heavily armored, it could absorb a lot of small arms fire.

"Heaters and Beatle Two, we'll set up a racetrack pattern for close air support. Fire Zunis while they are still far enough away from him, then strafe with the guns." Not wanting to betray Koontz' position, they orbited just above 6000 feet, out of range of any stray 57s, off to the side of the chute. They watched as the chute hit the brush close to a Karst ridge and saw the figure of Koontz with his helmet still on scrambling up the Karst.

"Beeper, Beeper, come up voice!" The skipper called, asking Koontz to turn his survival radio, automatically activated by the ejection to the emergency beeper position, to voice transmits.

"Roger. This is Beatle One. I'm in the Karst area and climbing. I'm taking some small arms fire from below."

"Roger. We have you in sight and will provide cover. Hang on, the chopper is on the way!"

"Heaters, we're in hot." He immediately pushed his F8 into a dive, heading for the area where he had last seen the chute. Small arms fire and tracers gave him a target and he pickled a Zuni right into where it had come from, pulling off into a sharp racetrack to get back as fast as possible.

Ray, watching the skipper, followed closely and fired on more troops he saw streaming up the ridge now.

Franconi, now right behind Ray, fired twice, but felt only one Zuni leave the rack. *Shit! I've got hung ordnance.* And he pulled off. Then he realized that his cockpit was suddenly quiet and no lights were on. As he pulled out, he realized that he had had a generator failure right after firing the first Zuni. Probably the wiring in the Zuni had shorted something out. His first instinct was to pull the handle to deploy the ram air turbine (RAT) that served as an emergency generator for the F8. *Can't do that, I'll lose too much range and I can't tank without a generator.* The turbine, a big flat wheel dropped into the airstream, cost the F8

28 percent of its range. It only ran critical electrical circuits; neither ordnance switches nor the circuit for the refueling probe was on it.

"Beatle Two, this is Heater One, you're hit! Go feet wet!" Dan Prescott, looking back at the area where Koontz was down, had watched Franconi make his run, watching black smoke pour out just as the Zuni had left his port side rack. With no radio, Franconi didn't hear the call. He hated to leave the fight, but heading back over the Karst, he realized his only option was to head back to the ship and hope that he had enough fuel to make it—and hope that he could find the ship without navigation gear.

"They are getting closer. Strafe right on me!" came the frantic call from Koontz.

"Hang on. I'm rolling in again now." Prescott called.

He targeted the area where he had last seen Koontz, hoping he had climbed a little higher, and began to strafe. Wanting to linger as long as possible over the target area, he flew a low, slow pass, working the 20mm cannon over the whole area. Ray followed him, flying the same low, slow profile, carefully working his guns over the black figures pouring up the ridge toward Koontz' position.

"Good shooting. That slowed them down some. Where is the chopper?" Koontz scrambled higher, trying to keep cover between himself and the North Vietnamese.

"Beatle, this is Quick Draw. We're about one minute out. We have the Heater flight in sight. Can you pop a smoke on your position?"

Koontz thought a moment and then realized that the enemy troops knew where he was anyway. He pulled one of the smoke flares off his survival vest as he keyed his mike, "Roger. Popping smoke."

Yellowish gray smoke began to drift from behind a rock area where Koontz had hidden himself. Heavy fire immediately poured into his area as he crouched as low as possible. The first A1 rolled in, firing rockets followed by cannon. The firing slowed down at Koontz' position, but the A1 began to absorb heavy hits. The second A1 then rolled in, peppering the area as close as possible to the smoke. The big SH3 rescue helicopter moved in behind the A1s, maneuvering their machine guns to bear on the now dug-in North Vietnamese troops. Heavy return fire forced the pilot to back out of range, just away from the smoke.

Dan Prescott varied his roll in now, crossing the hill below where he thought Koontz was, as he attempted to keep fire on the area as the A1s circled back. He knew that the troops were keeping down as they strafed and moved up while they were in the pattern. The only hope was to keep constant pressure on them while the chopper came in. Ray stayed in trail, doing exactly what the skipper was doing. Koontz, during the strafing, kept moving higher, but he was running out of room as he almost scrambled up the top of a Karst pinnacle. Holding his radio up to call the helicopter, he was stunned to feel a bullet rip through his shoulder. He struggled to keep his feet, but felt the radio drop down the ridge, as control of his arm was lost. In a frantic attempt to get the helicopter in, the lead A1 came in at no more than 100 feet above the ground, firing guns and rockets. The helicopter followed, the gunner pouring fire into the area.

"Beatle, this is Angel. Can you give me a vector? We do not have you in sight." There was no response. Over the intercom the helicopter pilot screamed, "Does anyone see him?"

"Negative." Was the reply as each crewman checked in.

"Quick Draw, do you have him, over?"

"Negative, Angel. I'm rolling in for another pass and will check it out."

Reluctantly, the helicopter pilot pulled back, again out of range of the small arms fire. He saw several troops moving relentlessly up the ridge as the A1 made another run, but he could not see Koontz.

After he was hit, Koontz went into shock. He hid on the ground, hoping somehow that the A1s would drive the troops back. Through the fog of shock, he heard the A1 begin the run and then felt the pain of a hard kick to his ribs. After the kick, as he rolled over, the first troops delivered a series of rifle butts to his head and body, quickly causing him to pass out from the pain.

"This is Quick Draw One. I think they got him. I see them moving back down the ridges, looks like they're carrying him."

"Roger, this is Two. I saw the same thing."

"I am going to make one more pass over the area where the smoke was. Let's roll in together, Two, and you open up on anything below to cover me, while I do a quick 360 over that area."

"Roger One."

Quick Draw Two joined one in a loose deuce, flying down the ridge from one. As they neared the spot, he laid covering fire on the lower area of the hill, receiving only a token small arms fire in return. One orbited the area, finding it deserted. There was no hostile fire and also no sign of Koontz. He climbed up to a safe area further over the ridges and waited for his wingman to join him.

"Angel and Heaters there is no sign of him. Without radio contact I think we should call it off and go feet wet."

"Roger Quick Draw. Think we have done everything we could. Let's all go feet wet. Heater two, we're going feet wet. Mother Cow, Mother Cow, this is Heater One, holding hands with Two. We will need a drink as we go feet wet. Are you up, over?"

"Roger Heaters. We're orbiting on the Sandbox 320 just 20 off the beach at base plus eight, over."

"Mother Cow, is there a chance you could meet us at the coast? We are really thirsty."

Looking to his two crewmembers, having heard the request, they both gave him a thumbs-up. He knew that the doctrine of the det was to remain at least twenty miles off the beach, out of SAM range. Still, he knew that the F8s would not have asked unless they were in danger of flaming out.

"Roger, we'll put out the welcome mat. See you at the coast."

As they crossed the beach, CDR Prescott signaled Ray to move into close formation by waggling his wings. When he was close enough, he signaled him to give his fuel state. Ray quickly replied with four raised fingers, indicating four hundred pounds. They were tight but should just make the tanker. Although he also had about four hundred pounds, he decided to give Ray the first shot at the tanker.

As he cruise climbed with his throttle set at three thousand pounds per hour, he spotted the tanker just where he thought it would be.

"Mother Cow, we are closing on your six. We're a little tight so I would appreciate it if you could stream now."

"Roger Heaters. We deployed." Was the call as the skipper and Ray saw the drogue come out.

Now at three hundred pounds, CDR Prescott called, "Two, you plug first. Take about one thousand pounds and let me in." He hoped his nugget wingman could get in fast. It was easy to refuel when you didn't really need it. Not so easy when you were desperate.

Ray moved into the lead, as the skipper dropped back. He concentrated as hard as possible on flying good form on the tanker, and just began his move into the drogue when he heard, "Two, it will probably be easier if you put your probe out."

Shit! He quickly reached the probe toggle switch and cycled it out. With the probe out, he smoothly moved into position and easily plugged on his first pass. Pushing the hose in, he saw the green light and watched his fuel gauge begin to move up. Reaching one thousand pounds, he pulled the throttle back and disengaged quickly and moved to the right side to watch the skipper tank.

"Red Crown, this is Heater One, over." CDR Prescott called as he was watching his fuel gauge climb after successfully plugging in.

"Heater One, Red Crown, go ahead."

"Red Crown, do you have the status of Beatle Two?"

"Roger, The Barcap was vectored to pick up Beatle Two as he came feet dry. They escorted him to the first available ready deck on the America. He trapped aboard safely."

"Roger, Red Crown. Heaters out."

As soon as the skipper finished refueling, Ray went back in. As he backed off the drogue with enough fuel to make the ship, the skipper called, "Mother Cow, this is Heater One, thank you much."

After the hectic pace of the Alpha strike, entering the break at the ship should have been mundane. A VFR pattern, work to maintain the interval, fly the ball, and trap aboard. However, nothing was mundane when flying with CDR Prescott. A former Blue Angel, he missed no opportunity to showcase his skill. As he checked in with the ship, the air boss called "Charlie on arrival" for the Heater flight. Ten miles out, they had been given a green light to enter the break as quickly as they could and trap aboard immediately. The deck was ready or would be on their arrival. Pushing the nose down, he accelerated to over five hundred knots and descended to 1000 feet with Ray in tight formation. Five miles out from the ship, he motioned Ray away and rolled inverted. Ray immediately knew what he was doing and rejoined. The skipper was going to enter the break inverted and do a little show for the troops. Inverted, all the controls moved backward. To break left, the stick had to be moved to the right, but the skipper had done it so long it was like second nature to him. He pulled the nose down lower, visibility severely hampered by the gunsight, and descended to flight deck level. Screaming down the starboard side of the ship, he keyed his mike and called, "Two, fan break now!" and rolled vertical and pushed against negative G-force to cause Heater One to turn across the bow of the ship to the one-eighty position abeam. As he cleared the ship, he extended his speedbrake and pulled the throttle back, decelerating rapidly. Abeam the ship he was slow enough to raise his wing and drop the gear.

Ray, on hearing the call, turned with the skipper's inverted F8, but gained separation by pulling less on the stick. As he separated, he also put out his speed brake and decelerated, carefully monitoring his interval with the skipper. He knew that the skipper would fly a perfect break and didn't want to screw it up by getting out of position. Hearing nothing from the LSO beyond the "Roger Ball," he knew the skipper had flown his normal excellent pass. Concentrating hard, he maintained the ball centered until just before touchdown when it went slightly up. He was afraid he would bolter but was relieved to feel the cable catch. From the runout he knew it was the four wire the last one on the deck. After that there was nothing to do but taxi forward, shut down, tie down, and jump out up on the bow. Finishing with a post flight inspection of Two Twelve to check for battle damage, Ray dragged his way exhausted from the stress and heat, back to the Ready Room, his first combat mission over.

Chapter Five

MUSIC 5

Ray taxied forward after landing as directed by a yellow shirt to a spot on the bow and shut down the engine in a daze. Opening the canopy and securing it with its strap, he heard and smelled the flight deck. Loud noises of engines and the arresting gear. The smell of exhaust mixed with jet fuel and his own sweat.

Sitting in the cockpit, not moving, Airman Mears clambered up the side of 212 to put the safe pins in the ejection seat and help him unstrap. "How did it go sir?"

"Tough Mears. It was just tough. We lost Koontz from VA 18."
"What about that Lt from 123? I didn't see him trap aboard."
"He was hit but managed to land on the America."

Climbing out of the cockpit, carrying his helmet by the strap, he and Mears inspected the plane for battle damage. Satisfied that he hadn't been hit, he jogged to the island, entered through a hatch and descended down the ladder inside to the level of the Ready Room just below the flight deck.

Still wearing his torso harness, the G-suit, and survival vest he entered the Ready Room and plopped down in his chair, the marks of his oxygen mask on his face, sweat streaming down his forehead and dripping off his nose.

"Hey Ray, sign in your bird and wait for me in the Ready Room for debrief. I have to go report to CAG. Should be back in half an hour. You did a good job." Cdr. Prescott called from the flight gear locker at the back of the Ready Room.

"Aye, Aye Skipper."

Commander Prescott removed his survival vest, torso harness, and G-suit in the flight gear locker next to the Ready Room. With his survival pistol over his shoulder, he walked through the Ready Room and out into the passageway heading for the airwing spaces.

Ray wearily got up and hung his helmet in the helmet bag on the peg designated for him. Sitting on a bench, he removed his pistols, checking that the safeties were on, and removed the bandolier of bullets that he wore across his chest. Still sitting, he pulled off his camouflage green survival vest, the gray torso harness, and his green G-suit. He then hung them all on his designated peg. His pistols slung over his shoulder in their harness, he carried his two PRC 90 survival radios to a table at the end of the locker room and placed them in chargers. His flight suit had dark stains of sweat under the arms and at the neckline.

Only then did he return to the Ready Room. Twain, who was the squadron duty officer, was in the back of the Ready Room putting tapes in the music system.

"What happened Ray?" Twain asked.

"When we got to the target, I rolled in after the Skipper and dropped. There was a lot of AAA and flak but we avoided it and flew to a high perch for Mig Cap or Rescap while the A4s dropped their loads." He sighed heavily as he recalled the mission. "Koontz was flying the iron hand with Franconi from 123 escorting him. The flight got lit up by a SAM site and Koontz hung in to the last second with his shrike. He had to split-S to avoid the SAM but on his pull out he got hit by AAA, either 37s or 57s. He stayed with the plane as long as he could and punched out over some Karst ridges not far from the coast. We followed him out along with Franconi to do Rescap. He had a good chute and we saw him get out of it and run up the ridge, but the NVA immediately started swarming the place. Skipper set us up in a racetrack to keep them back. All three of us kept strafing their positions but they kept coming. Franconi got hit and was streaming black smoke. Skipper made him bingo to the nearest ready deck. The chopper came in and almost had Koontz until the NVA overran his position and the helo had to back out. They almost got him out. It really sucked." His shoulders dropped.

"When you were rolling in on the main target did you see much flak?" Twain asked.

"It was so thick I don't see how they missed us. I just had to concentrate on the target and pulling off. Feel like the Skipper and I just got lucky."

"Also, we would have run out of fuel if Frank in the whale hadn't come into the beach streaming the drogue for us. Skipper let me tank first but I know he was as low as I was or worse. Frank really saved our bacon."

"Well, scuttlebutt is that LCDR Hart has put Frank in hack for breaking protocol by entering a SAM zone," Aggie said, shaking his head.

"That really sucks."

"What sucks?" CDR Prescott asked as he returned to the Ready Room.

"LCDR Hart has put Frank Potter in hack for tanking us inside a SAM zone against protocol. He won't be able to go ashore next time we are in Cubi." Ray explained.

"I know what hack means. That does suck. It also means that no tanker pilot will ever take a risk to save our ass. I will talk to Chuck. He is not a bad guy. He is just trying to protect his people. If he won't listen, I will go to CAG.

In fact," Speaking as he thought, "think I will go to CAG and recommend Frank and his crew for the Navy Commendation Medal with combat V. Chuck won't be able to put him in hack if he is getting that medal. I want you guys to understand, Rescap is the most important mission we have. If it means we have to go below Bingo fuel to do it, so be it. Also, I think CAG will agree that if it takes breaking protocol to save one of our pilots, then so be it." He stood near his ready room chair, lost somewhat in his thought, considering the write up he would do for Frank.

"Hey Twain, notify all officers that there will be an AOM at 1800. Tell them to all bring copies of music they want to be playing as they man their aircraft," skipper said as he returned to the Ready Room. "Ray, come on up by my chair and we will debrief."

As the adrenaline rush wore off, Ray began to relax although he could not stop replaying the mission in his head. Still sitting slumped in his Ready Room chair after the debrief with the skipper, Chief Morgan approached him. "Mr. Rhodes, sorry to disturb you, but do you have a minute?" he asked politely as Ray was obviously not actively doing anything.

"Sure Chief, what's up?"

"Well sir, you know that your line division is on the flight deck for all twelve hours of flight ops and one hour before and one after."

"Yes. They work their asses off!"

"Yessir. But the boat doesn't appreciate that. Petty Officer Pearson and I work a schedule to get them all a half hour to an hour for chow in a rotation, but the damn ship chow line is sometimes an hour long. Then our guys don't get to eat. I went to the supply chief in charge of the enlisted mess and asked him if he could maybe make a special line or extend hours for flight deck personnel, which would include the ship's own Aviation Bosuns. You know the yellow shirts and the guys working fuels and cat and arresting gear. But apparently, they have enough workers to give them the time to eat. We don't. That SOB chief said that he could not change anything for our men and that he didn't think he should have to do anything for the Airwing as the men we sent him for mess duty weren't worth a shit."

"Well, there is some truth to that. We did send the worst of our sailors to them." Ray said. When the Airwing came aboard the carrier, each squadron was required to send a certain number of airmen or sailors to work in the mess or laundry. Typically, those were the enlisted men they could most afford to do without. Basically, the bottom of the barrel. "Still, we have to figure out some way to get our guys chow. I will get with LCDR Johnson and see what he can do." Ray added.

With a nod of appreciation, the chief left Ray alone with his own thoughts again. But Ray had never been one to sit around and stew over things he couldn't control nor change. So, he got up and decided to tackle one thing he knew he could contribute to and headed to the squadron maintenance office, which was a small cubicle in one of the maintenance spaces supplied to the squadron by the ship. There was a standard, small gray desk, filing cabinets filled with records on each aircraft. A bookcase full of manuals detailing maintenance repairs on every aspect of the planes was against the bulkhead.

"Preacher, do you have a minute?" LCDR James "Preacher" Johnson was the squadron maintenance office and Ray's direct boss.

"Sure Ray, or should I say Dusty per the Skipper's call sign for you?" He Pointed to the chair next across from his desk and said, "Sit down."

As he sat down, he said, "Ray is fine, Preach. Chief Morgan just came to see me and explained that our line crew is not getting enough time for chow during Flight Quarters. They schedule them for a half hour or hour, but the chow lines are so long they often have to get back on the flight deck before they can eat."

"I am aware of that problem, and we have to figure out how to solve it on our own. I went to the ship's supply officer in charge of the mess. He was no help. In fact, he was belligerent about not helping the Airedales. Complained that we sent him the worst sailors to work in the mess and what did we expect? I think it will be time for you to learn the fine art of cumshaw, Ray."

"Cumshaw, sir?"

Preacher began gesturing with his hands apart like a history professor, "From Moses' time to now and every war in between, supply and those running it have been the curse of all war fighters. So, we who fight the wars have to find a work around. Cumshaw is the navy term for going outside the system to get what you need from supply. Basically, bribe or steal what you need. Last cruise we could not get a new engine for one of our planes. I think it was Gunny Arancio who heard about the problem and was able to obtain through cumshaw an engine, which was brought to the flight deck by a helicopter. As I recall, several flight jackets and pairs of aviator sunglasses were passed to a supply chief warrant officer in exchange for his expediting our engine."

"How will that help our guys get chow? Just give the mess bosses sunglasses or flight jackets?" Ray asked.

"Nope. That won't work. They won't budge. So, what I am thinking is that we could set up an informal mess in the line shack. Have you seen Warrant Arancio's saltwater aquarium?"

"Yes. It's incredible that he can do that on the ship."

"Right." He leaned back in his seat and smirked. "If he can do that, I don't think setting up a little sandwich shop in the line shack would be a problem. When we get into Cubi next, I am going to have you go with him to get a small refrigerator to put in the line shack. We will get money from the mess, with the Skipper's blessing, to stock sandwich stuff initially. We will keep it stocked by requisitioning hams and other foodstuffs every time we help with high lining supplies."

At sea, replenishment of all stores, ammo, and even priests were done by high-lining goods from a supply ship to the carrier. Squadron personnel were required to assist. It was often known that a certain number of items such as hams and other food or snack items would disappear as the goods were passed from one sailor to the other on the way to the storerooms of the carrier.

"We will make sure that we can get our guys fed."

By 1800 the Ready Room was full. Twain, as the duty officer, was manning the tape deck in the back, ready to play whatever the skipper wanted. All pilots had brought in the songs they wanted to hear while getting ready to man aircraft for a mission.

Troy Davis, sitting in his Ready Room chair next to Ski, turned to him and said, "What difference does it make what music is played. Won't affect the flight"

"You boat school guys do not understand. At Meecheegan, when we stood under the stadium, waiting to run on the field, playing someone like state or OSU, the band played the fight song, and we were totally pumped up. That is what this is about. Skipper wants us to be pumped up by the same fight song!" Ski responded, turning to Troy and holding him by the shoulder.

"Alright men, listen up," skipper called their attention. Standing in front of his chair, turned around to face the officers he said, "I am sure you have all heard about what happened on the strike today. We lost a good man in LT Koontz. Also, a 123 bird had to land on the America and it looks like it will be struck due to battle damage. Ray and I did the best we could on Rescap. I want to emphasize the importance of doing our utmost to help with Rescap. I do not care what other mission you are on. Rescap is the most important thing we can do out here. Understood?" Hearing cumulative *Aye Ayes*, he continued. "CAG has informed us that for the remainder of this line period we will fly photo escort, A4 escort on road recce missions looking for trucks, Barcap, and Mig Cap. No more flak suppression this line period per the admiral's orders at TF 77.

In order to get max crew rest, we will stand alert five in the Ready Room in your flight gear. If the call is made to launch the alert, get your asses up and man it within five minutes. Regarding your jobs, the chiefs and warrants are going to take most of the load for your division and department jobs for this line period. Now, no more bullshit music as we man our planes for Alpha Strikes or Mig Cap, or photo escorts. We need battle music. For night Barcap, the leader can decide on the music to man aircraft. Twain, start playing the tunes. But now we are going to vote on our go-to battle music. Since we are a democracy you all get a vote but mine is the only one that will count, understood?"

"Aye Aye, sir."

"First, from Troy Davis." The Rolling Stones' "Can't get no satisfaction" blared through the speakers. "Troy, speak for yourself, we get satisfaction when we kick ass." "Light my fire" from Ray Rhodes. "Not bad. We will consider that." From Ames, "I feel good" by James Brown. "Also, something to consider." "Downtown" from Casper. "We will use that when we hit Hanoi." "Ring of Fire" by Johnny Cash from Twain. "Not bad for a redneck cowboy." "Country Road" from Preacher. "OK for night flying, not strong enough for Alpha strikes." Finally, from John Phillips, Aaron Copeland's "Fanfare for a Common Man."

The sound of horns and drums rose to a crescendo in the room. "That is perfect, Poet! We will use that to go to battle because we are a classy squadron. Should have known an ivy leaguer would have come up with something classy."

Chapter Six

CAG 6

The airwing - 14 March 1967 Over North Vietnam

Although working with the ship, the airwing operated semi autonomously with the Carrier Air Wing Commander, Cag in charge. He was an equal in rank and in all ways to the captain of the ship.. The ship operated as a runway and base while the airwing was responsible for all air operations. The ship's own air boss, normally an aviator of commander rank, was essentially the tower operator in charge of controlling the take offs and landings on the ship. However, the ship in general deferred to the airwing commander in decisions regarding missions. Every navy airwing operated under standardized carrier operating procedures (SOP) which were modified to fit their own particular aircraft and mission. The airwing made and continually revised the SOP, which ensured an efficient, orderly, and safe as possible operation around the ship and in combat. Procedures covered everything from entering the Marshall pattern for instrument approaches to tanking procedures after low fuel state bolters

Unlike the combat infantry of the army or marine corps, the CAG was expected to lead his pilots into combat. While his high-ranking counterparts made plans and monitored the operations of their troops from the relative safety of bunkers behind the lines, CAGs flew the most difficult and dangerous missions and were frequently shot down and lost.

NIGHT CAT NIGHT TRAP

Captain Everett Wilkins was happy. After twenty-one years in the navy, he still was fortunate enough to be able to do what he loved most: flying the A4 Skyhawk off an aircraft carrier. His poor counterparts in the army, full bird colonels, mainly pushed desks in their combat commands. Even the marine corps colonels seldom were in actual battles. He, on the other hand, led his men in combat as the point of the spear. Qualified in all the aircraft in the airwing, Captain Wilkins could choose any plane to fly. His choice was simple: he loved the Scooter. The tight cockpit fit him perfectly. He loved the feel of the stick, the quick roll rate of its delta wing, and the deceivingly cute look of its design. With more than two thousand hours in the A4, he could feel exactly what the aircraft could do, the limits of the airframe and engine, and all the subtle nuances of the systems. The little plane was simple and honest: it went exactly where it was pointed, stalled when it was supposed to, and recovered rapidly. On the glide path it was stable in pitch, with good engine response. If the small delta wing made it a bit wobbly in heading control while landing that was a tradeoff of high-speed roll rate against stability that he would take any time. His first fleet aircraft after receiving his wings at Whiting Field had been the propeller driven A1 Skyraider. He had liked the big old beast with its huge reciprocating engine, but as soon as the opportunity presented itself, he transitioned to jets and the then-new A4. After several tours including XO and CO of an East Coast A4 squadron, he was promoted to captain and had been selected as the commander of airwing 9, currently embarked on the USS *Adams*.

To all the men he was simply known as CAG, and any aircraft in the airwing was his to fly. He occasionally would fly one of the A1s, mainly for the memories, off the ship, but only flew the F8 Crusader and A3 Whale from the beach. He saw no reason to risk bending one of his precious airwing assets on a personal ego trip.

Captain Wilkins also chose his own missions, with the approval of the captain of the Adams. Typically, he gave himself the toughest missions. He led all the rough Alpha Strikes, but he also flew the boring night tanker hops and routine road reconnaissance flights, where targets of opportunity were attacked. Today's mission was the latter: fly down Route One just South of Vinh and hit any trucks or other targets that looked promising. Of all the flights over North Vietnam, he preferred these road recces: with no briefed target, the lead pilot had a great deal of latitude and the opportunity to bomb something that might actually make a difference to the poor grunts down south.

As his flight of two approached the coast almost even with Vinh, he looked over to his wingman. His second mission over the beach, LTJG Fredericks had moved out to the loose deuce position and begun to jink. His plane was moving jerkily and rolling too fast, like some high-speed moth. Although he had no combat experience prior to this cruise, Captain Wilkins had flown hundreds of practice missions and read every briefing book possible about flying over the beach.

"Trombone Two, this is One. Try to move it smooth and easy. Watch my movements and copy me. You don't want to bleed off too much speed." Captain Wilkins, using his personal Trombone call sign, coached Fredericks. He acquired the call sign during his first cruise on the Roosevelt in the Med. At a bar in Palma de Mallorca, he had jumped in with the band and played a few tunes on the trombone. As a navy ROTC student at the University of Nebraska in the '50s he had picked up extra money playing in a band on weekends. Ever since that night in Majorca, he was Trombone. He liked the call sign. It fit his midwestern disposition.

"Roger Lead." Fredericks responded.

He began to concentrate on moving in sequence with CAG but couldn't match the smoothness that Captain Wilkins had acquired over the years. Also from the Midwest, Fredericks had used the navy to escape from life in a small farm town in Iowa where his father owned and ran the pharmacy. Although he loved flying, he was not a natural pilot and had struggled to make it through flight training. As a result of mediocre grades, he had no choice when it came to aircraft and had been assigned to A4s as the only choice available.

Flying over the beach and flying with CAG made him nervous. Perspiration poured down from his helmet and ran into his eyes. He pushed his visor up and rubbed the moisture out with his flight glove. Of German ancestry, his eyes were bright blue in contrast to hair and brows of dark brown. His skin was pale white and his nose was thin. Probably due to the thin face, his oxygen mask never fit correctly. Dry, cold, pure oxygen blew into his eyes constantly, always irritating. Fighting to maintain position, he checked his bomb switches on and nervously scanned his instruments.

Captain Wilkins had insisted that VA 18 give him one of their new pilots, a raw nugget as first tour pilots were called, as a wingman. He wanted the opportunity to help break in the rookies. He didn't want the A4 squadrons to pamper him by wasting experienced pilots on his wing. As he watched Fredericks struggle, however, he hoped that this wingman was the worst of the group.

As they had briefed, after crossing the coastline south of Vinh, CAG put the flight in a shallow dive, descending to 8000 feet and moving the speed up to 450 knots. That provided sufficient airspeed to avoid any SAMs and from that altitude they could easily spot any trucks moving on the road or hiding nearby.

"Two, check switches hot." CAG called.

"Roger Lead." Came the response. Fredericks quickly moved his master arm switch on and selected bombs for the multiple racks. They each carried four five-hundred-pound bombs loaded with daisy cutters—bomblets which were designed to rip through trucks, guns, and men.

Captain Wilkins, checking his map for landmarks, easily found Route One. With only a few scattered clouds, visibility was almost perfect. One of few paved roads, the black asphalt was easy to spot. As they flew north parallel to the side of the road an occasional 37mm or

57mm anti-aircraft gun would open up on them, bursting below their altitude. There was no SAM activity.

For several miles they flew, seeing no signs of life except for the water buffalo and farmers working in the rice paddies. They also heard little activity in their headsets. No other flights were up on their frequency. Radars and SAMs were relatively quiet. Overall, it was a slow day over the beach.

Flying a loose wing, Fredericks was fascinated by the lush, green peaceful countryside of rice paddies contrasted with occasional lines of trees or small tropical forests. The road ran past small villages. The only signs of war were a few hulks of bombed out trucks and craters occasionally in and around the road. No vehicles except for oxcarts moved on the road due to the constant threat of bombs.

"Trombone Lead, this is Two. I thought I saw something in the trees on the West side of the road that we just passed." Fredericks had spotted what he thought was a truck hidden under the trees. The Vietnamese would hide in trees during the day, only running the road at night without lights.

"Roger Two. Let's go back for another look." As they turned back to check the grove, CAG pushed the nose down and took the flight down to 6000 feet in order to get a better look. As they circled back, he saw square shapes camouflaged among the growth. What was obviously the side of a truck was uncovered in signs that it had been hastily hidden.

"Two, I have at least one truck and what looks like a truck park down at two o'clock low, just west of the road."

"Roger Lead." LTJG Fredrick's began to excitedly scan the cockpit, gripping the stick tighter. Perspiration flowed heavily down his face and he finally unhooked the right side of his oxygen mask in disgust as the blowing in his eyes began to distract him. For at least the fifth time he checked his bomb switches and was again comforted to find them armed. In a quick movement he reached out with his left hand

and touched the picture of his wife and new baby that he had carefully taped to the instrument panel.

"Two, I am going to roll in when we cross the road. Wait until I start pulling out to roll in. Pickle two bombs and we'll pull off and see how we did."

"Roger Lead." Fredericks moved in a little tighter on Trombone One in order to get better position for his own bomb run. As they crossed the road, CAG broke left and pushed the nose down to a 45 degree angle. He smoothly and quickly centered the bombsight on the exposed side of the one truck and watched the altimeter unwind. At 4500 feet he hit the pickle switch twice, releasing two bombs and pulled back hard on the stick. Approaching 600 knots in the dive, the little jet required at least 1500 feet to pull out. The Vietnamese gunners had set a perfect flak trap. As soon as they saw the bombs release, they began firing. Completely ignoring the flight of the plane, they merely fired into the space through which they knew any bombing aircraft had to fly.

Seeing the nasty blasts flashing around his cockpit, Captain Wilkins knew they had been trapped. Frantically jinking, he hit his pickle two more times to drop any remaining bombs. If an anti-aircraft round hit a bomb there would be no chance to escape or eject. As he continued the pull out, he called, "Two, break it off and pull out. This is a flak trap. I repeat, break off, break off!"

For Fredericks in Trombone Two it was too late. Committed to his dive and concentrating on working the bombsight toward the target, he never saw the gunfire. Just above his drop point he flew into a deadly crossfire of 57mm guns. As he prepared to press the bomb pickle, one round burst under the belly, setting off one of the bombs, almost vaporizing the aircraft. The force of the explosion instantly killed Fredericks although the ejection seat was fired in the blast and carried its now dead human cargo clear of the falling, burning debris that had been Trombone Two. Working as advertised, the pilot was separated from the seat and the parachute deployed automatically. In sequence, a lanyard connected to the seat pan activated the emergency beeper. As Fredericks' body floated toward the ground, the beeper sounded on guard channel for anyone within range to hear.

Captain Wilkins heard the beeper and knew Fredericks must have ejected. He felt his airframe shake as it flew through the shrapnel. A solid thud somewhere in the left wing root violently drove the plane up and hard right. Applying left rudder and as much aileron as possible, he stopped the right roll and continued to pull. Almost simultaneously a fire warning light began to flash and several other warning lights came on.

Keying the mic again, he called "Trombone Two this is the lead. Do you read?" There was no response. He had no feedback from the radio in his helmet and suspected that, in addition to everything else, he had a radio failure. Looking in his left mirror he saw smoke pouring out of the wing. Checking gauges, he noted that the generator was still functioning, the engine was running at a high exhaust gas temperature, and he was losing hydraulic pressure. As he pulled up above the flak he headed west toward the sea, hoping to make it feet wet prior to ejecting. Struggling, he rolled the aircraft again to the right in hopes of seeing Fredericks. He was sickened to see black smoke billowing from what appeared to be aircraft wreckage. There was no sign of the parachute. Switching his radio to the emergency position, CAG broadcast "This is Trombone One broadcasting in the blind on guard. A flight of two A4s twenty miles South of Vinh on Route One. My wingman is down, and his status is unknown. I am hit and trying to make it feet wet."

Making lazy oval patterns over Red Crown, Dick Knowles, upon hearing the transmission on guard, was instantly alert, quickly shaking off the lethargy he had felt flying a solo Barcap. His wingman had gone down on startup and there had been no spare due to a shortage of aircraft. To make matters worse, after the catapult launch his wing light had stayed on, indicating that the variable incidence wing had not properly locked after he had lowered it. He had cycled it several times, but the light had stubbornly refused to go out. Limited to 220 knots, he had elected to proceed on to the Barcap station and at least give the impression to the North Vietnamese monitoring the radar and radios that the fleet was protected.

"Red Crown this is Heater Seven, did you copy Trombone One?"

"Roger, Heater Seven. We tried his tactical frequency and got no response. We will try on guard now." Red Crown was the call sign for the destroyer stationed far north on Yankee Station just off Haiphong. Its purpose was to provide radar coverage early warning of any potential Mig attacks to the fleet as well as the rescue of downed pilots who made it to the ocean.

"Roger Red Crown. Give me a steer to his position. Do you have him on radar?"

"Negative Heater Seven. We will give you a steer to his reported position. Come left heading Two Four Three."

"Roger. Two Four Three." Knowles responded.

"Trombone One, this is Red Crown on Guard. Do you read, over?"

There was no reply. In Trombone One, CAG was fighting to control the damaged aircraft. After the loss of all hydraulic systems, he had extended the stick with the manual pull-out that allowed the A4 to be flown without hydraulic assist. Using all his strength, he was barely able to keep the nose up and the wings somewhat level. Unknown to him, his transmissions were going out, but his receiver had been knocked out, preventing him from hearing Red Crown's response.

Looking out of his mirrors he could see that the fire was worsening. Despite his efforts, the plane was losing altitude. Initially he had been able to coax it up to almost ten thousand feet. Now he was descending below seven thousand. To make matters worse, in his struggle to maintain control, the aircraft had wandered to a more northerly heading, making it even more difficult to reach the relative safety of the ocean.

Passing four thousand feet, as it became obvious that he would not make it to the water, Captain Wilkins quickly went through the ejection checklist. Making sure that his straps were as tight as possible, he removed his knee board from his leg and placed it on the console next to the windscreen. Studying the ground as he passed three thousand feet, he found himself over a coastal mountain range with a large tropical forest. With no hesitation, thinking that there might be a chance to evade capture in the woods, he positioned himself in the seat and reached up with both hands, pulling the ejection face curtain. Although his hands were only off the stick for a fraction of a second, the aircraft immediately rolled hard right. As a result, when the seat fired, he was shot out at a forty-five-degree angle.

The rocket-powered ejection seat pushed Captain Wilkins out and away from the rolling aircraft on a low arc. In perfect sequence, air bladders activated, forcing him out of the seat. As he separated from the seat, a lanyard connected to the parachute was pulled, activating the chute and the emergency beeper stowed in the seat pan. A small charge explosively opened the canopy of the parachute, allowing it to cushion the descent.

Due to the low altitude of the ejection and the angle at which the seat fired, CAG only had two swings in the parachute before landing in a huge tropical tree. The canopy of the chute stuck in the very top branches of the tree, leaving him dangling some 80 feet above the ground. In the combination of shock and adrenaline rush from the ejection, he reached to the left side of his torso harness for the razor-sharp shroud cutter tool used to cut away the chute. Fortunately, he looked down before beginning to cut and realized, contrary to training doctrine, that ridding himself of the parachute was not his first priority.

Turning to the heading provided by Red Crown, Dick Knowles cycled the wing another time, willing the incidence lock light to go out. If the wing were not locked, exceeding 250 knots or pulling more than two Gs would make the wing come off. Supposedly when the wing came off the pilot would most likely be instantly killed by a negative G-force capable of breaking his neck. The separation of the wing from the fuselage at high speeds would create a snapping motion in the cockpit.

"Heater Seven, this is Red Crown. Your steer now Two Two One. The Big Look aircraft has reported two beeper signals south of Vinh. Contact Big Look now on Three Two One point Three."

"Roger Red Crown. Switching to 321.3." The lock light remained on. In frustration, Knowles took his survival knife out of the scabbard on the front of his torso harness and pushed the end of the blade into the plastic cover of the light until the bulb popped and finally the light was out. He then reached to his right and changed the channel of his radio.

"Big Look, Big Look, this is Heater Seven. What do you have, over?"

"Roger Heater One. This is Big Look. We have two emergency beepers broadcasting south of Vinh. Believe that to be Trombone flight. Squawk Ident and we will give you a steer." The Big Look aircraft was an air force EKC135 outfitted with massive antennae and radars to monitor all activity in North Vietnam. The relatively weak portable survival radios and beepers were easily picked up by their sophisticated equipment. Using radio direction finding equipment, they could provide rough vectors to downed pilots.

"Roger Big Look. Squawking Ident. Do you have contact with Trombone?" Dick asked.

"Negative Heater. Neither beeper has come up voice. We have you in radar contact. Now steer Two One Eight for the nearest beeper. Suggest you increase your speed to 450 knots."

"Roger Big Look. Heading Two One Eight. Increasing speed at this time." Dick had pushed the speed up to 250 knots, hoping the wing would stay on. He had heard of two accidents where the wing had come off. One in the break at Cecil Field and one at an air show off

Rota, Spain. Both pilots had perished. Now he increased the throttle tensely waiting for the wing to come off. Wondering if he would get a warning or if it would just come off and crush him with negative Gs.

Sweat got in his eyes as he watched his speed go past 300 to 400 then .92 Mach, about 500 knots. When the wing did not come off, he was convinced that the warning light was faulty, not the wing lock.

In the tree, CAG had made an appraisal of his situation. Checking his body parts, he found that he was relatively unscathed from the ejection. Except for scratches from the branches as he had crashed through and a pain from the area of his left ankle, which he thought had probably hit something on the way out of the aircraft, he was in good shape.

The parachute seemed to be firmly fixed in the tree, so he had no immediate worry of falling. Looking down, he seemed to be relatively well hidden from searchers looking up. The tree he was in was one of the tallest in the tropical forest. The thick growth of lower-level trees and bushes almost completely prevented anyone below from seeing him. He was tempted to pull out his survival radio and attempt contact but decided that the risk of dropping it was too great. If he lost the radio, he would have little chance of getting picked up. Reaching out with his right leg and foot he tried to swing himself to the branches near the center of the tree. Even at this height, the trunk was massive. He could touch the tips of a branch with his foot, but there was nothing to hook onto to pull himself over.

As Dick Knowles approached the coast, hearing the Rescap aircraft check in with their flight, he eased back on the throttle hoping to conserve fuel long enough to hold over any downed pilots until they arrived. While a flight of four A4s had been launched and should arrive on site within thirty minutes, the rescue helicopter and its A1 escorts could take up to an hour. Flying the heading provided by the Big Look EKC135, he rolled from side to side scanning the jungle below for any sign of a parachute. He first spotted black smoke and the remains of

CAG's aircraft in a clearing. Then, about a mile to the Northeast, he spotted the chute in a tall tree. Apparently in the ejection the pilot had been shot out at an angle keeping separation from the crashed A4.

Maintaining 10,000 feet, Knowles set up a racetrack pattern a mile in the opposite direction from the crash site, hoping searchers would think that he was over the downed pilot. Now flying at 250 knots, maximum endurance to save fuel, he smoothly jinked back and forth to keep the anti-aircraft gunners from getting a good bead on him.

From his position in the tree, CAG saw the F8 fly over and continue. When he first flew by, he thought that the pilot had not seen him, but when Knowles started orbiting about two miles south of him he realized he was flying an offset to keep the NVA from finding him.

"Big Look, Big Look, this is Magic flight. A flight of four A4s on Rescap for the pilot down south of Vinh."

Knowles was relieved to hear that Commander Rob Spooner, CO of VA 11 was leading the Rescap effort from the Adams. Magician, as he was known, was a solid pilot and known for his willingness to take any mission no matter how tough.

"Magician, this is Heater Zero Seven. I have sight of one chute. No one answers on guard. I am orbiting nearby. Suggest you get a vector from Big Look to my position"

"Roger Heater, will do. Big Look Big Look, this is Magic One. Request vectors to the Heater aircraft."

"Roger Magician, steer heading 238. Be advised, there is potential SAM activity in the area once you go feet dry."

"Roger. Magic One out."

Hearing the possibility of SAMs in the area, Rick Knowles eased his F8 into a climb, still maintaining 250 knots to conserve fuel. At 20000 feet he would have a much better chance of evading any SAMs.

From his perch he could see trucks loaded with troops pulling up near the downed A4. The soldiers immediately dispersed in all directions looking for the pilot. As he watched, he searched for the second

A4 but was unable to find it. Vaporized by the bomb blast, there was not much left of it to find.

Suddenly in his headset he heard the *deedle deedle* of a SAM radar on his ALQ 100 gear. First in low pitch it now began *deedle deedle* in high pitch indicating that a SAM had been launched.

Immediately Knowles pitched the nose down and hit the burner to get enough maneuvering speed to dodge the SAM. Following the strobe light on his consul he quickly spotted the missile flying at him. Waiting until the last moment, he did a high G barrel roll and the SAM flew by detonating once it was well past him. Scanning the ground, he picked up the mobile van that housed the SAM radar and, charging his guns, immediately dove on the site. Then, 37mm guns opened up on him as he dove. He put the nose of the plane with the piper of the gunsight on the SAM site and fired a mixture of armor piercing and high explosive shells.

Pulling off, he saw the radar van now burning. Having burned much of his fuel load on the dash down from Red Crown, afraid that the Rescap flight would not find the chute, and now having spent about 500 pounds of fuel attacking the SAM he pulled the throttle back and slowed down to the maximum endurance speed.

When the fuel gauge went below 2000 pounds, he decided to stay until he could make it out to the ocean and hope to find a tanker. But 2000 pounds came and went. He then decided to go as low as 1000 pounds and hope that he could coast out to feet wet before ejecting. He knew the Rescap had a much better chance of success if he directed them to the chute.

"Magician, this is Heater Zero Seven. I am low fuel. What is your ETA?"

"Heater, hang on as long as you can. We are about five out and have a buddy store orbiting."

"Roger that. Any chance that Texaco could come to me. Not sure I can make it feet wet."

"Roger. Will do. Keep the site marked. We will see you in five."

At that moment, a black puff of anti-aircraft burst about 1000 feet below and to the port side of the F8. Apparently the NVA had been listening and were letting him know they were there. To reach that altitude, the AAA gun had to be an 85. While radar guided, they were largely ineffective. Armed only with sidewinder anti-aircraft missiles and 20mm guns and at a low fuel state, Knowles knew that he could not take on the gun. He just kept jinking and varying his altitude while the gun would fire sporadically. Finally, with almost no fuel on the gauge, Magic flight arrived, and Knowles led them to the chute. Plugging in to the accompanying A4 Buddy stores tanker, he took on fuel while the tanker led him feet wet, setting up an orbit off the coast in case the Rescap flight needed him.

With enough fuel to make it back to the ship, Knowles left the area. Magic flight set up bombing runs over the downed A4, scattering the troops and setting the trucks on fire. When the Rescap helo arrived, the A1s took over, liberally hosing down with their cannons anything in the area that might remotely threaten the helo. The helo crewman descended on a jungle penetrator to CAG, hooked him up while cutting away the chute. While still dangling from the cable of the penetrator, the crewman and CAG were hauled aboard the helo as it made its way feet wet, another routine Rescap for the helo and A1s.

Chapter Seven

CUBI 7

"Sir, can I see you for a minute?" Chief Lester, knocking gently on the stateroom door, stood in the passageway outside. He was dressed in the tropical khaki uniform with an open collar. With almost thirty years in the navy, his brown hair was starting to turn gray, his stomach was showing the effects of the good and greasy cooking in the chief's mess, but he carried himself well and looked neat in his uniform. In his right hand he carried a covered black metal file with the numbers 207 stenciled in gold.

Recognizing the voice of his leading chief, CDR Prescott said, "Come on in." When Chief Lester opened the door and entered, he gestured to his neat bunk. "Sit down. What's on your mind?"

"Sir, I thought you should see this." He handed him the file, the maintenance log of Heater 207. "Look at Mr. Knowles' entry and what we found after his Rescap of CAG."

After opening the file and reading for a few moments, CDR Prescott said, without looking up, "Damn! Dick not only flew that mission solo, but he flew the whole thing with a bad wing light. Chief, I guess you know what happens if the wing comes off?"

"Yessir. I was at Cecil Field when that air force exchange officer lost his wing in the break. That's why I thought you should see this. Apparently, he got tired of seeing the light and broke the bulb. I'm sure he had to exceed the wing speed over the beach, that's why he writes that it had an apparently faulty warning light. He knew the wing stayed on above 250 knots. Also, he only had about 300 pounds of fuel when he trapped. There were no tankers up due to the divert to Danang of the whole airwing. He almost ran himself out of gas helping CAG." Chief Lester added.

"Chief, thanks for bringing this to my attention. Let me keep this log. I want to show it to CAG I'll get it back to you tomorrow." Standing up, he reached out to shake his hand.

"Yessir. No problem." Their meeting obviously over, he said, "Sir, may I be excused? I need to get back to maintenance. We have to get the birds ready to fly off tomorrow."

"Right Chief. That's more important than any combat mission. You are dismissed, and thanks again."

"Aye, Aye sir." Turning, he opened the door and walked out. CDR Prescott picked up his room phone and quickly dialed a number.

"CAG, this is Dan Prescott. Hope I am not disturbing you, but could I come by your room? I have something to show you." Receiving an affirmative answer from Captain Wilkins, with the log in his hand he left the room, walking down the passageway to CAG's larger stateroom. It was on the same level, nearer midships.

When he knocked, he heard CAG's familiar voice. "Come on in, it's open." The stateroom was only slightly larger than his own but had room for two chairs. There was, however, a small office with a desk and two additional chairs through a door to the right of the wardrobe. The room was perfectly neat, painted in the military gray and green. The only personal touch was a picture of CAG's family on the desk. CAG was seated at the desk with his injured left foot, wrapped, resting on the second desk chair. Crutches were leaning against the chair. An open bottle in his hand, he was refilling a glass as CDR Prescott entered.

A pen and a partly written letter lay on the desk. Gesturing to one of the chairs in the stateroom, he said, "Drag a chair over, Dan. You want a scotch? I'm only taking it for medical purposes. Rookie Doc's orders."

"Yessir, I wouldn't turn down a drink. Of course, for medical purposes. I've had a little cough." Pulling a chair near Captain Wilkins, he coughed twice quietly, proving his point. He watched CAG pour two ice cubes from a large glass into a drink tumbler and then fill it with scotch. CAG then handed it to him.

"Thanks. I see you'll do anything to get a Purple Heart. How's the ankle?" Dan Prescott asked.

"Just shitty enough that I can't make the fly-off. I thought about bouncing one of the E1 boys out of their seats or riding the Whale in, but I decided it won't hurt me to ride this tub in. I have to stay on the crutches for the whole time in port, but it is just a sprain, and I should be up by the time we get back out of the line."

Noting the scratches on his face, CDR Prescott said, "Those scratches give you character. Makes it look like you lost a sword fight. What happened?" He had heard the story that had been going around the airwing, but he wanted to hear it from the man himself.

"Dan, I fucked up and got that young Fredricks killed or at best captured. I flew us right into a flak trap. I got hit on the pullout and he got it at the pickle point. I briefly heard a beeper after he got hit, but he never came up voice. Nobody ever heard from him and the gooks won't tell anybody anything." Indicating the paper on the desk, he continued. "I have just been writing the letters that we all hate to write to his wife and parents. What a fucking waste!"

"I know exactly what you mean." He paused a moment long enough to let the memories of the letters he had to write over the years remind him they're still there, but not long enough to let the memories overcome him. "What happened to you?"

"I tried to make it to the water, but it was obvious she wasn't going to make it. That reliable scooter carried me as far as she could, but she just took too many hits, and I knew I was about to lose control. I saw a thick tropical forest just south of Vinh and decided that was my only chance to evade. Everything else around there is heavily populated. I set up for the ejection and pulled the seat handle with my left hand, keeping my right hand on the stick. When I punched, as soon as my hand left the stick, the plane rolled hard, and I went out at an angle like an artillery shell. The seat worked perfectly. If it hadn't, I was too low to do anything about it. I got about two swings in the chute and crashed down through a tree. The branches got my face. Thank God I had my visor down. The chute caught in the top of the tallest fucking tree in the whole forest, and I was left dangling over the other trees. I was lucky as hell!" He exhaled in relief. Or perhaps it was disbelief. Taking a long drink of the scotch, he continued, "I was lucky to get shot out at an angle and lucky to land in the tree. The ejection took me well away from the crash and you know the gooks were looking for me to be somewhere near that site. The tree hid me from any searchers on the ground and made it easy for Dick to spot my chute. The rescue chopper was a little afraid of pulling the chute into his blades, but it was really stuck in that tree and no threat of getting sucked up."

"How did the gooks get you?" CDR Prescott asked, knowing CAG wanted to talk about it. It would obviously be the topic of future airwing intelligence briefings, but he wanted to know personally.

"I have gone over it in my mind time after time. I fell for a sucker trap. I don't know what I could have done differently and I'm not sure I would do anything differently in the future, but I got suckered. We were cruising down route one. Fredericks spotted what looked like a truck as we went by a grove of trees. We circled back and I saw it. One side of what seemed to be a truck was just slightly exposed under the trees. It looked like it had been hastily camouflaged. Whoever had done it hadn't quite gotten the whole truck covered. Looking deep in the trees there appeared to be other square-like shapes. I thought we had found a truck park. I set up to make the first run-in, telling Fredricks to follow me. I guess in the future I would make the run and have the wingie ready to cover me and then have him go in while I covered."

"That might work," Prescott interjected, "but usually it is better to hit them hard and fast before they get ready."

"Yeah, I know. That's why this is so damned hard. The fuckers are good. I have to hand it to them. They keep us guessing. Anyway, as I said before, I made my run, pickled on the dummy truck. They had their guns set up perfectly. I was caught in the crossfire on the pullout. There was no way I could avoid flying through it. They knew exactly where I would be. With Fredricks I assume he got hit at the release point. As soon as I saw the flak I called for him to pull out, but I guess it was just too late. The bastards were smart enough to let me fly through and then blast both of us at the same time." Now looking away from Prescott, his eyes heavy with burden, he added "You know, they don't make any attempt to track you. They just fill the sky where you have to fly with flak. I am sure they had the release point dialed in. They waited until poor Fredricks was committed, then opened up. Like shooting ducks coming in for the decoy. I let the kid down and lost two of Bob Jeffries' precious A4Es. What a dumb ass!" He drained the rest of his drink and then refilled his glass from the bottle. "Anyway, what do you have there? You wanted to see me about something." He motioned to the log in CDR Prescott's lap.

Clearing his voice, he said, "This is the log of Two Zero Seven, the plane Dick Knowles was flying when he came in on your Rescap."

"I hate to admit it, Dan, but I owe that little fighter puke. Without him I doubt they would have found me." CAG enjoyed Dick Knowles' bantering and the constant teasing that went on between the attack and fighter pilots. "What's in the log?"

Opening the log, CDR Prescott handed it to him with the latest entry visible. "Sir, I am sure you remember from your F8 check-out how critical the wing lock is."

"Damn right! They drilled into us that we better get that wing down and locked before 220 knots or the sucker would come off, leading, if I am not wrong, to instant death."

"That's right. If the wing comes off, the negative G-force will almost undoubtedly kill the pilot. It is a serious downing gripe. Getting back to Dick, we didn't have any planes to cover Barcap and neither did 123 because the first launch was diverted. Dick's wingman went down on start-up, so he went up alone. Off the cat, he couldn't get the wing warning light to go out. If you read the write-up, he kept his speed down and cycled the handle several times, but never got the light to go out. Since there was no one else to do it, he apparently decided to go on up to the Barcap at 220 knots, and fly the hop anyway, hoping nothing would happen. When he heard that you and Fredricks were down, he asked Red Crown to vector him to your position. I got that from the Red Crown tapes. Apparently, he was maintaining 220 knots because an air force Big Look airplane asked him to speed up and he told them he was unable."

"So he chugged in over the beach at 220 knots," CAG furrowed his brows as he looked at the log.

"Not exactly. In order to get to you in the time he did he had to be going at least 500 knots. Think he eased the speed up and then decided the light was bad, realizing he needed to get to you ASAP."

"Hey, when he got near me, he took on a SAM site. I heard the SAM go off and warned him. He called back that he had it and had some business to take care of. I couldn't see, but it sounded to me like he strafed the site. He sure as hell didn't do that at 220 knots."

"Then, he held over you for as long as possible. He went way below bingo and was almost certainly going to flame out before he got feet wet. He might have been able to glide to the water, but it would have been real dicey. Red Crown said he called them and told them that he was going to eject and to fix the position. Spooner and his wingman arrived just in the nick of time with the buddy store. As it was, they tanked over the beach while the Magician took on another SAM. Dick told me that part, but none of the rest. He gave Spooner all the credit, saying he really had big balls to take on the SAM site with bombs."

"God damn! If anybody had big balls it was little Dickie! Spooner did a great job for me, but I can't believe what Knowles did. To sit there and watch your fuel go down below feet wet. I don't know if I could do that for someone." CAG leaned back in his seat and glanced at the ceiling. "Now I really owe him. Guess I'll have to buy him a bottle when we get in. What does he drink?"

"CAG, I brought this to you because I thought maybe a Silver Star would be appropriate. It certainly was bravery above and beyond."

"Damn right! I'll endorse it but understand that they probably will play politics and kick it down to something lesser. They'll say that he just did it because of me, because CAG was down. If it had been a JG he saved, then we might have a chance. Still, you and I both know he would have done the same thing for anyone, but that's probably not the way the desk pushers will see it."

"I know. Still, he deserves the Silver Star for this a lot more than I did for lucking into a Mig." Dan Prescott insisted.

"I don't disagree with you, but you and I don't write the rules. Write it up as well as you can and let's see what we can get." Changing the subject, he said, "This was a really shitty line period. I am glad it's over. We lost Scott, Koontz captured, and now Fredricks. Plus, we lost my plane and three others so shot up they may never fly again. You were here last cruise; will it get better?"

"CAG, I hope we have seen the worst, but I am afraid if the politicians don't let us hit some decent targets, if McNamara doesn't drop this progressive involvement, that it is just going to get worse and worse. We are just cannon fodder as long as we fly into this AAA and SAM environment. We need to cut off their supply. Bomb and mine the ports, cut the roads from China. Then we need to hit the AAA hard until we knock them on their ass, and they run out of ammo.

Then, and only then, can we go after some of the hard targets in the infrastructure."

"Dan, I couldn't agree with you more, but the powers that be don't listen to us. Sometimes, especially when I am writing these letters,"—picking the pen up and dropping it on the paper for emphasis— "I don't think there is one fucking target worth our men or our planes. But we chose to be warriors. Warriors for our country. Serving our country. Our job is to do what our political bosses tell us to do to the best of our ability. We just have to hope and pray they know what they are doing." Waving his hand, he added, "Now get out of here and quit drinking all my booze. I need to write these letters and get some rest. Doctor's orders."

"Aye, aye sir. Thanks for the drink." CDR Prescott drained the rest of his drink, set the glass down, stood up, and walked out of the room.

Streaking in from the west, down runway 24 at Cubi Point Naval Air Station, Philippines, the two flights of four F8s each made an impressive sight. Barely 100 feet above the ground, the planes were tucked into perfect diamonds with the second flight only about 50 feet in trail and slightly offset from the first. Even from a distance the engines could be heard. As they got closer, a distinctive whine signaled knowledgeable observers that the speed was in excess of five hundred knots since only the F8 oil cooler door opened at high speed made that noise. Visually, it was obvious that they were entering the break at an extremely high rate of speed. Racing in from the Adams on the traditional fly-off after a line period, they had beaten VF123 and were the first aircraft from CVW Nine to arrive. The Black Wasps of VF 188 were back at Cubi. As the first flight reached the end of the runway, the leader suddenly pitched straight up, hitting the afterburner as soon as he was clear of the flight and continuing straight up. The effect was chilling. Suddenly the first diamond was now an inverted triangle, seemingly flying leaderless.

It was just the effect CDR Prescott had hoped for when he had briefed his pilots on the break. A special Missing Man for his friend and skipper, CDR Scott Huggins. Normally, a Missing Man was flown in echelon, with the number two aircraft pitching out of the formation and the flight continuing with a gap to honor the lost colleague. However, since CDR Huggins had been their leader, Dan Prescott thought that the leader should be the Missing Man as they flew into Cubi.

The seven remaining aircraft continued in formation into the break at the far end of the runway. The remaining three aircraft of the original first diamond, now led by LCDR Knowles, rolled hard ninety degrees at an interval of about two seconds with Ray Rhodes on the right wing breaking last. Taking interval on Rhodes, LCDR Ferguson led the second flight in a spectacular diamond fan break, with all the aircraft smoothly rolling ninety degrees to the left in formation, gaining landing interval only by varying the amount of Gs pulled during the maneuver. As the fan opened, Joe Ames, flying in the slot, or bottom of the diamond, smoothly moved outboard of Kowalski on the right wing in order to give him space to complete the break. The execution was nearly perfect. Only a slight bobble by Ames as he moved from the slot during the fan break kept it from being perfect. Still, only a trained and highly critical eye would have noted anything but perfection. Everyone watching was highly impressed. Even an F4 crew, at the Cubi flight line preparing to take a plane out to the Kennedy on Yankee Station shook their heads in admiration. The VF 188 maintenance crew on duty at Cubi cheered enthusiastically as their pilots showed their stuff. On the flight line, the other squadron maintenance men also applauded and flashed thumbs-up to their 188 counterparts.

Showing the skill of his days as a solo with the Blue Angels, CDR Prescott returned at an impressive high speed, extremely low altitude entrance into the break. Just barely above the runway and off to one side, when he pulled the nose up prior to rolling into the break, his jet blast threw up a cloud of dust. As the aircraft landed, they formed into sections and waited in the area just off the runway for CDR Prescott prior to taxiing. After landing, he taxied to the front of the line where Rhodes, his wingman, waited. In section formations of leaders and wingmen, they then taxied to the carrier flight line near the dock where the Adams would tie up. As they taxied in, VF 123 entered the break in a nine-plane echelon fan. Although impressive, it did not compare with the dramatic return to Cubi of the Black Wasps.

At the flight line watching them taxi in was Commander Richard Scampi. The only possible replacement for CDR Huggins, CDR Scampi had only six weeks of refresher training in the F8 at the Replacement Air Group, VF 124, at Miramar when the Huggins ramp strike occurred. He had been rushed into Field Carrier Landing Practice to get ready for the carrier. After almost night and day practicing of FCLPs with the VF 124 LSOs, CDR Scampi had been sent out with the first available Carrier Qualification Detachment operating on the USS *Hancock*. With priority in the pattern, he had quickly requalified and was on his way to Cubi Point and VF 188 the next day. As the only available F8 experienced, command selected officer to replace Commander Huggins; it was essential to get him out to the squadron as quickly as possible. With one tour as squadron ops officer for an East Coast squadron, he had made two cruises to the Mediterranean in Crusaders. Knowing a combat tour was essential for his career, he had lobbied hard during a Washington shore duty tour on Navair Staff to get assigned to a West Coast squadron bound for Westpac, the Tonkin Gulf, and glory. There were some who avoided combat but for Fighter Pilots there was little chance of promotion without combat experience. Of medium height, he worked hard to keep himself in excellent physical condition, running whenever the opportunity presented itself. In contrast to his hard drinking, hard partying colleagues, he believed in maintaining personal discipline at all times. With regular features, short sandy brown hair thinning slightly at a widow's peak, a strong jaw and straight nose, he would have been considered attractive. Originally

Italian on his father's side, his family had been in the United States for several generations. Only a slightly dark complexion gave any indication of Latin origins. While most of the junior officers and some of his senior contemporaries let their hair grow well beyond that mandated by naval regulations, he kept his neatly trimmed, with sideburns precisely cut midway up the ear.

As the aircraft taxied in, he waited patiently, chatting with the VF 188 maintenance check crew stationed at Cubi. When CDR Prescott taxied to the line, stopped, and shut down the engine, Richard Scampi walked over to the aircraft and waited below the cockpit. Saluting sharply, he said, "Richard Scampi, reporting aboard as ordered, sir."

Handing his helmet to the plane captain and pulling the fore and aft cap from a pocket in the leg of his flight suit, Dan Prescott returned the salute, stuck out his hand, and said, "Welcome aboard. I'm Dan Prescott. I got the word from AirPac yesterday that you were coming, but I didn't think you'd make it this fast. Glad to see you. How did the boys look in the break?"

"They were really shit hot! Just a slight bobble in the second diamond fan, but I have never seen a more impressive break! Looks like you have a squadron of real pilots. That break looked like something out of your days with the Blues."

"Richard, is that what you like to be called?" Receiving a nod in the affirmative, he continued. "I want to introduce you to the guys. We really have a great bunch of kids. Some of the best nuggets I have ever seen, and our second tour guys are first rate. Come on over and meet them." Together they walked to the line shack where the other pilots were already filling out the maintenance log.

As they walked in, Joe Ames yelled over to them, "Hustle it up Skipper, we want to get to the bar!" Although his hair was still fairly long, he had shaved, and his flight suit looked reasonably clean. He wore a sweat-stained "piss cutter" fore and aft cap that hadn't been to the cleaners since purchased. His contemporaries referred to the cover as old scuzzy, which he took as a compliment. As usual, he lit a cigarette immediately after climbing out of the cockpit and held the almost finished butt in his right hand.

"Hold your horses Aimless. We have a little business to take care of first. Gents, I want to introduce our new XO." Pointing to CDR Scampi, he said, "This is Commander Richard Scampi. Even though he is an East Coast Puke, he comes highly recommended." Walking down the line of pilots, he introduced each one individually to CDR Scampi, stopping to chat for a while with Dick Knowles.

"Dick, the XO is another one of your Boat School alumni, although I would guess he was gone before you got there. What class were you, Richard?"

"I was class of '54. I went to Pensacola straight after I graduated. What class were you, Dick?"

"Sir, I was '58. I just missed you."

"Richard, Dick is the Ops O. He does a great job for me and can fly almost as well as I do, right Dick?"

"Skipper, you know I could have your ass if I wanted to, but in deference to your age and seniority and my future fitness reports, I allow you to win, sir." Knowles responded.

CDR Scampi laughed at the comment and said, "I hope you will have the same deference for me."

Before Dick Knowles could respond they were interrupted by the high-speed approach of the navy-blue jeep emblazoned with the large letters OOD in white on the hood. As it drew near, they could see a LTJG in tropical khakis holding on for dear life as a full captain wearing a tropical white uniform drove the jeep with abandon through the flight line, screeching to a halt near them. As it stopped, the captain pulled his uniform hat out of the back seat, put it on and started for them with a scowl. CDR Prescott immediately turned to Dick Knowles and began to yell, "Knowles, if I ever see you pull a stunt like that again with one of my airplanes, I will...."

"Danny boy," the captain interrupted. "Can the bullshit! I know you were flying the lead. If that hadn't been such a shit-hot break I would have all your wings, including yours!" He pointed to the wings on CDR Scampi's khakis, indicating that, even though he obviously had not been flying, he would have been guilty by association.

Captain William S. Butler was an imposing figure. With his cover on, in the white uniform, he appeared much taller than his height of six feet. His left breast, below the Gold Wings of naval aviation, was covered with colorful combat ribbons. CDR Scampi quickly noted the Silver Star, three DFCs, and a multitude of campaign ribbons.

Noting Scampi's interest, CDR Prescott, saluting sharply, said, "Captain Butler, what a pleasure to see you. I didn't notice you pull up. Let me present our new XO. Captain Butler, this is CDR Richard Scampi. He's an East Coast Puke, but I am sure we can get him fully indoctrinated in the ways of Westpac." Completing the introduction, he continued, "Richard, this is the legendary Captain Wild Bill Butler. He was my CO in VF 194. He went on to be CAG on the Bonnie Dick with airwing 12. As CAG he bagged the first Mig shot down by a Crusader. As old and slow as he was then, we all assumed that a group of shit-hot nuggets must have pushed that Mig out in front of him."

Ignoring CDR Prescott's comments, Captain Butler held out his hand to Scampi. "Welcome to Cubi. I am sure Dan will show you the Westpac ropes." Turning back to Prescott he said, "If you think you are so shit-hot, how about taking on an old man while you are here in port. Do you think you can get four of these birds up?"

"Sir, you wound us, particularly maintenance. My boys in maintenance are doing a great job of keeping the Heater fleet up." Pointing to LCDR Knowles, Dan Prescott said, "You know Dick Knowles."

Quickly returning Knowles' salute, he offered his right hand in a handshake. "Good to see you again Dick."

"Well Captain, LCDR Knowles, just as you were pulling up, made some disparaging remarks about my aging abilities. How about CDR

Scampi and I take on you and LCDR Knowles in a little two on two. I'd like to give my Ops officer here a little lesson in humility and I want to see what our new XO can do."

Indicating Captain Butler, he continued, "Dick, do you think you can get this senior citizen, with nearly 2,000 F8 hours, Natops qualified?"

"Captain Butler, you are hereby Natops qualified. It will be a pleasure to fly your wing," Knowles responded.

"Roger that, Dick." Captain Butler answered. "You are going to have to agree that no matter how badly we beat these two, do not lord it over them in the Ready Room. I know your Skipper's ego would be too fragile to handle that." Then, he turned back to Dan Prescott. " In a more serious vein, I was really shocked and sad to hear about Scott. That was the most dramatic Missing Man I have ever seen, Dan. You and your boys really did an outstanding job. No more passes that low though. I don't want you fucking up my base by splattering your body parts all over it, not to mention the pieces of aircraft!"

"Yes sir!" Prescott said, "That was a one and only, sir."

"Good. Now get your asses out of here and to the bar. Dan don't get too loaded. I want to invite you and Richard here over to my quarters at 1800, dress casual. We'll burn some steaks, and you can tell Betty some of your bullshit. She wants to see you and find out all the news about the family."

"Yes sir! We'll definitely be there."

"Oh, and Dan, tell that walking group of flight violations you call a squadron,"—indicating the other pilots watching with interest from outside the maintenance shack—"not to get loaded and fuck up my officer's club."

"Sir, if anyone fucks up your club it would be 123 or the attack pukes. We are a classy squadron."

Chapter Eight

Olongapo 8
22 March 1967 Cubi Point Naval Air Station

The round table was close to the bar, overlooking the dining room, and beyond, through the huge, glass, floor to ceiling windows that comprised the back wall of the club, the base and runway that was Cubi. Beyond the carrier dock where the Adams would moor, across the bay, sat the massive Subic Naval Station with scores of docks, shipyards, exchanges, and housing. Barely visible past the military precision of the joint bases was the chaos and jumble of Olongapo, the Philippine town next to the base.

The club was built on a hill. On the top floor, at the street level, upon entering, there were phone booths on the right side to be used by officers to call home. Facing the entryway was a long bar with two Filipino barmen filling drinks. Several tables in the bar overlooked an even larger room below with dining tables, a substantial dance floor and a large bandstand. Below the main dining room, was the infamous cat room. An old F8 cockpit had been used to make a ride down a simulated catapult into a pool. Normally drunk pilots tried to "catch a wire" by dropping the tailhook with a handle. The margin of error was only about four inches and missing the wire resulted in a bath in the pool.

John Phillips and Casper had commandeered the table shortly after noon, ordering champagne and slowly sipping while watching planes land and take off and watching ships move in and out of the harbor. The new pilots in the squadron, along with Joe Ames, had joined them at the table. Contrary to posted club rules, they had passed time playing a leisurely, low stakes game of poker, concerned more with form than substance. Only junior officers were at the table, with Phillips in charge. John Phillips had been instructed by the skipper to watch over the nuggets during the in-port period. Casper and Ames, aware of Phillips' mission, were adding their expertise.

"Pace yourself." Ames warned Kowalski as the big man guzzled another glass of bubbly. "That is the secret to a good port call. Get a nice high, maintain it, but don't get knee knocking drunk early or the whole in-port period is wasted on a fucking hangover from hell! I know all too well. If you get yourself fucked up early, you'll never make it through the Dick Knowles fighter sweep through Po Town."

"Shit, Aimless, I can handle this stuff. Anyway, what difference does it make if I get totally wasted now or in two hours in Po town. I think I'd rather be wasted right here."

"Come on, Ski. For once Joe is right. You want to go with us, and we don't want to drag around 200 pounds of passed out drunk Polack," Ray added.

"Actually guys, new word from Dick. The fighter sweep of Olongapo will be tomorrow night. We are on our own now. Heard a new crop of teachers have come in. I want a chance at a round eye before the ship gets in. Thus, I, the Awesome Aggie, am going to reduce my alcohol input until dance time." LTJG Twain remarked.

As the ship steamed toward Subic Bay and the carrier dock at Cubi Point, Chief McDaniel called Petty Officer First Class Pearson to the small office he used in the airframe division. He was the division chief for both the airframes division and the line division. Pearson was the leading petty officer in the line division, which was composed of the most junior enlisted men in the squadron. They performed the duties of plane captains—pre-flights of the aircraft, helped the pilots strap in before a flight, guided the pilots through the start-up of the aircraft, and helped them out after the flight. They were responsible for servicing the air bottles and hydraulic systems of the aircraft. It was also their responsibility to pull the safety pins out of the ejection seats and reinsert them when the pilots returned. Although junior, these tasks were essential to the safe operation of the aircraft. Typically, the plane captains would do a tour in the line division and then move on to more technical jobs in airframes, engines, or other divisions in the maintenance department.

"Pearson," seated behind his desk, Chief McDaniel said, "Your kids will have Cinderella liberty while we are in port. And Cinderella liberty means you are back on the ship at or before 2400 not 0001! On days the duty section will be responsible for washing the aircraft and handling the plane captain duties for some flying the Skipper will be doing. Everyone but the duty section will have liberty while we are in port. You have a good bunch of kids on the line. They have been doing an outstanding job, but, as you know, once they get drunk anything can happen and most of it is not good. When we get in, take everyone but the duty section to the enlisted club, but do not let any of them go to Olongapo. You're pretty familiar with Olongapo, right?"

"I've been there a few times."

"Well, first night when we get into Cubi, take your crew over to the Enlisted Club like I said. Don't let them go to Po Town on the first night. Tell them you will take them over the bridge on the second night if they get the planes washed and serviced before liberty call."

"OK, Chief."

"Then I want you to be a mother hen for them on their first trip to Olongapo. I don't want to see any of your guys in Captain's mast or with problems with Shore Patrol. Got it?"

"Yes Chief." He wanted to say *Aye, Aye Sir*, but the chief was enlisted and would not appreciate it.

"So, you watch your boys, show them the ropes and do not let them get into any trouble or hurt in any way. They worked their asses off this last line period and deserve to blow off steam, but we need them back. It is a Cinderella liberty, so hit the bridge at 2330 and back aboard no later than 2350. I don't want to hear about any of our guys not making it across the bridge since it closes at 2400. Understood?"

"Yes Chief."

"Keep them together and don't let anything happen to them. Keep them from tangling with any marines, black shoes, shore patrol, or whatever. Try to keep them from the hookers but make sure they know to use a condom. I don't want them in the VD ward."

"Yes Chief." Though he knew that, regardless of how efficient of a supervisor he was, he was certainly no Saint. Therefore, he couldn't guarantee to keep his men from straying..

Chapter Nine

As agreed, Ray met Warrant Arancio as soon as the ship pulled into the Cubi Point Dock. The warrant carried one large cardboard box filled with leather flight jackets and a smaller box full of aviator sunglasses.

He greeted Ray, "Hey Mister Rhodes. Are you ready to learn how supply really works in the navy?"

"Yes, I am, but please call me Ray. Is it OK if I call you Tony?"

"Absolutely."

Grabbing the first available base jeepney, they loaded in, and Warrant Arancio ordered the driver to take them to the Subic Supply Center where he asked Ray to wait with the boxes in the jeepney. He took one flight jacket and one pair of sunglasses out of the box and walked into the office.

"Is Chief Warrant Officer Espolito in?" He asked the Wave manning a front desk. She motioned him to the passageway and said, "third door on the left."

Walking in the open doorway he said, "Hey Joe, I brought you a present." He dropped the flight jacket and sunglasses on the desk.

"Good to see you, Tony. How can I help? Did that engine work out OK last year?"

"Yes, indeed. Thanks to you we had another bird up for the gooks to shoot down."

"What can I help you with now?"

"Well, the Skipper asked if I could get you to help us get a small refrigerator to set up our own squadron geedunk."

"Do you have a Cadillac chit?"

"I do." He tossed the supply requisition used to purchase nonmilitary items on the deck next to the flight jacket and sunglasses.

"Great. I can have that item ready for delivery to you the next time the ship comes in."

"We really need it now. What would it take to get expedited delivery?"

"With five of those jackets and a box of sunglasses I can have it on the dock for you tomorrow."

"Done, thanks Joe. See you next time."

Meanwhile, the JOs returned to the Cubi O'Club. They had spent part of the afternoon at the BOQ pool, played a leisurely game of water basketball, and relaxed, drinking just enough beer and Cubi specials from the pool bar to maintain an alcohol high. The tropical rum drink was especially popular, priced at thirty-five cents. They had cleaned up and changed into—in Twain's mind, at least—their dancing clothes. He wore a pair of light blue bell-bottomed trousers and a wild patterned paisley shirt with the top three bell-bottomed.

Ski, dressed in a blue golf shirt and tan slacks said, "Aggie, I didn't know you were gay?"

"Ski, you just do not know or appreciate style."

By arriving at the club early, they were able to commandeer another round table with seating for six by the dance floor. Opposite the table, across the dance floor was the Filipino band setting up for the night. Behind the band stand the lights of Subic and Olongapo were visible through the floor to ceiling windows. Soon after their arrival, four young women came in and sat at a table next to the band and across from them.

"I see a nine, eight, and a couple of fours," Ames said to no one in particular.

"Hell yes. That's what I'm talking about. Come on Ski, let's go and welcome them."

"Damn Aggie, I just got my drink."

"Well, bring it with you. We need to strike before the rest of the airwing gets here."

Tall, skinny Aggie in his wild clothes made an interesting contrast to the large, muscular Kowalski dressed in a conservative blue shirt and tan trousers. The girls watched curiously as the two of them made a beeline for their table.

"Evening ladies, welcome to our club. I am Twain, also known as Awesome Aggie and this hunk is Ski Kowalski. And you are?"

A pretty blonde of medium height and a nice figure replied, "Twain, like Mark Twain? I am Lynn."

"Yes, miss. Like Mark Twain. In fact, he was my great great grandfather."

"Really? As an English literature teacher here at the high school, I thought that would be Samuel Clemons."

"Indeed. My great grandfather changed our name from Clemons to Twain to try and profit off his daddy's name, may he rest in peace."

The girl next to Lynn, attractive in a unique way, with more olive skin and dark black eyes said, "Since this is your club, what do you do?"

"I am glad you asked. We flew in from an aircraft carrier today. It is arriving tomorrow, and I am the master chef on the ship in charge of the gourmet meal selections."

"You are,"—she nodded toward Ski— "and what does your dark and silent companion do?"

"He is my taster. Providing useful insight on the menu."

"Miss, he is more full of shit than a Christmas turkey. We flew in from the Adams today in our aircraft." Ski remarked.

"So, none of what Awesome Aggie here has said is true?" Lynn didn't sound surprised nor upset. "So, you are pilots. What kind of pilots? And what is the Adams?"

"We are fighter pilots, Lynn."—Aggie puffed out his chest a bit—"Flying the magnificent F8 Crusader off the US aircraft carrier John Adams. I did state that we flew in, and I might have overstated my abilities as a chef. However, I am dynamite with a drink menu. May I buy you a drink?"

"Only if you take me for a spin on the dance floor first," she asked as the band struck up the Beatles hit. "Penny Lane."

As they danced, she asked, "why didn't you tell me you were a fighter pilot?"

"I figured you would be bored with pilots by now."

"I just arrived four days ago. You are the first pilot I have met."

"You do not need to meet any more."

As the Chief had instructed, Pearson took his line crew to the Cubi Enlisted club for the first night where they drank beer, shot pool, and just relaxed after a tough line period.,

The next night Pearson took his group of five young airmen to the Enlisted Club first for a beer. Then they all piled into a base Jeepney to ride to the main gate at Subic. From there, they walked across the bridge connecting Subic to the Filipino town of Olongapo.

"Hey guys, watch this," Pearson said as he pulled a quarter out from his pocket and threw it into the squalid, brown, polluted waters of the river separating the Subic Bay Base from the town of Olongapo. Several young boys quickly dove into the water fighting to be the first to find and claim the quarter.

"That is what Olongapo is like. Now mind your Ps and Qs. I am going to take you to one of the classier joints here, but the girls still all have butterfly knives so don't try anything cute, or they will cut you up.

Also, make sure you use a condom. There is some nasty VD here. If you get VD, the chief will restrict you to the ship for the next in port period." He raised his eyebrows to mark the severity of the consequence.

They walked as a group down the main street in Olongapo. Groups of sailors and marines were going in and out of various bars. Bright neon lights, blaring rock or country music, or scantily clad girls sought to pull them in.

After two blocks, Pearson led them into the Satisfaction Club. Dimly lit, a bar of at least 20 feet stretched across the back wall. In the left corner of the room a quartet was playing a mix of Beatles and Rolling Stones songs. In the right corner several girls were seated at a large round table. Other tables surrounded a small dance floor near the band. As they were early arrivals, two uniformed marines were the only other patrons. Pearson instructed his men to sit at a table far from the bar. He wanted no trouble with drunk marines.

"Men, the girls will come over soon. They will want you to buy them a drink or two before you take them upstairs. Don't buy too much. They call it a cocktail, but it is really just juice and they charge the shit out of it."

Turning to the waiter who had appeared at the table he said, "Give us a round of San Miguels and a pitcher of Mojo." Mojo was a powerful mix of cheap rum, vodka, and just enough pineapple juice to cover the taste of the liquor. Pretty young girls dressed mainly in slips or night gowns moved over the table. Pearson pulled a chair out and motioned for one of the pretty ones to sit. "What's your name?"

"I am Sally. Buy me a drink."

"OK. But just one. Then we go upstairs. Good?"

"Good."

Pearsons winked to the men as if say, *and this is how it's done, boys.* One by one three of the other sailors followed Pearson's lead. After buying one or two drinks for the girls they also went upstairs, leaving Mears and Walker, a black airman from inner city Chicago.

Talking to a young, pretty girl, who was standing at the table, Mears asked, "Where are you from?"

"I am from the mountains. Bagio. Do you know it?"

"No, I don't."

"Buy me a drink"

"OK, but just one"

"Then you take me upstairs?"

"Nah, not my thing."

"You gay?"

"No."

Walker asked, "Mears do you like this shit?" He shook his head no.

"Well, let's get out of here then."

"Just let me buy this girl one drink and I'll leave with you."

"What is your name?" he asked, turning to look at her. She was beautiful, he had to admit it, but to him she looked no more than fourteen or fifteen. "Emma," she answered. That was clearly not her name, obviously.

He looked at her and for a moment pondered on whether he should take her up or not. Given the way she moved and interacted with them, this was certainly not her first night at the club. Finally, he decided to go for it. "Why do you do this?"

"I have to help my family," she said in a whisper, looking down at the floor. Had it not been so dark in there, he might have seen her blush. Instead, he sensed her embarrassment.

"Fuck this. I joined the navy to get away from this shit. I am going back to base and the club. You staying or going, Mears?" Walker asked.

"I am with you, Walker." He got up and looked into the girl's beautiful eyes that betrayed her innocent façade. She'd seen too much for her age. "Goodbye, Emma." He offered her a smile. "May you find healing." His thin voice was lost in the loud music.

The days in port had been good for the squadron. As the ship departed the port, Ray went

up on the flight deck to watch. It had been a good in port period. None of his sailors had gotten into trouble. He and the other JOs had consumed their share of booze. Aggie had apparently fallen in love. They seemed to have put the death of the skipper behind them.

He had spent his third-class cruise as a NROTC midshipman on an old destroyer. Having spent a brief period in the deck division with the bosun mates, he enjoyed watching the expeditious way they handled the lines. The captain of the ship, on the bridge, had carefully maneuvered away from the dock. It was impressive how he handled such a large ship. Ray hoped that in his career he would have a chance to do the same. After watching the ship depart from the Cubi Point dock, Ray went down to the "line shack" to work on evaluations of the line crew.

As he was just starting, Mears came in through the hatch. "Oh, hi Mr. Rhodes. I didn't know you were here. Sorry." A bit uncomfortable speaking to an officer he swayed back and forth a little, uneasily.

"No problem, Mears. How was your liberty?" Ray sensed that Mears was not comfortable being around an officer. The navy did maintain strict separation of officer and enlisted.

"I liked going to the E club. We drank a little, played some pool, then went to the pool."

"Did you go into Po town.

"Yeah, Pearson took us in."

"How was it?'

"Sir, it is fucked up! Kids diving in that shit river for quarters, young girls selling themselves. Like high school age. It ain't right." Surprisingly animated, he shook his head in disapproval.

Ray nodded his head in agreement, surprised to hear both anger and sadness in Mears' statement. A statement loaded with hurtful memoires of a past life that was hurtful.

Chapter Ten

Rescap

5 April 1967 Yankee Station

"What a shitty night!" LCDR Jackson exclaimed as he entered the Ready Room in his flight gear, helmet in hand, dripping water from his torso on the floor.

"Preacher! Did not know you could swear." Aggie said from behind the duty officer desk.

"I think even God would agree that this was one shitty night," he said, plopping into his Ready Room chair near the front.

Almost simultaneously Joe Ames entered the Ready Room from the passageway while LT Casper came in from the opposite end of the Ready Room where the flight gear was stored. Ames dripped water from his head and flight jacket. Casper still had his helmet on with water dripping into a puddle on the floor. He plopped down into a chair next to Preacher.

"Preach, I didn't pick you up until about twelve seconds before you hit the deck. I could hear you coming, and you did an outstanding job, given the conditions of almost zero visibility. Outstanding job but I have to grade you a Fair, Two wire. You dropped the nose just a touch in close, but overall, an outstanding job."

"Then why didn't I get an OK Two, Joe?"

"Because of your wingman. Ghost, I did not pick you up either until you were almost over the ramp. You had a smooth three wire, OK pass. How the hell did you do it?"

"Just lucky I guess."

"Luck has nothing to do with it, Ghost. Got to admit, you are really good around the boat. But beat the Skipper on the greenie board and he may have your ass. It is a real pleasure to fly with you." LCDR Johnson said.

The greenie board was the large board in the front of the Ready Room where every pilot's landing grade was displayed as either OK green, Fair yellow, No Grade brown, Cut red. The F8, if catching the first arresting gear wire, the one wire, had only eighteen inches of clearance over the deck. Thus, it was essential to stay on glide path in close.

Having avoided the foul weather, rough night flight followed by even more difficult night landing, Aggie was relieved to be on a day flight with Dick Knowles.

"OK gents," LCDR Knowles began, "This will be a standard day Barcap. I, of course, am the lead. Aggie, you are the wingman. Ski, you are the spare. In the unlikely, and God forbid, circumstance that my bird goes down on start, Aggie you will be the lead and fly the hop just as I brief it, clear?"

"Clear. But does that mean we can still do a tuck-under break when we get back to the ship?"

"Under no circumstances can you do a tuck-under break, or a low pass or anything that is not standard."

"We rendezvous at 20000 feet off the port side of the ship and head for Red Crown at buster (fastest basic engine speed) so that the guys we are relieving from 123 can make their Charlie time at the ship. I will call a frequency switch to Red Crown on 239.5. Once over Red Crown, we will slow down to about 350 knots to loiter. I expect we will tank at least twice during this hop to keep a full combat fuel package. Remember to keep your eyes open on Barcap. Skipper just told us about the Chinese Migs shooting down that air force F4. Don't count on Red Crown to pick up all the bogeys. Use your Mark One eyeballs at all times. Finally, our job on Barcap is to protect the fleet from any crazy Mig pilot that might get the idea of attacking our ships. I know it can get boring, but you have to stay alert. Got it?" A sea of nodding heads followed. "However, while our main mission is to protect the fleet, we also will go in and assist with any Rescap—navy or air force. Understood? That is truly our most important mission."

"Yessir!" Aggie exclaimed.

As they went back to the equipment room to put on their flight gear, Ski frowned. "What the fuck is a tuck-under break?" he asked.

"Easy game Ski. We come into the break in echelon. Then I do a normal fan and you would roll 270 degrees to your right and pull into the break. The Blues do it all the time." Always talking with his hands, he tried to show how the break would work with his right hand but could not get it all the way around.

"Is that what happened to that guy in VF15 at Rota?"

"Yeah. Seems he got a little disoriented in the roll and ended up only going about 180 degrees. He pulled it right into the ground."

"And you expect me to do that? Screw you!"

Aggie's and Ski's planes were parked next to each other on the port side just aft of the island. Dick manned his plane on the starboard side of the ship also aft of the island. After careful pre-flights, each pilot started their aircraft, master switch on, throttle up around the horn hitting the igniters as the engine spooled up from the huffer turning the J57 jet's blades. Once they were up and running, each went through a series of movements of the controls as indicated by their plane captains. Once all controls were working properly, they keyed the mike on the ship's departure frequency and called: "Heater Two up". "Spare up." Hearing nothing from Dick Knowles, Aggie again said, "Heater Two up."

As Ski and Aggie watched, Dick's canopy popped open, and he frantically waved a flight deck troubleshooter over. He motioned with his thumb to his ear and then gave a thumbs-down. The green-shirted troubleshooter climbed up the side of the aircraft and pulled out the helmet plug, cleaned it and reinserted it. Dick tried it again but still got no feedback. Totally frustrated, he looked at Aggie, pointed to himself with a thumbs-down, pointed back to Aggie and gestured to him that he had the lead.

"Heater Two now has the lead."

"Roger, spare is now two," Ski replied.

After downing his aircraft, LCDR Knowles climbed up the ladders to the pri fly platform outside of the air boss' chair. On seeing him arrive, the boss asked, "What happened, Dick?"

"Just a radio failure. I wanted to come up and see the two nuggets launch."

"Hey Dick, what is it with that LT Twain? He looks like a tall, skinny, Pancho Villa when he goes out to man, black mustache, wearing that felt hat and a bandolier of bullets."

"Boss, you know how it is. When I first came into our old squadron as a nugget, I had plenty of quirky habits." Dick answered.

"Yeah, but you didn't dress like a bandido."

After the yellow shirts directed him carefully over the shuttle, Aggie gave a thumbs-up to the weight board and holding the throttle at full power with the T handle in front of it with his left hand, saluted the shooter (catapult officer) with his right hand. A perfect cat shot, in full power the F8 hit 180 knots by the end of the ship. Accelerating to 350, he did a spiral climb to 20000 feet watching the launch of Ski, his wingman.

Once Ski joined up, they began the high-speed dash to Red Crown.

"Heater flight go to 239.5." A double click of the microphone by Ski was the only acknowledgement of the frequency change.

Day Barcap to most of the pilots was plainly boring. They flew around the Red Crown ship up near the North Vietnam border in a generally oval pattern. The purpose was to prevent any attack by Migs on the fleet. However, in the history of the war, the Migs had never ventured out to attack. If they decided to attack in numbers, the Barcap would only be a minor obstacle. In reality, the North Vietnamese knew that not only would a massive number of fighters be launched to meet any threat but that the ships also had ground to air missiles that were quite effective. In fact, one of the carriers had downed two Migs with anti-aircraft missiles from a distance of over fifty miles at a time when the Migs were flying, and no navy or air force aircraft were airborne. On Yankee Station, the fighter squadrons of all the carriers shared the Barcap duty. It was not unusual for F8s to relieve F4s from another ship. Although boring, on Barcap the pilots needed to be alert.

"Red Crown, this is Heater flight checking in."

"Roger Heaters."

After checking in with Red Crown, they flew a lazy racetrack pattern over the radar picket destroyer. Aggie was daydreaming with thoughts of Cubi and Lynn when the controller interrupted him, "Heater lead I have your wingman one mile in trail."

Looking to his left he saw Ski exactly in the proper position of combat spread at 1000 feet directly abeam. Immediately he called, "Heaters break left!"

Pulling hard he strained to see behind them where the bogey should be. "Two, do you have him?' Selecting after burner, he pulled the nose up into a high yo yo. Straining against the g forces, he looked at Ski, who per prescribed tactics, was executing a low yo yo. Aggie then pulled down hard turning left, covering Ski, as he selected burner and flew up into the high yo yo. Each pilot perfectly positioned to protect the six of the other.

Do you see him now?" Straining, back and forth they went continuing to look for the bogey while covering the other's six.

"Red Crown. Where is that bogey now?"

"Belay that Heaters. It was a surface contact. Sorry about that."

Looking down, both Aggie and Ski saw what appeared to be a trawler of some kind heading for Haiphong. "Red Crown, confirm, there was no radar contact with an unknown aircraft"

"Roger. The contact was on the surface."

In the squadron ops office LT Casper (Ghost) was writing the schedule for the next day. Commander Scampi entered the small office.

"Mr. Casper."

"Yessir?"

"I want you to write me in for every Mig Cap to be flown with Davis as my wingman."

"Sir, are you aware that per the Skipper, I try to balance all the points so that everyone has an equal opportunity for hops over the beach and fly their share of Barcaps, both day and night?"

"Mr. Casper. Understand you are a NROTC graduate, correct?"

"Yessir."

"Well, I don't know about ROTC but at the Academy we were taught to respond to an order by a senior officer with Yessir or Aye, Aye Sir!"

"Did you run this by the Skipper, sir?'

"Don't question me, just do it."

With that, Scampi left Casper to deal with a brand-new type of headache.

On barcap, just after they had tanked from the duty A3 tanker, Red Crown called. "Heater flight. An Airforce 105 is declaring an emergency and attempting to make it feet wet just north of Than Hao. Your steer for Rescap is 249."

Aggie immediately responded, "Roger Red Crown, coming to 249. Flight Buster now." But he thought to himself, *Than Hoa, must have been part of a strike on that bridge.* Every pilot knew of the numerous attempts to bring down that bridge leading from Hanoi and Haiphong to Vinh, carrying weapons and troops down south.

"Heater flight, switch to 238.3 and contact Rescap lead."

"Roger."

After tightening his shoulder harness and checking his switches, Aggie called, "Rescap lead, this is Heater flight responding. We are two F8s armed with 20 mm and sidewinder missiles."

"Roger Heaters. This is Sandy One. We are over the site now and have eyes on the pilot in the water. Do not think we will need you but keep it coming."

They arrived just as the Helo was leaving with the downed pilot, escorted by a pair of the Sandy A1's. "Sandy One, Heater One, just passing above and to starboard of you. Looks like you have everything under control."

"Roger Heaters. Thanks for the effort. Sandy out."

After returning to the ship with the normal, pre-briefed fan break, Aggie was telling his version of the Rescap when CDR Prescott entered the room.

"Attention on deck."

"Seats, gentlemen. I have an announcement. I just came from a meeting with CAG. As you know, the ship's movements are secret, known only by the mission planners in DC and the hookers in Olongapo." A subtle but noticeable laugh echoed in the room. "However, due to the necessity to clear visits ahead with the British, CAG has confirmed that we will be going to Hong Kong after our next line period. The ship must go to Cubi first as the Brits do not want ships coming directly from the war zone as that could cause problems with the Chinese. We will have five days in Hong Kong before returning to the line via Cubi. As a result,"—he paused— "Poet?"

"Yessir." John Phillips answered.

"I am ordering you to go to Hong Kong directly from the line with other airwing personnel to set up the best Heater Admin ever in the Hong Kong Hilton. Understood?"

"Yessir. I think I can handle that."

"Commander Spooner will fly the Air wing advance party to Hong Kong in the COD. Now Ray, roll the flick."

"Sir, before we roll the flick, did you hear about my lead with Ski in the Rescap of that air force pilot? Think our action is worth at least a DFC." Aggie said.

"Aggie, what I heard was that you arrived on scene in time to watch the helo pick up that pilot after the A1s had taken care of any boats in the vicinity. If you deserve anything, it is a bill for the JP you burned."

"However, you did follow our orders to assist in any Rescap. Good job, but if anyone deserved a medal it would be Preach or Ghost for their night landings in the middle of that thunderstorm. Most of the airwing had to bingo to Danang. Good job, Preach and Ghost."

Aggie had no other option but to grin and bear it.

Having switched to the midnight-to-noon schedule, the four nugget pilots went directly to their stateroom to try and sleep before their flights began at midnight. Lights out in the room, in complete darkness at that level of the ship, Aggie said quietly, "I am going to get killed tonight. Did you see how shitty the weather was last night?"

"Shut up Aggie." Ski said firmly.

"No. I know that I am going to buy the farm tonight on the ramp."

"You are not. Supposed to be a nice night with a moon. Not like the weather two days ago."

"I don't care. It will still be dark."

"I get your stereo."

"Shut up, Ray. You are good at night."

"I get your shit kickers."

"Shut up, Troy. You aren't even flying. You have the duty."

"I get Lynn," Ski whispered.

"You bastards. Have no sympathy. Maybe my plane will be down."

As they all tried to sleep, the catapult shuttle slammed into the stop at the end of the ship. It was an ominous reminder that launches would proceed that night as scheduled.

Chapter Eleven

Astrud

15 May, 1967 Yankee Station

"Now hear this! On the ball we have the COD with 4,500 pounds of mail." Over the 1MC came the voice of the air boss. A muted cheer was heard throughout the ship. Mail was the touch of home, the contact with lovers and family, the connection with the real world. Soon mail clerks from all the departments and squadrons were hustling to the ship mail room to pick up their respective mail. All nonessential work was halted for mail call. "Mail Call! Now Mail Call!" the bos'un called. The sorting was over, mail was ready for delivery. Mail clerks were now carrying the coveted cargo to their respective areas.

The Ready Room, as the focal point of all squadron activities, was the designated space for the pilots to receive their mail. Every pilot and officer was there for the mail call whenever a COD or helicopter-delivered mail. At the announcement of mail call, the room quickly filled.

In Ready Two, the skipper, when available, had traditionally passed out the officer mail. Like a junior Santa, he called the names, enjoying the moment.

"Aggie!" He called, tossing a wrapped shoe box to Twain. "Looks like your mother has sent more chocolate chip cookies. Are you going to share it with your loyal squadron mates?"

"Skipper, you know I will, at least you'll get your cut." Twain answered.

Continuing with the mail, the skipper lobbed letters and packages around the room, commenting at times about wife and family, teasing recipients of perfume-soaked love letters. John Phillips, the SDO for the day, was razzed heavily about a lavender colored, heavily scented letter he received from, as he put it, an old college friend. Ray Rhodes watched as the mail was dispensed. When everything was passed out and he had received nothing, he walked quickly from the room without saying a word.

The skipper watched him leave and called John over quietly. "Go down and talk to Ray. He looks a little down. He hasn't gotten a damn thing in the last four mail calls except from his mom."

Phillips quickly got up, asked Casper to cover the duty desk for him, and followed Ray out.

"What's up Ray?" John quietly said. He had entered the four-man stateroom without knocking, following Ray directly from the Ready Room after mail call.

"Oh, hi Poet." He called from his top bunk where he had plopped down, still dressed in flight suit and boots from his stint as the alert pilot. "Just doing a little thinking. A little decompression."

"You seem a little down." John grabbed a desk chair from the built-in unit nearest the bunk, turning it around and sitting on it backward with his head facing Ray on the bunk. He was wearing his short-sleeve tropical khaki uniform without his cover. As usual, he was perfectly neat in contrast to Ray's casual wearing of any uniform item.

"Well, I just haven't heard from Astrud in a while. It kind of pisses me off and worries me that she hasn't written."

"I'm sure it's nothing to worry about. The mail really gets screwed up out here. You'll probably get a bunch of letters all at once."

"That's bullshit, John. Everyone else gets mail. Somehow my mother manages to get letters to me. I just don't understand. With all the flying, briefing, watches, and my regular job I don't have time to spit, but I manage to jot a note to her every single day. You would think that if she cared, if she loved me, that she would be thinking of me enough to write."

"She's in graduate school, she may be doing some massive paper or getting ready for some exam."

"Still, she ought to at least get a note out!"

"First of all, the mail does really get screwed up out here. Once I got about six letters completely out of order. The first ones had gone to the Enterprise or Danang or God Knows where. Probably some yeoman mail clerk on a Tin Can is throwing your letters in a bag, waiting until he has enough to forward. Second, some people don't like to write. She's probably afraid to send you something unless it is perfect. Remember, English isn't her first language. She is probably writing letters and tearing them up, embarrassed about how they sound. Afraid to tell you the wrong thing. Afraid to depress you by telling you how much she misses you. Afraid of sounding trite. She is a great girl, and I am sure she loves you."

Ray lay still for a while, looking up at the white pipe thickly coated with insulation that ran above his bunk, wondering idly what it was for, before answering. "Thanks John, you're probably right. It is just that I love her some damn much. Every day I think about what she is doing at that moment. I remember our last times together. I think about how beautiful she is, how I feel when I am around her. Shit! I'm getting too fucking sentimental." He swung his legs over the side of the bunk and sat up, ducking his head and slumping to avoid hitting that same pipe.

"Hey, Ray, it is acceptable for fighter pilots to fall in love. It is more than acceptable, it is inevitable. But you have to learn to prioritize. Here in your room, or in the mess, or in the Ready Room, it's alright to think about her and home and the future. But when you are up there, you have to pay attention to your job all the time. You and whomever you are flying with have to be 100 percent all the time."

Staring down now directly at Phillips, Ray answered with emphasis. "John, I know that. I work my ass off in the cockpit to be good."

"I know you do, Ray. But just remember that if you want to survive and see her again, you have to concentrate on what you are doing. It can be tough to love some of these girls. They don't understand what you are going through, and you can't tell them or you sound like a wimp. Accept Astrud for who she is: a beautiful, free spirit. Maybe you should ease up on the letters to her. Maybe you are putting too much pressure on her."

Ray looked at him with uncertainty. "I don't know. I feel like by writing her, that I am somehow with her. But maybe you are right. I'll try to give her a little space. You know I wanted to marry her before cruise, but she refused. She said that she was too young to be a widow and that if I wanted to get married when I made it back that she would consider it then."

John looked straight back at him. "Well, if you truly love her then that should be plenty of incentive to concentrate on what you are doing. When we're flying, we don't have time for sentiment." He paused as he thought, *and when we get in port we just stay drunk trying to avoid thinking about coming out here again or what we are missing back home.*

"That's pretty depressing. I hope there is more to it than that." Ray stared back at him, locking on his eyes, changing the subject, "Do you worry about buying the farm?"

"Not that much. After the last cruise, I think I can handle anything. I took Skipper Prescott's philosophy: I try to be the best damn fighter pilot I can be. I am confident that I am good enough to survive. I know I can fly the ball with the best of them. I also think I am pretty damn good over the beach. What I am most afraid of is being captured. I would rather be dead. When I am out here, I just try not to think too much." He stood up and cleared his voice. "You know I like to write. I can't do it out here, however. Being in this war changes you. I don't feel any poetry. I don't feel like writing. As much as is going on, as much emotion as we all feel, it is just too close for me to think about it, much less write. Thinking too much out here just makes you dead or crazy." He paused, obviously absorbed in thought, disregarding his own advice. "I have to get back to the duty. Turn on some tunes and get your head right." He reached out and gently slapped the side of Ray's head to emphasize the thought. As he opened the door, Twain bolted in.

"What's up?" he asked Ray and John. Without waiting for an answer and offering the shoe box he was carrying, he said, "Have one of the best damn cookies ever to come out of the state of Texas!"

Both John and Ray took a cookie.

"How could a mother who can cook like yours produce such a skinny shit as you?" John said.

"It's not for lack of eating. I just always get lots of exercise. I have a real high metabolism, mainly due to the high level of screwing I participate in."

"Ray, you're his roommate. Hope you're not participating in his sex diet."

"Shit, Poet! You know Kowalski is his lover!" Ray answered, as the big Pole came through the door.

"The only love he is getting is with his right hand. Notice how those muscles are built up." Kowalski answered.

"My wrist muscles, as handsome as they are, are a result of my careful exercise plan of cycling the stick several times every hop." Twain responded.

"That's your excuse for killing snakes in the cockpit when you get in close?" Ray added.

"Shit! I'm so smooth on the ball they could call me butter!"

"How come it doesn't show on the greenie board?"

"I attribute it entirely to LSO prejudice against Texans in general and Aggies in particular."

"This is getting too deep for me. I'm out of here and back to the duty desk." Phillips said as he left the room.

Now alone, Twain said, "Are you all right, Ray?" As he sat down on Troy's lower bunk, chewing on a cookie.

"Yeah, John and I were just shooting the bull."

"You didn't get any mail yet, did you?"

"No, but it's all right." Ray turned away, pulling himself up on his upper bunk above Ski.

"No it's not all right. She ought to write. Ski and I saw the Skipper send John after you. Did you hear what happened to John last cruise?"

"I guess not. What happened?" Looking down at Aggie from his perch on the bunk

"He married some hippie college girl just before he went on cruise. They had a fast, hot love and sex affair just after he got to Miramar. He talked her into going to Vegas before the cruise. On the third line period, he got a literal Dear John letter from her. She said she didn't like the war and couldn't love a military man. She also told him that she was screwing one of her professors and that they had gotten married too fast. John, Poet, was really down and damn near bought it on the ramp one night after that. Skipper Huggins grounded him. Knowles and Prescott were barely able to talk him out of his depression. That's why the Skipper sent him to talk to you."

"God, that really sucks! I didn't know about John, but Astrud is not like that. Something is wrong or she would have written by now. But I do think I may have put too much pressure on her. Poet is right, he told me to ease up on her."

"Fuck 'em!" Kowalski said. "There are women everywhere. She's a great gal, but you can find any other one you want. Why get all hung up on one? Fuck 'em!"

"That is just what I would like to do right now. I'm so horny I could screw the crack of dawn! Will this fucking line period ever be over?" Twain asked.

"Twelve days and counting," Ski replied.

Returning to Ready Two, John Phillips found Casper working on something at the SDO desk and asked, "Dave, can you hold down the desk a few more minutes? I have to do something."

"Sure, John. Take your time. I am through flying for the day and am just working on the schedule here. Nothing is going on."

"Thanks."

He went directly to the two-man room he shared with Casper. Taking out stationary, he wrote:

Dear Astrud,

Ray does not know I am writing to you—he definitely would not like it, so please do not tell him. Things can get pretty rough out here, especially for a first-cruise pilot. I'm sure they are not easy for you either. For Ray to survive he needs all the help he can get. He doesn't need to be worrying about you and whether you have found someone else.

Write to him. Even if you are tired of him or don't care about him, write to him at least twice a week. He's worth it!

If you don't, I will be extremely disappointed.

Thanks,

John Phillips

He took out an envelope, looking up her address from a squadron roster that included wives and significant others, addressed, and sealed the letter. He then took it to the first-class yeoman who served as the squadron mailman, instructing him to get the letter out on the next COD and to California as soon as possible. He was assured that she would have it within three days.

Chapter Twelve

WOXOFF Happy Hour

11 January 1967

She hadn't wanted to go to the Friday Happy Hour on the base, but her friend Susie had insisted, telling her that she had to get out and see something besides the UCSD Student Union. Susie told her that it was necessary for her education in American culture to experience the WOXOFF room in the O'Club at Miramar. Happy hour was in full swing when they arrived. Wild drunks were happily trying to dance to the heavy beat of The Doors. Pilots in their khaki uniforms blended with obviously military men in civilian clothes. Tables of squadrons were engaged in contests to see who could drink the most tequila shooters. Hands imitated airplanes in conversations all over the room as Crusader and Phantom pilots argued about wins in practice dog fights.

Abandoned by Susie who was dancing with a pilot, she nursed her margarita and deftly dodged the passes of a lot of friendly drunks, rejecting them all. Bored, when one mellow, well mannered, handsome guy came by and just wanted to talk, she quickly agreed. Lanky, with long sideburns and dark hair well beyond any acceptable military length, he seemed different from the others. For almost two hours they chatted easily, and she told him of life in Rio, the beaches of Ipanema and Copacabana, and her childhood in Rio Grande de Sul. He, for his part, talked passionately of the hard life on the family ranch in Southwestern

Colorado, of growing up around animals and mountains, and of hard winters and short springs in the San Juan Mountains. It was obvious to her that he loved his mountains as much as she loved her ocean. The cowboy from the mountains and the Brazilian ocean girl had an immediately easy communication. When he asked, she quickly jumped at the chance to escape the wild, noisy bar. Flagging down Susie to let her know she had a way home, Astrud and Ray left the club.

They went for coffee to a small diner in La Jolla. Talking quietly, before they knew it, hours had passed. They walked to the Cove, and there, watching the dramatic white foam of the breakers on the night rocks, he kissed her. The connection and chemistry between them were instant. She was tired of arrogant professors and insecure graduate students. Typical of the UCSD graduates, she was opposed to the war, but intrigued by the fighter pilot, the contrast between words and action.

For his part, he was bored by the typical girls who came to the O'Club, looking for husbands with a future, attempting to turn the sex of a one-night stand into forever.

She was so different, so sensual with graceful, elegant, and easy movements. He was overwhelmed by everything about her: the soft and rhythmic accent, the golden color of her skin and hair, and the unusual light brown of her eyes. She had a natural approach to life, consisting of no makeup, no preconceptions, and accepting life as it came to her. Effortlessly, she dressed in a stylish and comfortable manner, never seeming to worry about her appearance. She didn't seek approval in the mirror. In many ways, the Brazil Girl was the California Girl, at least what Ray had always imagined a California Girl to be as he replayed the Beach Boys' hit in his head. Combined with the exotic beauty was her quick mind. She was obviously independent and intelligent, leaving the security of a wealthy home in Rio to study for her PhD in Marine Biology at UCSD's Scripps Institute. She talked passionately of the ocean and its marine line. If possible, she was even more passionate about Rio and the rest of Brazil.

He was fascinated by her stories of Brazil, to him exotic and mysterious. A land of oceans meeting mountains, samba and mulattos. Caipirinhas and Ipanema. A big country that she obviously loved as much as he loved America.

They argued about the war. She quickly perceived that she should not press too much as he was obviously sensitive about it. They argued about socialism and Latin America, the influence of the United States and her feeling that the objective of US policy was to exploit the locals, to make Latin America a mercantile colony of the United States.

An aero engineering major at Utah State, Ray was hopelessly outmatched. She was gentle with her arguments, not wanting to attack the sensitive, almost vulnerable, warrior whom she was growing to respect and genuinely care for. As it grew very late, he reluctantly took her back to the graduate student housing at UCSD, but only after she promised to join him for a late brunch the next day.

He picked her up promptly at eleven. Unlike most of the single fighter pilots, he didn't drive a corvette or other sports car. He had no motorcycle, but instead coveted an old, open jeep his father had given him to take to Utah State. He took her to a Champagne Brunch at a beautiful little restaurant overlooking the Pacific in La Jolla, where they ate Eggs Benedict in a crab sauce and drank California Champagne. After lunch they went to Torrey Pines and hiked the trails, ultimately kissing at trail's end on the promontory overlooking the Pacific.

In a cold, January fog they built a fire on the beach below Torrey Pines, thrilled by the sight of a Gray Whale breaching near them. They cooked hamburgers and beans, drank Paul Mason Crackling Rose, and talked until dusk. Lying on a blanket on the beach, Ray kissed her again, gently touching firm breasts, bare under her UCSD sweatshirt. As they became more passionate, she asked, "Shouldn't we go somewhere more private, preferably with a bed?"

He gathered the picnic and wine as quickly as possible and drove fast, her hand pressing his leg tightly as he shifted gears, back to the apartment on Mission Bay he shared with Kowalski. He hoped that the big Polack would be out partying. As he opened the door he was distressed to find Ski, dressed in his favorite Michigan Football T-shirt and workout shorts, spread out on their couch. Coors in hand, he was idly watching Roller Derby on their television.

"Hey, Cowboy, what's up?" a slightly inebriated Ski asked.

Making introductions, Ray presented Astrud to Ski. Obviously embarrassed by an awkward situation, Ray was relieved when Astrud said, "Ski, it is great to meet you and I look forward to seeing you in the future. I do not want to be rude, but Ray and I have plans."

"No problem, Astrud. It's definitely a pleasure to meet you and I would certainly hope you have plans. For my part, I was just heading out as soon as I finished this beer." With that, he chugged the rest of the Coors down and said, "I'm outta here." Then headed for his room to change.

Embracing Ray tightly, she asked, "Where is your room? I am starting to get tired."

Unlike other girls he had known, Astrud was not at all embarrassed to undress with him for the first time. Ray helped her pull the sweatshirt over her head while she unbuttoned his shirt, revealing an almost skinny body, but rippled with muscle. She ran her hands over his chest and stomach, then pulled him into a tight embrace, pressing her now bare breasts against him as her shirt came off. Instinctively his hands were all over her and she kissed him deeply on the mouth and lightly on eyes, nose, and ears.

She reached down, feeling him, and began to unbutton his Levi's. Soon they were frantically throwing the rest of their clothes off as passion drove them into a frenzy, kissing and touching each other hungrily. He was naturally gentle, and slow with everything he did. Surprising to him, she was in a rush, anxious to take everything from him as quickly as possible. It was also apparent to him that she, for all her exotic ways, had less experience than him. That night they made love until exhausted, then fell asleep. Wakening the next morning, they drowsily made love again. To Ray, each time was better as each learned the needs of the other. Falling in love, Ray wanted more than anything to satisfy her, to make her happy.

Astrud was confused. Obviously, the sex with this skinny cowboy pilot was great. She wanted him so much, and loved being with him, but was afraid of mistaking sex for love. Without realizing it, she had been extremely lonely, needing more companionship than Susie or any of the new friends at UCSD could offer. She decided to just let the relationship develop, vowing not to let it affect her plans.

Days merged and they spent every minute possible together. Walking on the beach, eating in the cozy, quaint restaurants nearby, they talked constantly, hungry to learn as much as possible about each other. Although it was obvious that he loved flying, he spoke mainly of the ranch and life in the mountains, preferring not to think about the looming separation caused by the cruise. As often as possible they made love, he was always ready, only waiting for her to give him a signal.

She essentially moved into their apartment, using the jeep to commute to school while Ray caught rides to the squadron with Kowalski. Ski, cursing his own bad luck in love, frustrated by the frequent sight of the beautiful Astrud at their refrigerator clad only in a Utah State sweatshirt, drinking his milk, designated Ray the Luckiest Living Cowboy.

As time for him to go on the cruise drew closer, he pressed her to marry him. He felt a need to marry her before he went to combat, afraid that he might lose her while he was gone, and afraid that he might not make it back. She brushed him off, telling him that it was too fast. Hearing of the last cruise from wives and girlfriends at numerous squadron parties, she told him that she was too young to be a widow. Not wanting to hurt him, she also began to realize that her feelings for him, while growing, were not as strong as his for her.

Conning his boss, LCDR Robinson, into giving him a few days of basket leave, he took her to Cortez and the family ranch for a long weekend. He rented a fast Mooney Ranger at Gillespie Field, and he flew it to its maximum range in order to reach the dirt strip at the ranch where he had first learned to fly the family Piper Cub.

His family, obviously doting on their only son, took her in as one of their own. She was overfed with the local beef, comparing it favorably to the meat from her grandfather's fazenda in Rio Grande de Sul. Ray drove her through the ranch to the mountains near Cortez, and she found the San Juan Mountains to be overpowering in their winter beauty. Nothing in Brazil compared, she had to admit.

On a cold morning, he put her on their gentlest horse and together they rode to the end of the ranch. In the family since the start of the century, it had been settled first by Ray's grandfather. It was very large, as the dry ranches of the west had to be in order to graze any cattle but was not rich. His parents worked very hard to make it with the uncertainty of rain and harsh winters. Still, it was Ray's dream to return after the navy and split time between flying for an airline and ranching.

Astrud loved the natural beauty of the ranch, but knew that she could never live there, so far from the ocean and so isolated. Not wanting to hurt Ray, she said nothing.

"*Um beixo!*"

"That's not enough. I say I love you and you wish me a kiss. I need more!"

"Ray, you have to be patient. Don't push me too fast. You want everything too fast." She teased.

"Because I don't have time. I have to compress everything. The time goes too fast. Yes, this is happening fast, but I know it is right for me. Is it right for you?"

"It feels right, but everything is so complicated. I have my life, my family, and what I want to do. You have to be patient. You have to give me time."

"I don't have time to give."

The night before they had taken most of his things to North Island and the ship, eating the traditional pre-cruise dinner at Mexican Village on Coronado with the rest of the pilots. Everyone, attempting to avoid the tension of separation, had consumed too many margaritas. Slightly drunk, he knew he did not want to spend their last hours arguing, so he simply pulled her in in a tight embrace, trying to implant that feeling of her body close into his memory forever.

When he had finally gone to sleep at almost three, she had remained awake, looking at and gently touching his semi-nude body, thinking. She knew her feelings were strong for him, but she wasn't sure it was love. Was she caught up in the emotion of war, sex, loneliness, and separation or did she truly love him? She had had a multitude of boyfriends and a few lovers in Brazil. At one time she had been pressured, both by her *novio* and her family, to marry a handsome surfer who was studying law at the university. While she thought she loved him, she had not been certain and they finally had broken up, arguing over her pursuit of a career. Certainly, what she felt now for Ray was stronger than any other emotion she had ever felt, but she was still confused. Cruise would be a good test. If they both could wait for the almost nine months of cruise and still have the same feelings, then it must be real. It would also give her the opportunity to get back to working hard on the dissertation. He would fly and fight, she would put all her energy into her research. The time would pass quickly, but in her stomach, she felt the aching fear that she might never see him again.

It isn't fair, she thought. They should have more time. But maybe the intensity of time pressure had created this emotion. Maybe without the war and cruise there would be no love. Maybe they were lucky to have this short, compacted period of pure joy and passion. Certainly, most people had never experienced that high of total passion. She rode with him in the jeep to the ship, Ski sitting in the back since his car was already in storage. Astrud was charged with driving and guarding the precious jeep while Ray was gone. As always, she reached over and clutched his leg tightly while he drove. On the ferry to North Island, they got out, leaving Kowalski, semiconscious from his hangover, immobile in the back jump seat. As the ferry crossed the bay, he held her tightly, not wanting to let her go, wanting to go AWOL and stay with her more than anything.

"Um beixo," he said to her, lightly kissing her lips.

"I love you!" She replied, herself shocked at what she had said.

He heard the words and was stunned. Pushing her back to see her face, he laughed. "It worked. Um beixo brings love. Astrud, I love you so much."

"Um beixo, Ray, and I love you too." The emotion of the moment, the beautiful morning on the sea, the carrier with the planes already aboard looming in the background had been too much for her. She wanted to send him off with hope and love.

Like hundreds of others, they had remained on the dock, embracing and kissing, until the last moment before the gangplanks were raised. Tears pouring from hundreds of eyes, wives and girlfriends stood on the dock and waved as lines were removed and the tugs began to pull the John Adams from its dock. Unable to watch any longer, Astrud returned to the jeep and drove to the parking lot near the Hotel Del Coronado where she walked for hours, watching her ocean, thinking.

Chapter Thirteen

Blue Tree

16 May 1967 Yankee Station

Back at sea heading for Yankee Station, Dick Knowles sat in his Ready Room chair looking at the flight schedule that Casper had just brought him. He always checked it out before he took it to the skipper for his signature.

"Hey Dick. Glad I caught you. Is that your schedule?" Chuck, the officer in charge (OINC) of the F8 photo detachment asked.

His six pilots and four aircraft took photos of all the Alpha strikes as well as flying reconnaissance over some of the roads. Unable to evade by jinking while on their photo run, they flew as fast as they could, using speed to defeat most of the anti-aircraft. However, they still were very vulnerable while over the target. The F8s who escorted them, calling out anti-aircraft fire and SAMs while looking to intercept any Migs could jink but were also in a vulnerable position.

"It is. Do you have something to add?"

"Dick, we have just been tasked with a road recce South of Vinh. Supposedly there is a big buildup of NVA troops and materials on Route Pak Two heading South. It should be a piece of cake since the Migs hardly ever go that far south and usually there is little triple-A and no SAMs."

"I am giving it to my nugget and thought you might want to have one of your nuggets take it."

"We are short of aircraft. I can squeeze in the flight but won't be able to give you a spare."

"That will be alright, Dick. I think I can get 123 to handle the spare."

Once Chuck left, Dick called Ski. "Hey Ski, this is Dick Knowles. Can you come up to the Ready Room for a minute?"

"Yessir."

Ski, who had been resting on his bunk, hustled into his tropical khaki uniform and made his way quickly to the Ready Room.

"What's up, Dick?"

"We have been tasked with an extra hop for tomorrow. The photo beanies have a need for an escort for a job they have just been handed. Do you know Craig McSherry?"

"Yessir. I knew him both in flight training and in the Rag."

"Well, he is flying the mission. It is a Blue Tree route South of Vinh. Supposed to be a big buildup of troops and supplies heading down Route Pak Two that CAG wants to confirm. It should be a cakewalk as they normally don't have SAMs or much triple-A that far south. However, be prepared for the worst."

Though he looked unmoved by the statement, Ski was excited to be chosen for the mission. His leg twitched uncontrollably just as it had when the coach had told him that he was going into the game. Excitement at escorting the photo alone but aware of the responsibility he had for the photo pilot.

Now flying on the midnight-to-noon schedule since arriving on Yankee Station, the briefing held in Air Intelligence was at 0930. Half an hour before manning aircraft. Ski and Craig met with Charlie Wilson, the photo det commander and CDR Dawkins in Air Intelligence for the briefing. Dick also attended.

"Craig and Ski, this is an important mission so listen up carefully."

"Aye, Aye Sir!" they responded in unison, listening intently, their total attention fixed on Cdr. Dawkins.

Pointing to a very large map of the area of North Vietnam from Vinh south to the border with South Vietnam near Hue, he said, "This is the North Vietnamese highway 1a as designated by the French who built it." CDR Dawkins pointed to the road on the map. "We have intelligence to lead us to believe that the North Vietnamese Army (NVA) are running a large group of troops and equipment down this road as a buildup to an assault on Hue. They always run some troops, trucks, and equipment down this route, but usually at night and not in the numbers that are presently indicated. We cannot confirm the source of this info from AirPac, but I assume it is human intel. In order for us to launch a major strike on this buildup, we need photo proof of it. With that we can go to AirPac who will get DC to approve the attack. Thus, it is imperative that you get good pix." He looked each pilot directly in the eyes to ensure they were paying attention. Once satisfied, he proceeded. "There should be no SAM activity. We have not seen Mig activity South of Vinh in several months. However, there will probably be triple-A, mainly 37s and 57s. As long as you do not go below 10,000 feet, that should not be a problem. Understood?"

"Yessir!"

"CDR Dawkins, let me jump in here please." Receiving a nod of acceptance, Charlie went on. "Craig, you will cruise into the beach right here."—pointing to the map— "See this lagoon and riverlike area just South and East of Yen Dinh on the map here?"

"Yessir," Craig answered while looking at the smaller version he had neatly folded to fit on his kneeboard.

"If you follow that water heading basically Southwest, you will hit the highway. It is a mostly paved major road compared to the other roads in the area. You will make your turn in to fly directly down the center of the road. Until you get there, don't go into the viewfinder. Once you locate the road, then get in the viewfinder and follow it exactly."

Craig nodded.

"Cruise in at 10000 feet at your maximum basic airspeed and keep it there for the whole flight. Ski, you will probably have to be in burner some to stay up with him." The photo, with no gun ports or missiles was "clean" and therefore slightly faster than the fighters. "Weather is supposed to be about 20000 overcast, around 15000 broken ceiling and clear at 10000 feet. Ski, keep your focus on calling triple-A for Craig. You are his only eyes."

"Yessir."

"Craig, if possible, make the run all the way down to the area where the road runs along the beach at a town called Mui Doc. Of course, if something happens, break it off and head east to the water as fast as you can. We will have a Texaco tanker orbiting offshore for both of you. Good luck."

As they left the briefing, Craig said to Ski, "Standard rendezvous, 10000 feet off the port bow. We will be switching to the strike frequency of 231.7 from departure."

"Roger, see you there."

As they made their way back to Ready Room Two, Dick called Ski and whispered, with direct eye contact, "Always be skeptical of what the spooks say. They tend to sugarcoat things. Keep your eyes going and expect SAMs and Migs and whatever. I am not saying that will happen. All I am saying is that you are flying your plane, and you are responsible for yourself and Craig. Do whatever is necessary. Also, remember the rules of engagement: if they fire at you, you can fire back."

"Yes sir." And with that, Ski went to get ready for the mission.

"Bottle Cap One up."

"Heater up."

After a routine catapult shot, they rendezvoused at 10000 feet just off the port side of the ship. The weather was overcast at about 20000 feet with a broken cloud layer at 15000 feet. The photo run was to be at ten thousand feet to stay clear of all cloud cover.

Craig in Bottle Cap One headed into North Vietnam just South of Vinh at Trung Thuy with Ski in Heater 203 flying on his port side, almost in combat spread but slightly behind and slightly higher.

Finding Vietnamese Highway 1a, known as Route Pak Two, McSherry turned to fly directly down the road. On the photo run he had to fly with his head in the viewfinder of the camera. It was up to the escort to call out triple-A fire, SAMS, or Migs or any other threat.

"Bottle Cap, Heater. I see little puffs of black smoke just behind your exhaust."

"Is it triple-A ?"

"Doesn't seem to be. It is in exactly the same spot each time."

"Yeah. Think that is this engine. For some reason it does that."

They flew along for what seemed like ten miles seeing nothing but road with an occasional vehicle and more ox carts. Rice paddies, villages, ox carts, and water.

Suddenly, looking ahead, Ski could see trucks, troops, and weapons carriers moving down the road. "You aren't there yet but just coming up will be the motherload of photo ops."

"Roger. Just came into view. Wow! We hit the jackpot. Air Intel is going to love this."

Camera rolling, they flew down the column at 10000 feet for at least half a mile with the end of trucks, troops, and guns not in sight. Occasionally Ski could see what he thought were bursts of 37mm trip-A fire, but the flak was well below them.

Just then he heard, "Migs, Migs South of Vinh. This is Big Look on guard. Migs, Migs, South of Vinh." Big Look was the air force EKC 135 radar plane that monitored all activity, especially of Migs and SAMS in North Vietnam. They typically flew a racetrack pattern just off the coast. One of the responsibilities of Navy Barcap was to protect them.

Instinctively Ski searched up above them starting at one o'clock high. Then he spotted flashes of light off a wing going in and out of the broken layer of clouds above them and slightly ahead.

"Bottle Cap break hard left. I have the Mig 17s at two o'clock high just in and out of the broken cloud layer."

As he watched the photo break hard, up, flying in afterburner up into the heavy cloud cover in burner, heading out into the gulf, he was on his own. The Photo, as he should, was heading for feet wet and safety as fast as possible.

Focusing on where he had seen the Migs, although he was already flying fast, he moved the throttle handle into the outboard detent to cause the afterburner of the J57 engine to light. He pulled up in a climbing turn heading directly to where he had seen the Migs. Before he reached the clouds the Migs broke out and were headed down toward him. He had armed his guns when they went over the beach, and flying directly at the Migs he fired a short burst at the same time one of the Migs also fired. Almost head on closing faster than twice the speed of sound, all shots missed. The Migs seemed to be flying in some sort of cruise formation or flying wing. At any rate, it evened the odds for him as, unless they broke up, he would fight them as one on one. Ski was a good tactics pilot. Of the nuggets, he was one of the best and often beat some of the more senior officers in practice dogfights. Sticking to his training and the F8 dogfight doctrine, he began to do a series of what were called high and low yo-yos while the Migs were turning hard, trying to get on his six for an atoll missile or guns shot. He knew better than to try to get into a turning battle with the Migs. They could out turn the F8 but could not climb as well or roll as fast. If reinforcements did not show up for them, he was confident he could beat them.

"Heater 203. Bottle Cap 101."

"Roger Bottlecap. Little busy right now."

Each time they circled around each other, as he climbed faster and higher than they could, he was able to get more behind them. It was only a matter of time before he would get a sidewinder shot. Finally, he caught the Migs in a climbing turn. With a good tone from the sidewinder missile indicating it was locked on, he pulled as many Gs as he could to get a good lead and fired. His heart sank as the missile flew straight for the first one thousand yards before arming. Then it began to track as the Migs climbed. Obviously having seen the sidewinder launch, the Migs, having passed through the broken layer, kept climbing straight up into the solid overcast before the missile caught them. Staying below the overcast, Ski circled the area, hoping to see the Migs, a parachute, or pieces of an aircraft falling to the ground, but saw nothing. The Migs had disappeared. Looking at the ground, once again he saw the line of trucks, troops, and guns. He also noticed flashes of small arms and an occasional 37 tried to reach him. With his guns still charged, he dove toward the center of the road and flew straight down it, strafing everything in sight until he ran out of ammo. At that point he climbed out of their range and flew as fast as he could to the ocean and safety.

"Texaco, Texaco this is Heater 203. I need a drink."

"Roger 203. I am an A4 streaming on the 235 radial of the Home Plate tacan orbiting at 35 miles."

"Roger Texaco. Be there in five."

"Bring cash. We do not accept credit cards."

While tanking from an A4 was a bit more difficult since the large F8 rudder was in the turbulent jet blast of the A4 exhaust, Ski had no trouble getting in. Since he was only down to 1000 pounds on fuel, he only took 2000 more to be at the optimum landing weight.

"Bottlecap, say your position."

"Roger, I am orbiting above Texaco."

After joining again on Bottle Cap 101, they flew into the break at the ship, executing standard break with the lead breaking first and Ski waiting ten seconds to break and take interval on the lead. As he put down his gear, tailhook, and raised the wing he fully concentrated on maintaining altitude and airspeed. He knew the whole ship would have heard of the Mig engagement and would be watching his landing either on the Plat TV or from Vulture's row above Air Ops. Working hard, when he rolled into final, the ball was centered, and he was exactly on speed.

"Heater 203, Crusader Ball, 2.7."

"Roger ball." He heard Joe Ames respond.

Hearing no other transmission from the LSO, he knew he had nailed the landing.

As he entered the Ready Room, Troy, the current SDO, said, "Routine Hop you big Polak?"

Craig, who had landed first, came in from Ready One, still dressed in all his flight gear. "Thanks Ski. You saved my butt."

"Craig. I almost let us down. Big Look saved both our butts. I was keeping too much focus on the ground and did not look up until they warned us. We would have flown straight into their trap. They were going to let us go by, concentrating on the line of troops while they slipped in behind us and toasted us. Got to buy whoever is in the big plane a bottle of their choice."

Dick Knowles, who had been waiting in the Ready Room said, "Ski. I am proud of you." Slapping him on the back. " When you had to you did great! Now tell us about the Migs."

"And capped it off with the best trap I have ever seen you make. OK 3. Way to go Ski!" Joe Ames who had just come in from the LSO platform added.

"When I heard the Big Look Aircraft transmission I immediately looked up to the right. We weren't that far from the water, and I figured they had to sneak down low level below our radar until they got near the convoy. They had to be inland. There was a broken layer of clouds at about 15000 feet. I caught the sun reflecting off something in just a flash. Then I saw the first Mig 17 coming out of the clouds followed by the second one. They were concentrating on Bottle Cap who was breaking speed of heat for the water. I had plenty of speed up, but I hit burner anyway and flew straight at them. I had charged my guns going over the beach, so I fired a short burst at them, but it was a high deflection shot and missed, but it got their attention and one of them fired back. As we passed, they turned just like we do in tactics, and I went up into a turning high yo-yo. They kept turning, trying to get on my six, but I kept going up and down until I was getting close for a shot."

"What was the wingman doing?" Troy asked.

"Lucky for me, the wingman was just flying a loose section or the old flying wing off the lead. For me it was like a one on one. Early on I had turned nitrogen cooling on and selected the winders in the master arming switch. I pulled the nose hard to get it in front of the Mig even though I had a good tone and fired. At first, I thought it was not going to track, but after those thousand yards of straight flight to arm, it turned directly toward the wingman's tail. I had fired as I was climbing just at the broken cloud level. Before the winder hit, they went up into the overcast. I never saw a flash. I circled under the overcast looking for anything, a parachute, pieces of a plane or the Migs to come back down, but they just disappeared. I think the clouds must have made it break lock."

Just then, CDR Dawkins came into the Ready Room. Perturbed, he said, "LT Kowalski, did you strafe that column you were sent to photo?"

"I wasn't sent to photograph. I was sent to escort the photo and got jumped by Migs you said would not be there."

"Did you strafe that column?"

"Sir, that column shot at me and the photo. Under the rules of engagement, I shot back. I think if you check my gun camera film there was plenty of fire coming up from the column. I also shot at the Migs. Is that all right?"

Dan Prescott, hearing this having just entered the ready room from the central passageway, said, "CDR Dawkins, if you have a problem with one of my pilots come see me about it. Otherwise, we can go to

CAG together and discuss the quality of intelligence we are getting from Air Intelligence."

"No problem. I just was trying to confirm the facts Dan" With that, he turned and left the room.

"Dick, will you come down to my stateroom and bring Ski with you please."

"Yessir."

The only place for the squadron commanding officers to have private meetings were their staterooms, which doubled as their offices. Cdr. Prescott indicated to both Dick and Ski for them to sit on the single bunk while he turned the desk chair backwards and sat on it with his arms folded over the top of the chair.

"Ski, I caught the tail end of what happened, but I just want you to know that in my book you did nothing wrong and a hell of a lot right. The gooks are planning something big and are sending everything they have down that road to hit our marines and army guys in Hue or Khe Shan. This could be the most important target to hit for this cruise but the puzzle palace at the Pentagon keeps from hitting what we need to and frustrates the hell out of me, and, by the way, CAG and the Admiral. Just wanted to tell you well done. Sorry I can't give you a medal for it and screw that spook. Oh, and by the way, don't forget, as a bonus for your action against the Migs, you have won the 0200-night launch with me. Get some rest."

"Thank you, sir," Ski said leaving the room as Cdr. Prescott motioned him out.

"Ski, this will be a standard night Barcap. Luckily, the weather doesn't look that bad. We will rendezvous at 20000 feet off the port side. I will have my form lights on on my aircraft." The F8 was equipped with small lights visible to wingmen to assist with night formation flights. "We will switch to the Red Crown frequency as we depart from the ship. On Barcap, fly a loose form on me. Even with decent weather, stay fairly close. Standard Cat shot. Emergency procedure for the day is generator failure. On this hop what would you do in case of a generator failure?

"I would pop the Rat," Ski said, referring to the ram air turbine that worked as an auxiliary generator. Once popped, it dropped from the fuselage into the airstream, which turned a turbine providing back up electrical supply.

"And what do you lose on the Rat?"

"Probably most importantly on Barcap is that we lose our refueling probe. Also, weapons will not work. Lights are OK as is the fuel pump, etc."

"Roger. Have a good flight and work your ass off on the approach and at the ball."

On the flight deck, Ski went through the preflight with Walker as his plane captain. He strapped in and after going through the start-up, taxied up on the port catapult. Adding a little power to go over the shuttle, he was given the signal to go to full power. With the throttle at full power, he looked at the lighted weight board and turned on his external lights to indicate that he was ready to launch. The Cat and Arresting gear officer leaned down and touched the deck with his lighted wand and the catapult immediately fired, launching Ski and his F8 Heater 209 off the bow of the ship.

As usual, the F8 took a good cat shot and was immediately flying. However, just as he was airborne, all the instrument lights went out. With one hand on the throttle and the other on the stick, Ski had no way to control the red lens flashlight attached to his torso harness. With the gooseneck lens ninety degrees to his body, swinging, it sporadically shined a light across the attitude gyro, altimeter, and the other instruments. Ski lowered the wing and raised the gear. Remaining at full power, he pulled back on the stick and climbed, knowing that the altitude was his friend as he tried to sort out the problem.

"Sandbox. This is Heater 209. I have had an instrument light failure on launch."

"Roger 209. Standby for instructions."

"Roger," Ski answered. He climbed until he felt he was well clear of the water, leveling off at about 20000 feet. Hands now off the throttle, he was able to focus his light on the instruments. He already knew that there was no circuit breaker or anything else he could do to get the lights back. With the luxury of altitude, he was able to strap down the flashlight so he could see his instruments. As far as he could tell, everything but the lights were working well.

The air boss called out to Pri Fly. "Who is the F8 rep?"

"I am Boss." Preacher answered, "There is no way in the aircraft for him to reset the lights. They must have shorted out on the Cat shot."

"Could it have been a generator failure?"

"I do not think so, sir. He had his radio working."

"Roger. We will have to bingo him to channel 77. Hey departure, give me a steer for Heater 209 to Danang."

"Heater 209. Sandbox departure. Your signal is Bingo. Steer 218 for Danang. Contact approach control on 235.9"

"Two-O-Nine, this is the air boss. Don't even think of drinking a beer there. Be overhead for the 0600 recovery."

"Roger boss, 209 out."

Chapter Fourteen

.

LOOSE DEUCE
20 June 1967 Yankee Station
0400 hours

After returning from a standard night Barcap on the midnight-to-noon schedule, Ray headed down to the line shack to do more paperwork. Supposed to fly with the XO, he ended up with Casper, the spare. CDR Scampi had downed his plane on startup.

"Sir, do you have a minute?"

"Sure, Pearson. What's up?"

"It's CDR Scampi, sir."

"What about him?" Ray frowned, not wanting to get into a conflict with the XO.

"Sir, he not only treats the plane captains like shit when he is manning, he has been shorting out his instrument lights and downing his plane on night flights."

"Do you have any proof of this?"

"Yessir. He has had four instrument light failures before night flights. The rest of the squadron has none except for LT Kowalski's off the cat."

"He carries a little screwdriver in his flight suit and jams it into a bulb to short out the lights."

Seven hours later, in the Ready Room, Casper answered the phone. "VF188."

"Ghost, this is the CO. Would you send the XO to my room ASAP?"

"Yessir. He just came in from his flight. Now or after his brief?"

"Get his ass up here now!"

"Yessir!"

Casper called out to CDR Scampi and said, "Commander, CO wants to see you in his stateroom ASAP."

"Tell him I will be there after debriefing the hop with Air Intelligence." He turned to talk away, but Casper stepped in front of him, blocking his way.

"Begging your pardon sir, but he insisted you see him before the debrief."

"OK. I will go right down to his stateroom."

Relieved, Casper stepped aside and let him walk away.

After knocking on the stateroom door, Scampi heard the skipper call, "Enter."

Commander Prescott was sitting at the desk in his small, single stateroom. The room was immaculate, but sparse. One bed neatly made. Gray walls. Gray straight chair. He turned in the chair and said in a very firm voice, "Flying Wing. Did I hear right that you were having Troy Davis fly a Flying Wing formation on you over the beach on Mig Cap?"

"Yessir, but I can explain."

"You can explain how the fuck you were totally disregarding F8 doctrine by flying a formation that has been out of the tactic's manual since World War Two. Are you that fucking stupid? Now you almost got Davis killed and lost one of our precious aircraft."

"If you are in the soup or flying a flak suppression hop, you close in and fly closer. But if you are planning on jumping Migs, you better be in combat spread."

"I have half a mind to ground you and put you in hack or send you home. I won't do it because we need an XO and a pilot." By now, Commander Prescott was red in the face, obviously furious. "I understand Davis is medically down from injuries he suffered in the ejection. For now, I am going to keep you off the schedule and we will discuss who will be your wingman in the future."

"Sir, if I can explain. My last tour in the Med in VF15 I was the Ops officer and tactics leader. We found that the Flying Wing with a Thatch weave was the best formation for our patrols contrary to the tactics manual."

"Shit. That might work against lumbering Bear Russian bombers, but it will just get your wingman shot down here. Do not consider using it in the future." He was fuming. "Additionally, did you know that, after my tour with the Blues, I had a tour in the Med with VF 64 as the senior Lieutenant. We did tactics by the book. Combat Spread and once the fight was on, you went to Loose Deuce for mutual support. Whoever saw the bogey first called the fight. That is what you will do in the future, understood?"

"Yessir."

"Tell me, what is the proper and accepted tactical move to make when targeted by a SAM?"

"You wait until it gets close, then at the last minute you perform a high-G maneuver, usually a barrel roll ending up in a split S down."

"And that is what you did, right?"

"Yessir."

"And where did that leave Troy, flying behind you in a flying wing? He had to wait on you to execute his defensive maneuver, right?"

He nodded.

"As a result, his plane got hit. Thankfully he was quick enough to at least avoid most of the blast and was able to get feet wet. When we fly off after this line period to Cubi you will ride the ship in. I order you, in any future hops, to follow tactical F8 doctrine. I do not want to hear anything about East Coast doctrine. Understood?"

"Yessir."

"Furthermore, how is it that you now are on the schedule for all the Mig Caps?"

"Did LT Casper talk to you about that?"

"No, he did not. I read the schedule. Not only do I read the schedule, per regs I sign off on it. I can see who has whatever hop. I saw that you were scheduled for the last three Mig Caps."

"Yessir. It is my belief that one section, highly trained, should always do the Mig Cap. Protecting the fleet from Migs is our most important task. So, by having two or three highly trained pilots working as a team would be the most efficient way to do that."

"And you would be that highly trained lead? It is not a question of you using junior pilots as bait and flushing the Migs in front of you like a bird dog? Our doctrine, I repeat, is that we fly combat spread and use loose deuce tactics. That every pilot in the squadron is capable of dog fighting the Migs using F8 doctrine. Understood?"

"Yessir."

"By the way, whatever you were doing when we went two on two with Dick and Captain Butler did not work out that well, did it?" No reply. "As I recall, Dick shot your ass down." Still no reply. "I want you to know that no one came to me with this. I can read the schedule, and I get reports every time a plane is down. I see that on the last four night hops you have downed your aircraft and the spare has had to fly the flight. I do not care about what the reason is. You will fly what you are scheduled for. If that engine starts you better damn well fly the flight. Dismissed."

Totally humiliated, Commander Scampi turned on his heel and left.

After ringing Dick Knowles' stateroom, CDR Prescott told him, "Dick, get up to my room ASAP. We have a major fuck-up to work around."

The three roommates and John Phillips crowded into sick bay to see Troy Davis. Troy had two black eyes and lacerations on his face. His neck was held in suspended traction with a cervical device connected by cables to an anchored system on the overhead.

Sick bay on the aircraft carrier looked just like a hospital room in critical care in any major hospital. The ship had several Doctors and a Dentist. The Doctor in charge was a full Captain. The air wing had their own Flight Surgeon who was attached to the ship once the air wing came aboard.

"How are you doing roomie?" Ski asked.

"I am OK. Lucky to be alive." Troy mumbled. His mouth also had been bruised in the impact with the water from the ejection.

"What happened?" John Philips asked.

"XO had me flying in a formation one hundred to 200 feet out on his wing on Mig Cap over the beach at 20 grand. I heard the *deedle deedle* on the ALQ 100 of a SAM radar. Then I heard the high pitch of it locked on and launched. I was stuck on the XO, but I tried to look down the strobe to the SAM and next thing I knew the XO did a split-S and shouted, break now! I broke down as hard as I could but apparently the SAM exploded behind me and caused damage to the PC system. I was losing control, but I just put the nose down and headed for the water." He sighed heavily while recalling the events. "I did not have much control, and I was afraid the PCs would go completely out. I got over the water and rode it until I felt the nose dropping hard. I punched out hunched over with the D handle between my legs. I felt one swing of the chute and smashed into the water face first."

"What does Rookie Doc say about it?" Twain asked.

At that moment, navy LT "Rookie" Doctor Pete Williams, Flight Surgeon, walked in on the group. "What about Rookie Doc?" he asked.

"When will this sloucher be back up and flying? He is using this lousy excuse to get out of night flying." Aggie asked.

"He has a severe neck sprain. We did not find any damage to his discs or back, but I want to be cautious for a few days until the swelling goes down. I do not think he will be up in-flight status for a few weeks. Since the X-rays did not show damage to the discs, we are going to take him out of traction and put him in a hard neck collar. We will keep him here under observation for a few days."

"I don't think you get a Purple Heart unless you bleed. Can you cut him somewhere?" Ski asked.

Laughing, Dr. Williams answered, "No. But I understand that you do get a Purple Heart for any injury caused in combat."

"Troy, you are such a slacker. You boat school guys will do anything for a medal. But thanks for becoming our new, permanent SDO." Ray added, patting him gently on the shoulder. "Glad you will be OK. How did you get picked up?"

"I heard the A4s overhead running a Rescap. Think maybe I heard some Spads coming in to strafe around me and then the last I heard were the blades of the helo before I passed out. They said that I lit smoke, but I don't remember that."

"Man, you are really going to owe those helo guys a lot of drinks."

Troy began to close his eyes and blink back open, obviously feeling some sedative he had been given. "Guys, think we need to let Troy get some rest. We will get out of here." John Williams pushed the others out. "Troy, just sleep for now, but we will be back."

"Is that a threat?"

They smirked as they left to let him rest.

Back in their stateroom Aggie said, "Man, Troy was just lucky he made it. What the fuck was the XO doing putting him in that close formation?"

"He was doing exactly what happened. Covering his own ass with Troy." Ski said.

"Did you notice that Troy did not say anything about the XO or any F8 being in on the Rescap. A4s and maybe Spads. But no F8s. I don't know if 123 was flying then but I sure as hell know the XO was." Ray added. "This sucks."

After briefing Dick on what he had learned about the Davis shoot down, Commander Prescott told him, "Get me a Purple Heart and let me know when Troy will be awake. Then let's go down and pin it on him, OK?"

"Aye, Aye Sir."

CDR Prescott didn't waste any time calling the Duty Desk.

"Ready Two, VF 188, how can I help?"

"Ghost, I want everyone in the Ready Room at 12 hundred before the movie for a brief AOM. Also, have sick bay let me know when Troy will be awake. I need to go see him." Prescott said.

"Aye, Aye Sir."

Everyone was in their assigned chairs when Commander Prescott entered the Ready Room. "Attention on deck!" Dick Knowles shouted.

"As you were." Most were dressed in the tropical khaki uniform of the day, but Preacher and Joe Ames were still in their flight suits having just landed after the last flight of the day.

"As I am sure you have heard, LT Troy Davis was shot down today by a SAM near Haiphong. He is doing well in sick bay, but they are going to keep him for a few days to make sure that his neck and back will be alright. He will be bored. So please go down and see him and, Aggie,"—he nodded toward him— "do your best to keep him entertained with your bullshit."

"Aye, Aye, Sir. But I only spread the utmost truth."

A quiet but audible laugh spread among those present.

"Now Troy probably could not evade the SAM because he was flying a tight formation on his lead." Prescott said, turning and glaring at the XO. "As long as I am Skipper of this squadron no lead is to brief or fly any two plane in any formation other than combat spread per the established doctrine. First one to see the Migs calls the fight. And then you fight in Loose Deuce. Is that understood?"

All answered. "Aye, aye."

"Now, some better news. You probably heard me say, LT Troy Davis. That is because the Lieutenant list has come out. All our JGs, including Aggie, have been promoted to Lieutenant. Therefore, I expect one tremendous wetting down party next time we are in Cubi. Understood?"

"Yessir! I personally will take charge of it." Aggie said.

"Finally, Gunners Mate Warrant Arancio has something to say."

"Gents, two items." The gunny warrant officer has a very large Italian. He had risen through the ranks starting as a gunner's mate in the Korean War loading 500-pound bombs on F9s and Corsairs by hand using a "hernia" bar. As were most Gunner's mates, he was tough. He had been in bar fights in bars throughout the world in his career. The broken nose and scars on his face and hands showed it. However, he thought of the young pilots as his friends and felt the need to protect them like a Mother Hen. After almost thirty years in many squadrons, he had personally felt the pain of losing pilots in combat or carrier accidents. He was especially upset when the guns would jam, a problem with the Colt 20mm feed system. He prided himself on making sure that when they fired, they were bore sighted to hit whatever they were aiming at. "First, if you need anything at all for your personal defense, please see me. The day before the fly off to Cubi, meet me on the fantail at 1600 hours to fire out your survival pistols. We will have plenty of rounds and the ship will be dumping trash over the stern, which we can use as targets. Again, if you want anything for your personal defense, I can get it for you."

"Gunny, is it safe to have Aimless walking around the Ready Room with a grenade?" John Phillips asked.

"Poet, that was his choice. It will not go off until he pulls the pin." The gunny replied. "Next, as some of you know, I have a hobby of keeping clown fish in my aquarium down in ordnance. Somebody, who I will throw overboard once I find them, put JP in my water and killed all the fish."

The squadron's gunner's mates, whose duties included loading the guns, locking in the highly sensitive and dangerous sidewinders by hand on the fuselage mounts, and hand lifting as a team the bombs onto their mounts, respected the Warrant, but liked teasing him about his fish. "Next time we are in port I am looking for volunteers to go out on a special services boat and help me to catch more clown fish snorkeling. It will be a few hours of shooting our pistols and fishing a little."

"The three amigos are in." Aggie shouted, with nods of head from Ray and Ski.

Technically, Warrant Arancio reported to Ray Rhodes, since Ray was the designated gunnery officer. However, while not officially, everyone knew that warrant officers ran things even more than the chiefs did. The chance for the three JOs to be invited to go with him was guaranteed to be a good time. Undoubtedly Warrant Arancio had a connection in Special Services that would hook him up with a boat, snorkeling gear and anything else he wanted.

Chapter Fifteen

DUSTY RHODES

23 June 1967 Yankee Station

The last mail call before returning to Cubi, Ray received a package from his mother that looked suspiciously like cookies.

"Hey Ray,. Your package looks a lot like cookies. Are you sharing with your roomies?" Aggie asked.

"Aggie, I don't know, after I give the Skipper his cut, if there will be enough for you." Ray laughed and tossed him a brownie wrapped in Saran Wrap.

John Williams had received another suspicious letter with a woman's handwriting. After opening the envelope and reading it, he approached the skipper at the front of the Ready Room where he was busy reading his mail.

"Skipper," he said quietly. "Don't mean to intrude but have something we need to discuss."

"Saw that letter. Is it from who I think?" The skipper said without even looking at it.

"Yes. It is from Astrud." The skipper could hear the tension in his voice.

"What does she say?"

"She doesn't come right out with it but I think she is pregnant."

"Wow." The skipper leaned back in his chair. "That changes the ball game. Did Ray say that he wanted to marry her before cruise?"

"He did."

"I want to get you and Dick together and see what we can do. Bring me some ideas. Make it 1400 in my quarters."

"Yessir. I will tell Dick."

At 1400 exactly, Dick and John Phillipps knocked on the door of Commander Prescott.

"Enter."

They entered the stateroom and, directed by Commander Prescott, took a seat on the single bed. Dan Prescott sat facing them on his desk chair.

"I think I have a solution if our boy and his girl are open to it."

Bending over to get his face closer to them, his hands on his knees, he said in a confidential tone, "I can send Ray back to the Rag to get an update on the latest tactics for fighting both SAMs and Migs. They have gun camera film and detailed updates from an Israeli pilot who fought both in their recent war with the Arabs. That will be my justification."

"Then, if she agrees and he still wants to, they can get married."

"When would this happen?"

"We can get away with it easier with CAG and the powers that be if I send him TAD during our Hong Kong visit. He can leave when we get to Cubi and be back before we return. That way he won't miss any flights on the line."

"Can they get the marriage license, etc. in time without him being there?"

"I will sic Sandy on it. She will get it done if Astrud and Ray agree. Probably must execute some kind of power of attorney. I don't want this to get beyond us and Ray, so I don't want to try anything with our legal officer on the ship."

"I think Sandy knows a lawyer there who can help on the QT."

"First things first. Poet, tell Ray about the letter and tell him to call Astrud as soon as he lands after the fly off to Cubi on Wednesday. Let him know that we are working on a way for him to get back there and marry her if she agrees but tell him to keep quiet about it."

Poet nodded, and once dismissed, he began taking action.

"Hey Ray, how are you doing?"

"I am doing OK. How goes it with you, Fred?" They had been in the same training squadron in Meridian and many of the same classes in Flight Training. Fred had gone to A4s, and they had lost touch until they both were sent to squadrons on the Adams.

Fred, who was from a small Kansas town, had always wanted to fly. As a boy he had made models of almost every plane the United States flew in World War Two. He read books like *Thirty Seconds Over Tokyo*, *The Bridges of Toko Ri* and anything dealing with the Battle of Britain. In his teens, he hung around the local civilian airport until they gave him a job washing aircraft, fueling, and assorted other tasks. Occasionally, a pilot would take him up for a short flight and let him fly a little. After college, he entered the navy via the Aviation Officer's Candidate program (AOC). Completing advanced jet training in the F9 Cougar in Kingsville, Texas, he received his wings and commission as ensign at the same time. Before he entered the navy he met and married Jennifer, a girl he had known slightly in his church youth group. He had met her again after he returned from college and worked part time in the local drug store while he waited for his AOC class to start. While he, like many naval aviators, had wanted fighters, his instrument flying grades were not quite good enough and he had been sent to A4s.

"I am OK but flying tonight. A night bombing hop on combat sky spot. You know, I hate these hops. You have no idea what you are bombing. Just fly out on a radar heading and drop when the controller tells you and hope that you are over the trail and not dropping on some innocent family just trying to get by out there. I don't have a problem bombing triple-A sites or SAM sites. I don't have a problem with bridges, power plants, military convoys on Route Pak 1. Truck parks or even individual trucks. I just don't like to drop without knowing what I am dropping on."

"Understand. Glad we don't do that. Night all we do is bore holes in the sky and try not to kill ourselves on the ramp. Have a good hop anyway and nail an OK 3."

"What time do you go?"

"At 1930 and you?"

"Same launch. See you on the flight deck."

"Roger."

Later, when Ray was in the line shack in his flight suit doing more paperwork, the phone rang. "Hey Ray, this is John. I need to talk to you. Can you come by my stateroom before your hop?"

"Roger that. I will be there in fifteen. Just have to finish a couple of evals."

"Hurry," John said before hanging up.

Not even ten minutes later, Ray knocked on his door. John opened the door and motioned for Ray to sit on one of the two desk chairs. A two-man stateroom John shared with Casper, there was a double bunk against the port bulkhead, a sink mounted on the forward wall with a mirror above for shaving, and two identical pull-down desks side by side on the starboard wall.

"Ray, as you know the Skipper asked me to talk to you about Astrud."

"Yes."

"Well, I went ahead and wrote to her. Hope you didn't mind. I got a letter back from her today. From the gist of the letter I think she might be in the family way."

"Pregnant?" Ray asked.

John answered, "Yep. She wants you to call her. She said anytime day or night. So, Skipper says for you to get up to the phones at the club and call her as soon as you land on the fly off."

"This is absolutely confidential. If you and her decide to get married like you wanted before the cruise, Skipper will make it happen by sending you back to Miramar for updates on Mig tactics on a brief by an Israeli fighter pilot. However, the Skipper is sticking his neck way out for you. You cannot let anyone know what is actually going on. Understood?"

"Yes, I do." Ray had to really stop himself from hugging him. "John, I cannot thank you enough. You don't understand how much this means to me."

"Oh, I think I do,. Have a good hop and end it with an OK 3."

It looked like a good night. The seas were calm and the moon was out.

"This should be easy, Ray. Know you are pumped up but keep it under control. Smooth flight ending in a perfect OK 3. Right?"

"Yes, Skipper. But I do want to thank you for what you are doing."

"I am doing exactly nothing, understood?"

"Yessir!"

"This will be a standard Barcap. Join on me at 20000 feet off the port side. We will switch to Red Crown on 239.5. Plan on tanking two times. Concentrate on the approach and get that smooth OK 3. Concentrate. Do not think about anything else during the approach other than staying exactly on speed and on altitude. Understood? Won't help Astrud if you end up splattered on the ramp. Besides, I can't afford to lose any more aircraft."

"Yessir!"

On the flight deck in the calm before the launch began, he saw Fred preflighting his A4 with a heavy bomb load. The plane was a VA 18 A4, Number AH 304. He waved, and called out, "have a good flight, Fred."

"Likewise, Ray!"

After a thorough preflight, Ray strapped in, started the engine and went carefully through the preflight checklist. Night was no time for haste. Following the flashlight commands of a yellow shirt flight director, he taxied forward. He was trusting the yellow shirt for direction and speed. On the completely blacked out flight deck, the only lights were the flashlights of the yellow shirts and the dim aircraft lights. Carefully watching his flight director, he powered up just a little to go over the shuttle on the port catapult, applying the brakes just as the nose fell over the top. Holding the brakes, he advanced the throttle to full military, checked the lighted weight board, checked his engine instruments, and then turned on the exterior lights to let the cat officer know he was ready to go. The Cat shot was a bit more thrilling than usual when Ray was shot into a black night at 180 knots, but the climb rate of the F8 made it simple. As usual, the Barcaps were the first to launch. However, there had been a problem with the skipper on the starboard cat and Ray had been first to launch. Spiraling up to the rendezvous at 20,000 feet, he watched the deck in the dim light and finally saw the skipper go.

Just before joining in formation with Commander Prescott he heard the air boss call: "Aircraft off the port cat, keep it climbing. 304 keep climbing."

"I am trying boss" he heard Fred call.

"Skipper, as usual a smooth OK 3. I did not have to say anything. Nice pass!" Joe Ames debriefed CDR Prescott's landing.

"Thanks, Joe."

"Aimless, are you just brown nosing the skipper? You know I fly smooth as silk, but you keep giving me fairs." Aggie shouted from the SDO desk.

"I give you fairs because it looks like you are killing snakes in the cockpit. You are such a hamburger, and the lettuce and tomato are falling off your head." Joe replied.

"Ray, you also had an OK 3. Just a little tweak at the burble, but a good pass." Ames said.

"Joe, what happened to Fred, that A4 on launch? I knew him in flight training." Ray asked.

"Boss kept calling for him to climb but he flew into the water about a mile in front of the ship. He may have gotten a slightly weak cat shot but it doesn't appear so. All he had to do was jettison the bombs and that scooter would have jumped up in the air, but for some reason he did not do that or eject. Just a lack of concentration on his part."

"Did he make it out?"

"No and the helo didn't find anything."

"That's really shitty. He had a wife and a kid."

Later that night, knocking on the stateroom door, Ray asked, "Hey Preach. Do you have a minute?"

"Sure Ray, come on it." A standard two-man stateroom, which he shared with LCDR Ferguson who was in the mess. He motioned to one of the two chairs by the identical small desks against the bulkhead. "What's up?"

"I don't know if you heard about the scooter driver who went in off the cat."

"Yeah, I did."

"I knew him in flight training. He had a wife and a kid. I talked to him just before he launched on the flight deck. He was depressed."

"Oh?"

"He told me that he hated to do those night radar sky spots where they dropped their bombs and didn't know what they were bombing. That he was afraid of dropping on some innocent mother with kids like his." Ray sighed heavily. "I think he killed himself by not focusing. Makes me wonder what we are doing."

"Ray, you just have to focus on being the best you can be in each and every hop. War is not neat or pretty. To survive you have to concentrate all the time."

"Preach, I am sure you have heard about me and Astrud. The only thing we ever disagreed about was the war. I don't know how to handle that. How do you do it?"

LCDR Ferguson said, "You do know that I am not a preacher. It is just a nickname because I don't drink, seldom swear, and generally behave on liberty. I am a Christian. I do believe, no matter what the protestors say, that the war is just. I wish we would fight it to win. It frustrates me that we do this with one hand tied behind our back which results in more of us dying and more of the innocent civilians dying. I truly believe that the strong have a responsibility to help the weak. If you wonder about whether this is just or not, ask the people of South Korea. We saved them and could have saved the North also if Truman hadn't tied MacArthur's hands." He could see in Ray's eyes that what he was saying wasn't really helping soothe his soul. But there was nothing he could do. "Here we need to go full force after the docks in Haiphong. Destroy their SAMs and other arms before they are operational. By fighting this McNamara style war, more innocent Vietnamese end up being killed, more of our marines get killed, and our fellow aviators get killed. Not our fault and not the fault of your scooter driver friend."

Since they were on the midnight to noon cycle on Yankee Station, flight ops were secured at 1200 hours the next day. The ship began its voyage back to Cubi Point at that time. At 1600 hours, most of the squadron pilots had assembled aft on the flight deck fantail with their survival pistols. From open boxes of 9mm and 45 ammo supplied by Gunny Arancio they grabbed rounds to fill the magazines for their guns.

"All right. All of you, including Joe Ames, please use good safety procedures. Only shoot at targets I call out to you when I call your name. I will assign a score for each shot, and we will see who is the best shot in the squadron behind the Skipper."

"Hey Gunny. The Skipper isn't here."

"No, he isn't but I am sure he is the best shot. And, by the way, I am second best. Anyone disagree?"

Laughing, they all agreed.

After carefully firing a few single shots, Ski said, "Screw this" and rapidly fired off his whole magazine from his 45 after missing the target with the first round. After that, they all began firing out their pistols when the gunny gave them the target.

"Hey Aimless. Throw the grenade!" Poet yelled.

Warrant Arancio immediately said, "No way. He'll probably throw it backward."

With that, the shooting ended. Ray, due to his experience with firearms on the ranch, and Casper who had hunted as a kid, were declared the winners. Aggie, as usual, complained that he was discriminated against because he was a Texan.

Back on a normal schedule, the movie that night in the Ready Room was at 1800 hours, after dinner in the wardroom.

As the pilots milled around the Ready Room waiting for the flick, the skipper spoke to Dick: "Tomorrow the XO and I will be riding the ship in. Of course, Troy cannot fly yet so he will also ride the ship. I hope the Doc clears him to get off when we get to Cubi. The XO will handle the SDO duties, and I am going to catch up on some paperwork. Make up one four plane diamond followed by a three plane in echelon. We only have seven birds up after losing Troy's. I know it is hard for us to slow down when we are heading for port, but please escort VA 18 in as they will be doing a missing man for the pilot they lost last night. Orbit while they go into the break first."

"Aye, Aye Sir! I will fly lead for the diamond and have Preacher lead the echelon."

"Sounds good."

Chapter Sixteen

Sandy
28 June 1967 San Diego

"Hello." Sandy sounded groggy.
"Hi Honey, sorry to call so late but I just got in." Dan Prescott said, calling from one of the phone booths in the Cubi O'Club reserved for officers. Using that booth, he called his wife, Sandy, in San Diego.

"Oh Dan, I was worried! I thought you would call yesterday."

"I rode the ship in instead of making the fly off. Troy had to eject, and we are short of planes now. I wanted to let the nuggets have a chance to get in."

"I heard about Troy. How is he?"

"Looks like he is going to be Ok. Expect the Doc to clear him for flying in a few days."

"How are the kids? I know it is too late for them."

"They are fine, sleeping."

"I will call later tonight when they will be up. By the way, how do you know the ship's movements before we do? That is supposed to be a secret." Dan asked.

"You know, one of the girls has a friend from another squadron whose husband is now at AirPac. He tells her and she tells us. Not much of a secret."

"Figures. How is Pam Huggins doing?"

"She comes to all our squadron wives' club meetings and seems to be doing better, but it is really tough. You be safe. Let the young kids take the rough missions."

"You know I can't do that."

"I know. I just love you and miss you."

"I love and miss you too." He told her.

They had met when Dan Prescott was in his second tour as a Blue Angel solo pilot. After just graduating from the University of Miami in finance, she was working for a mutual fund company based in Fort Lauderdale. Her father, a retired airline pilot, recently widowed, had asked her to accompany him to a reception for the Blues prior to their show over Fort Lauderdale Beach. He had flown Hellcats in World War Two off the Enterprise and was a founding member of the Fort Lauderdale Navy League. Escorted by her father, she was a striking Florida blonde, tanned wearing a turquoise dress just low cut and short enough to be enticing without offending her dad. The minute they entered the reception, Dan saw her and moved toward her in order to cut off any of his Blues squadron mates before they reacted. Just under 6 feet tall, Dan Prescott, wearing his Blue Angel Flight suit, was ruggedly handsome. Dark hair, eyes almost black, a strong nose with high cheekbones giving him a hint of Native American in his background.

Reaching out to shake Sandy's father's hand, while keeping his gaze on Sandy, Dan said, "Hi. I am Dan Prescott. Whom do I have the pleasure of meeting?"

"I am Chuck Umstead, and this is my daughter Sandy. Wanted to see the current crop of naval aviators. Things have changed a bit since I flew the Hellcat."

"Wow, quite a plane. I would really like to hear about that."

"Bullshit! If you have any sense you want to sit down in that lounge area with my beautiful daughter and try to charm the heck out of her."

"Dad!" Sandy exclaimed.

"I may be old, but I still know how the game is played."

Dan and Sandy were patient while her dad told a few sea stories. Then they moved to the lounge and learned more about each other. Dan asked her to dinner the night after the air show. Completely smitten, he managed a long-range relationship with her until his tour ended with the Blues. Then, with a choice of assignments, he chose to be the senior lieutenant in a Cecil Field based F8 squadron, VF 64 in order to be close to her. For her part, she lobbied for and obtained a transfer to the Jacksonville office of the Mutual fund company for whom she worked. Together full time, Dan asked her to marry him before he left on his first Mediterranean Cruise.

"Sandy, I need you to help me with something," Dan said.

"Sure, what do you need?"

"You know Ray Rhodes, the one we call Dusty?"

"Sure. He is your wingman. He seems to be a great guy."

"He is and he is becoming a great stick. He is the best nugget I have ever seen. We are lucky to have him."

"What do you need?"

"Sandy, do you remember that dark blonde Brazilian girl he brought to some of our parties?"

"Sure, Astrud. For a few weeks she came to our squadron wives' activities, but I haven't been able to get her to come lately."

"Well, that is probably because it seems that Ray got her pregnant before the cruise. He wanted to marry her, but she wanted to wait until after the cruise. She went silent with Ray, but I had John reach out to her. She had quit writing to Ray and shut him out because she was pregnant and did not know how to tell him."

"Oh, that poor girl."

"She wants to talk to him now. He was supposed to call her yesterday and ask her again to marry him. I haven't heard yet, but I am pretty sure he did it as I ordered him to do it."

"Oh, that's good."

"Cutting to the chase, I am planning on sending him back to Miramar on TAD when we go to Hong Kong so they can get married, and she can get set up with all the dependent stuff. Can you help her set up the wedding, Sandy, get the license and whatever else needs done?"

"Will do, Skipper. I will get Pam to help. She needs a project but if Astrud agrees, we will plan her wedding."

"Thanks Love, I really appreciate it and miss you. Let me know."

"Call when the kids are up. I love you!"

The fly in to Cubi was uneventful. There were only a few broken clouds on an otherwise beautiful tropical day. After hanging back to allow the A4s to perform a very good missing man break, Dick led the Diamond Fan break followed by Preacher leading the echelon fan. After taxiing in, Aggie shut down his plane and unstrapped as fast as possible, telling the plane captain who was putting the pins in the ejection seat to hurry up. He climbed out of the aircraft and ran over to the ramp still with his helmet, G-suit, and torso harness on, and grabbed Lynn who was standing there. He picked her up and kissed her despite the oxygen mask hanging to the side.

"How did you get on the flight line?" he asked.

"I have a friend who works for Captain Butler. She got him to get me a pass. You need a shower!"

"I will grab one at the BOQ. Can I buy you lunch?"

"It will have to be dinner. I am AWOL from school and my friend Jane is handling both our classes for me. I just wanted to greet you."

"OK. Dinner it is. Think we better make it at the Subic Club with all those sophisticated ship drivers. Cubi club will be nuts. Pick you up at 6 at your quarters?"

"That will be fine. Do not get too drunk, Aggie Twain!" she admonished as she walked toward the Ops building and the base taxi.

"I promise not to drink more than five tequila shooters."

Since flight suits were not allowed in the club, Ray rushed to the BOQ with his flight bag and changed to civies to make the call to Astrud. Almost running from the BOQ to the club two blocks away, he was covered with sweat by the time he got into the phone booth.

The ringing stopped and she answered, "Hello."

"Hello Astrud. I am so glad to hear you. I love you so much and miss you!"

"Oh, I love you too, Ray. So happy you called. I am so sorry I did not write. I did not know how to tell you about the baby. Did you know?"

"Poet, John Phillips, told me that he thought you were pregnant but was not sure. You are, aren't you? And if you are, so am I. Will you marry me now?" he asked.

"Yes, and yes I will marry you, but how?"

"Skipper is going to send me TAD next month to Miramar while the ship goes to Hong Kong. We can get married then. Skipper said that his wife would help with the arrangements, and I can get Mom and Dad to help also."

"Oh, I know his wife, Sandy. She is great. You do not know what a load this takes off of me. I do love you so much. I worry about you. Please be safe. I heard what happened to Troy. Will he be OK?

"I think he will be fine. May have a kink in his neck for a while, but we think he will be back up flying before long." He heard Astrud sigh with relief. "Some good news. I got promoted to full Lieutenant. We are having a wetting down party at the Club once the ship gets in. That will give us a little more money for the baby. Do you need anything now?"

"No, not really. But I will need some baby stuff. What's a wetting down?"

"Oh, it's a naval tradition. Upon promotion, all officers throw a party for their shipmates with drinking being the primary activity."

"Sounds fun."

"Anyway, I am going to send you $500 now. Sandy can get you in the base exchange to buy baby stuff. Do you have a good doctor? She probably knows someone and once we are married, the navy will pay for the doctor. I think in San Diego they send you to civilian doctors. She will know all that. I will call my parents, and they will also help with anything you need. They will be so excited to have a grandkid. Have you told your family?"

"No, not yet. At first, I thought of not having the baby, but I am so glad I kept it. I really need and want this baby. I love you. I am so glad you want the baby."

"Of course I want the baby. I want to be a dad!"

"Have fun during your ceremony, my love."

At the wetting down, the new lieutenants had contributed a hundred dollars to Aggie to set up a champagne fountain, an open bar, and a food table featuring lumpia, wontons, chicken adobo, and lots of tequila shooters.

"What the fuck makes the F8 so special?" He slurred, obviously drunk, sipping from the delicate champagne glass.

"I'm Jim Kowalski, known surprisingly as Ski, pilot extraordinaire of the finest plane ever built, the F8 Crusader from Chancey Vought." Kowalski said, switching his champagne from right hand to left, and extended his right to the stranger. "Welcome to our wetting down party, who the fuck are you?"

"I'm Jake Williams. I fly F4s with VF 96 off the America."

"Well, Jake my man, the F8 is your red bicycle!"

"Yeah, that's right!" Aggie overheard, walked up and agreed with his roommate. "It's a fucking red bicycle!"

"I don't get it." Williams said. "What does that have to do with flying?"

"You don't get it because you fly a double-barreled shit can. You wish you could get it, but you don't. You wish you could fly the F8, but you can't." Slurring his words, Aggie chimed in, getting a little antagonistic.

"Hey, I love the Phantom. We can wax your ass any day."

"Yeah, always we, 'cause it takes two of you to fly the easiest flying plane ever made landing on those huge big deck boats." Aggie was not going to let up.

"The red bicycle," Ski continued, not willing to give up his point, "is what every kid wanted at Christmas! A red, three speed, Schwinn Corvette. The fastest, baddest, most beautiful bike in the neighborhood. That's what we got under the tree with the Crusader. Sometimes she's a mean mother dirty and at night, and you have to be the best to fly her, but she's the most beautiful and fastest bike ever built."

"Yeah! And you don't have to haul around dead weight in the back seat!" Aggie added. As he drunkenly attempted to drink his champagne, his huge hand slipped on the glass and in his attempt to grab it he snapped the round bowl off the top off the stem.

Seeing that, Williams said, "I can do anything a F8 driver can do." He proceeded to snap the top bowl off his glass, but when he did it the stem slipped and gouged a hole in the palm of his hand which immediately began to bleed.

"Maybe not quite as well as we can!" Ski said, pouring the contents of his glass on the bleeding hand. "Here, this will sterilize it."

In the meantime, Jake Williams pulled out a handkerchief and began tying it around the hand to stop the bleeding. Aggie went over to the champagne fountain and filled up three more glasses, bringing them back to the group.

"For a phantom puke you are all right, Jake my man." He said as he handed the glasses to Williams and Ski. "To all of us who fly off the boats!"

"To the beautiful Crusader!" Jake said. "You guys are right. I would love to fly her. I love my phantom, but I would just like one shot at your bird."

"To all our lost mates!" Ski, now somber, added with melancholy. Raising their glasses, they all silently toasted.

Just then, Troy walked in awkwardly wearing a hard neck brace, struggling to keep his head straight. He was followed by Rookie Doc. Together, they headed for the champagne fountain. "Since I paid for part of this, I wanted to get my share." Troy said.

"As your doctor, I am not sure you should be drinking, but I am open to bribes."

"Hey, Doc, perfect timing. This F4 Puke needs surgery. Do you have a needle and thread?"

Doctor Lieutenant Russell took one look at Williams' still bleeding hand and said, "I imagine the alcohol has sterilized it, but if you want to keep from getting grounded you need to head to sick bay and get it properly treated. Doesn't look bad now but if you hang around much longer with this crew who knows how it will heal."

Ray, who had just finished shopping at the commissary for the line shack kitchen, walked in and filled a champagne glass from the fountain. "All right, a toast: First, Astrud has agreed to marry me. Second, I am going to be a father!"

Aggie said, "Congrats Dusty! I am taking Lynn to Hong Kong!"

"Isn't that like taking hamburger to a steak fry?" Jake asked.

Before Aggie could do anything, Ski jumped in and said, "No. It is like taking the playmate of the month to your high school prom."

As they all raised their glasses, Aggie laughingly said, "Who invited the black guy?" pointing to Frank Potter who had just entered.

Ray said, "I did. I wouldn't be here if it wasn't for Frank."

"Well, I wouldn't be here either if it hadn't been for you and your skipper."

Frank Potter had been one of the few black midshipmen at the Naval Academy. He had wanted to be a Naval Aviator ever since he had been a child. He had wanted to fly fighters. At the Naval Academy, he played Lacrosse on the same National Championship team with Troy Davis. He graduated in the upper third of the class and was immediately sent to Pensacola as a new ensign. In the same pipeline as the four roommates, he had also made lieutenant on June 6. In flight training, with a few exceptions, he found that skin color really did not matter. What mattered was how you flew, and he flew well. Unfortunately, his good grades were not good enough for his first choice of fighters and too good for his second choice of A7s. Too good because A3 pilots were in demand and landing the big "whale" on any of the carriers took a highly skilled pilot.

"Frank, we are going out with our Gunny Warrant tomorrow in a special services boat to catch clownfish for his aquarium. Bringing beer and our pistols. We drink beer, snorkel and catch the little clownfish and shoot at sharks or anything else that moves in the water. Want to come?" Ski asked.

"Hey man, thanks for the invite but I have other plans. Getting a ride on the COD over to Clark where the round eye stews roam. Of all things, Charlie set it up for us. Kind of a peace offering after he wanted to put me in hack. After talking to your Skipper and CAG, his new rule is do everything reasonable to save your sorry asses."

"Doc here has a friend from Med School who is a Rookie Doc Air Force Flight Surgeon. His job has him taking care of all the stews from the charter flights taking the guys to Danang. They stop back in Clark for a few days before going back to the states."

"Yeah, my buddy Gene says he will give us the sevens and eights, but he keeps the nines and tens for himself." Doc added.

"We'll see about that" Frank added.

Chapter Seventeen

MIGS

5 July 1967 Yankee Station

Ray was in the line shack checking to make sure the groceries they had bought in the commissary were properly stowed when Mears came in, grabbed a can of coke from the refrigerator, and put a dime in the cash box to pay for it.

"Mr. Rhodes. Thanks for taking care of us with this." He gestured to the refrigerator and various supplies for sandwiches.

"Don't thank me. Thank the Chief and Chief Warrant Officer. They got it done."

"Sir, I went back to that club in Olongapo while we were in port. I saw that girl that I call Bagio again. She is really sweet. She can't help what she does. She has to help her family."

"I am not one to judge, that's for sure. Just be careful."

The line shack phone rang, and Ray picked it up. "LT Rhodes, can I help you?"

"Hey Ray, can you come to the Ready Room? I have another flight for you."

"Sure Dick." First day back on the line, he only had a night Barcap scheduled as they started on ten days of noon-to-midnight flying.

In the Ready Room, Troy was manning the SDO desk with his neck brace on. Aggie had written on the message board in the front of the room: HK 28 days. It was a countdown to the port call in Hong Kong.

Dick Knowles turned to him and said, "well, 123 needs us to supply a Barcap flight with LCDR Rames. They don't have enough up aircraft."

"Sure. It will be good to have a day hop before tonight."

"You brief with LCDR Rames at 13:30 in Ready One. He is one of the best, so try to learn something."

Flying lazy racetrack patterns of combat spread around Red Crown, he was suddenly shaken out of his lethargy by the call: "Half Dollar flight, we have Migs airborne south of Vinh, your vector is 243 for intercept."

Immediately, LCDR Rames answered in his Kentucky twang, "Roger 243, Dollars go full military." With that, both F8s made hard turns to heading 243 and went to maximum power without afterburner. Refueling quickly after arriving at the Barcap station, they had a good combat fuel package.

Ray checked his gauges again, although through his constant, unconscious scan he already knew he had over eight thousand pounds of fuel remaining. *How had Migs gotten south of Vinh without being spotted?* he wondered. Usually the Big Look' Air Force radar planes knew when the Migs were taxiing out for takeoff.

"Check Nitrogen cooling on. Switches hot," was the call from Rames. After double clicking his transmitter to acknowledge, Ray turned on the nitrogen cooling that would make the seeker head of his sidewinder missile super sensitive to heat, turned on the master arms switch, and then charged his guns. He heard a satisfying thunk as the twenty-millimeter cannons cocked with rounds in place. He was excited. Going into his first real air combat.

"Two, keep your head up and we'll fight 'em just like we briefed."

He was lucky, he thought, to be a navy fighter pilot. He had heard that the air force relegated wingmen to mere appendages of the lead. In Navy Combat Spread the doctrine was that each plane fought the fight in support of each other at a spread of approximately 1000 feet. If anyone jumped him, the lead could quickly turn behind him and protect him, while he could do the same for the lead. If the Migs fought in tight formation, they effectively reduced their numbers to one fighting unit and they would outnumber them, always the goal in air combat. You always wanted numerical superiority.

"Half Dollars, your bogeys now at 252 approximately 25 miles." Hopefully the controllers were vectoring them in behind the Migs, but sometimes they screwed up and had been known to put fighters in front of the enemy. He strained, looking through the gunsight to spot the bogeys. As they coasted in slightly north of Vinh he heard the growls of North Vietnamese search radars in his headset. *Shit!* The Vietnamese radar had them.

"Two, I've got a tallyho at one o'clock slightly high. It looks like two 17s. Hit chaff now!" He immediately banged the round knob on the wall of the cockpit slightly behind the throttle and heard the almost anguished call from Red Crown, "If you pop chaff, we're going to lose everyone!"

"No problem Red Crown, I have a visual. Just wanted to cause a little distress for our buddies. Two, call out when you have a tally. I think they were trying to set us up. I have two 21s now, about eleven-thirty and high. Looks like they wanted to have a go at us when we took the bait of the 17s."

Rames was legendary in the F8 community for his vision. He always saw the opponent in Air Combat Maneuvering (ACM) before he was seen and used it to tremendous advantage. He now made a gentle climbing turn to position them for an attack on the 21s who were flying a fairly tight flying wing type formation in a semi holding pattern. As he saw the 21s, he called, "Tally ho! Twelve-thirty, slightly high." At the same time, he began to get a growl in his headset.

"Two, you take the one to port and take the shot when we get a little more in range."

"Roger!" Rames was giving him the first shot. As they were about four miles, he saw the flash of burner coming out the tailpipe of both 21s. They both then began a hard turn to starboard.

Rames called, "Pull some lead on him and smoke that sucker. I'm crossing under."

"Roger," Ray groaned as he pulled Gs to try to get a lead on the nimble 21. Feeding in just a little rudder as he pulled hard on the stick, he saw the port twenty-one out of the left section of his cockpit. With that much lead and a good tone, he felt confident of the shot, hit the pickle button on his stick and heard the satisfying roar as the winder lit off. "Fox one," he called.

"Roger. Looks like a good shot." Rames called as the sidewinder started to track on the port Mig. The Mig seemed to ease its turn and then at the very last instant, made a hard, high G-barrel roll and the missile flew harmlessly by. "Shit, guess that guy has been shot at before. I'm at your three o'clock high. Cover me while I take a run at two."

Looking to the right, Ray saw Half Dollar lead rolling in from a high yo-yo position. He immediately selected burner, dropped the nose to gain a little speed as he overshot the Mig 21 he had fired on and climbed up to his own high yo-yo. Crusader pilots had learned early in the war that they could not stay down and turn with the more agile Migs, but they could roll faster and by combining climbing moves with high G-barrel rolls, they could maneuver behind the generally less skilled Mig pilots. The Mig he had fired on quickly came around and was climbing also, getting back in position to support his wingman. The four planes were flying around in a high-speed circle reminiscent of children's Ring Around the Rosey played out between 25000 feet and ground level at speeds exceeding 1000 miles per hour over one hundred square miles of real estate.

Before the lead Mig could get back into the fight, Rames shouted, "Fox One!" and launched a sidewinder at the second twenty-one.

Less experienced, the pilot broke early, and the winder tracked him perfectly, exploding on the tailpipe, severing the aircraft in two. Ray watched but saw no ejection and no chute. "Splash one. Dollar lead, you have the other bogey at four o'clock, break right!" Immediately he saw the 123 F8 come right, but not as hard as he expected. "Two, I'm going to try to sucker him in behind me. Jump on him hard and fast and hit him before he gets a shot on me. Do you have the section of seventeens?"

"Negative, but I think they beat feet."

"This is Red Crown. Confirm one flight of Migs is heading back to Kep."

"Roger."

As Half Dollar lead continued a relatively easy descending four G-turn, the Mig executed a port barrel roll in an attempt to get on his six. Ray was taken a little by surprise by the maneuver, but executed his own hard, high G-barrel roll to starboard to get a shot.

He saw he was too close for a missile shot and called, "Lead I'm too close for a winder, but I'm in hot with guns."

With that he started tracking the Mig with his gunsight, pulling hard to pull enough lead. When he thought he was in range he began to fire. The Mig suddenly rolled inverted and pulled down into a split-S. Ray followed, fighting to pull lead on him again.

"Two, break it off! He is pulling you into a flak trap."

Ray quickly released pull on the stick and rolled to within about thirty degrees of level and started a hard climbing turn, which he rolled back on, jinking his way back up gaining altitude. He saw splashes of black fall away to the sides of the cockpit as he flew out of the range of the thirty sevens. Just then he heard the disconcerting rattle of a tracking Fansong radar in his headset from the ALQ100.

"Pop some chaff 2. Get in burner and let's get feet wet. These boys are fixing to try out some Roman Candles."

Once again, he popped the chaff dispenser at the side of the cockpit. He then heard the high-pitched tone of a launched SAM. Craning his neck from side to side he strained to see it, continuing his jink maneuvers as he headed for the sea and safety.

"Two, the SAM is at your three o'clock and does not appear to be tracking. I'm at your eleven, slightly high."

"Roger, I've got a tally on both." He worked to get back in position on one, while carefully watching the SAM streak higher. Since the Alpha strike, it was the only one he had seen. He really did not remember the details on the SAMs that time since he had been so harried, struggling to fly and stay alive. This time he watched with fascination and the missile streaked above them, harmless. It did look like a big, yellow orange telephone pole flying. Thank God the small canards kept it from turning very well. He knew now that as long as he could see it, he could outmaneuver it.

The missile finally detonated well above them, raining debris on whatever was below.

"Two, check your fuel. Big Boy, Big Boy, are you up? Got two thirsty gators coming feet wet!"

As he checked his fuel gauge he felt a hard knot in his stomach. He only had six hundred pounds left. He didn't realize how much of the fight he had been in burner. He really hoped that tanker was handy.

"This is Big Boy. We're tracking on the Sand Box 342 radial on an outbound racetrack at 48 miles right now, angels base plus twelve."

"Half Dollar, this is Red Crown, squawk ident." Rames pushed the toggle switch up on the transponder located just below and right of the attitude gyro. "Radar contact. Your steer Zero Six Five for an intercept with Big Boy."

Ray breathed a sigh of relief. The tanker wasn't more than ten miles away at twenty thousand feet. "Two, what's your state?"

"Five hundred," he quickly replied.

"Roger. You plug first and take the lead, I'll join on you and look you over." Rames was really treating him right. Letting him lead would save him the fuel flying formation cost by constantly moving the throttle.

He saw him join easily in his mirrors as he turned gently to a heading of 065 on the RMI.

"Big Boy, I have a visual on you."

"Roger, I'm streaming the drogue and have a good light." Thank God! He knew that if he couldn't tank there was no way to get back to the ship. He was also glad it was an A3. The Whale, as it was affectionately called, was so much easier to tank from than the A4 with buddy stores. The tail of the F8 was right in the jet stream of the Scooters when plugging. Although Ray took pride in his ability to execute air to air refueling, the F8 was not easy since the probe came out behind the cockpit. The pilot had to trust his ability to fly formation and smoothly move the spot where he knew the probe to be into the basket of the refueling drogue. He stopped where he was behind the A3, reached over and flipped the probe toggle switch, glancing out to see that it had extended. He then smoothly moved in on the whale. With relief he saw the green light come on indicating transfer of fuel. Scanning his fuel gauge, he saw the needle start to move above five hundred pounds.

"Take about three thousand pounds and then let me have a drink. You can get back in after I top off."

He clicked his mike key twice in acknowledgement.

After uneventful tanking, Rames said, "Two, I'm going to have to do victory roll in the break. Instead of our fan brief, count five after I break and do your own break. You should see me and be able to do your own interval. Be sure you break up, as we're going to bring her in low and fast."

"Roger lead."

Since the Barcap were always the last to trap, it was their tradition to put on a show for the ship. All their crews generally watched them come in. On good days, the Crusader pilots did their best to impress all. Rames was one of the best, occasionally kicking up rooster tails of water with his low passes, sometimes stunting by entering the break inverted. Anything to spice up the end of a normally boring Barcap.

"Sand Box, this is Half Dollar One five miles out. Request a low, high-speed break with victory roll." Rames drawled out in his calmest tone.

"Roger, Half Dollar One. You are cleared low, high speed with roll. Nice shooting!" responded the air boss.

"Cooler doors, Two." Ray, flying as tight as possible, at least 3 feet of overlap on a step down, double clicked his mike in response. Without looking, he reached the cooler door switch with his left hand. The only reason to open the cooler was the noise it made over five hundred and fifty knots. *Shit Hot!* he thought, this was going to be a real high-speed break. On the right wing, looking through the lead, he looked up at the island of the ship as they roared down the starboard side of the Adams, then Rames gave him the kiss-off signal. He strained to keep level, low and fast while watching the breaking F8 do a series of turning, climbing rolls over the bow. He then broke up hard, pulling enough Gs to create white contrails off the wings. With the pure joy of the moment, he smoothly broke up to the same altitude and abeam distance as the lead. He thought he had a perfect interval. It would be a real shame to screw up the show by having a foul deck wave off or bolter. At the 180, he slowed enough to drop his gear and raise the wing incidence handle. He then slowed to approach speed and engaged the APC. Everything in the green, he concentrated on his turn into the ship, wanting to pick up a centered ball.

He heard Rames call, "Dollar One, Crusader ball three two."

"Roger, Ball."

When he heard no more comments from the LSO, he knew that LCDR Rames had flown his normal, excellent pass. As he rolled in, he saw the ball exactly in the center. His set up was perfect, he called, "Heater One Two, Crusader Ball, Three One."

"Roger Ball" was the only call he heard also during the pass as he flew one of the best approaches of his short career in F8s. He felt the satisfying pull of the tailhook and then felt the radar smash into his oxygen mask. He realized he had neglected to lock his harness before landing. Not a mistake he would make again. Thank God for once he wasn't tall. Aggie would definitely have taken a chunk out of his face on the scope. As it was, his upper lip was sore where the mask had been pushed back. The wonderful, damned Crusader always had a way of bringing you back to reality. It kept the best humble.

As he rolled back out of the wires, he raised the hook, folded the wings, and taxied forward to shut down. Climbing out of his plane, he saw LCDR Rames waiting for him below. Crews were gathered around applauding. He climbed down, helmet still on, and Rames shook his hand and said, "Well done Wingie."

"Congratulations sir! Great shot!"

"Hey, we were a team. You ought to get half the credit." But they both knew that the Silver Star for shooting down the Mig would only go to the shooter. Still, he was thrilled to have been part of a shoot down.

He and Rames separated at the rear of the island. "Stow your gear and meet me at Air Intelligence for the debrief."

"Yessir!"

As he entered the parachute riggers compartment at the rear of Ready One, Aggie, John, and Dave Casper greeted him.

"All right, we want a blow-by-blow description," John Phillips said.

"Sorry guys, I have to get to air intel for the debrief. I will come right back and tell you all about it."

"Nice job, Ray!" the skipper said as he entered the small compartment. "Heard you almost had one also."

"Thank you, Skipper. I thought I had him twice, but he broke away both times at the last second."

"Think you must have tangled with the Yellow Baron. Sounds like he knew what he was doing."

"Yessir. Wish I could have been with you, but LCDR Rames did a great job getting us in position. I do not see how he can spot them so far away. It was just awesome. Let me tell you all later. I have to get to air intel."

He pulled off his bandolier of bullets and pistol, removed the survival vest with the radios and nine-millimeter, stepped out of the torso harness, and unzipped the G-suit. He hung all the flight gear on the peg labeled LT Rhodes, among all the other flight gear, hung his helmet in the helmet bag over the other gear, and hustled out.

"Before the movie starts, gents, I want Ray to give us a quick debrief on the Mig engagement. However, before he does that, I think we need a little safety reminder," CDR Prescott said. "Ray, what happened to your lip?" Indicating his fat lip where the oxygen mask had been crushed against the radar screen.

"I forgot to lock my harness." He felt and looked embarrassed.

"Don't you mean, I neglected to do the landing checklist?"

"Yessir."

"Men, I don't care how exciting your hop was or how scared you are or whatever. Do that checklist or it can kill you. I am embarrassed to say that, for exactly the same reason as Ray here, I now never neglect to do my take-off and landing checklist." Seeing the nodding heads signaling their understanding, he said, "Roll the flick"

Chapter Eighteen

Countdown

1 August 1967 Yankee Station

Twenty-eight days and counting until Hong Kong. In the left-hand corner of the message board hanging on the front wall in the Ready Room, Aggie came in and wrote: Countdown and the large number 28 behind it.

As he wrote, LCDR Ferguson asked, "Is that the day we come off the line, or arrive in Cubi, get to Hong Kong, or the day Lynn tells you she has dumped you for one of those slick surface officers with good manners?"

"It is the date we hit Cubi going to Hong Kong. And you know better than to think any black shoe (surface officer) could have a chance with Lynn."

Countdown Day 18

LT Dave Casper was calm as he did the preflight of Heater 208 for a routine night Barcap. On the midnight-to-noon schedule, he would launch at 0200. Normal nights, he was not concerned about his flight. He would be flying wing on Dick Knowles, who made it simple. Like many of the squadron mates, he had received his commission through NROTC at the University of Kansas in Lawrence. His father had been an air force pilot in WWII. After the war, he went to work for Cessna

Aircraft in Wichita Falls, Kansas. His father had taught him to fly. Starting with the old Cessna 140, he had ended up learning to fly almost all the aircraft that Cessna had, including the multi engine 410. A natural pilot, he had had to learn the navy way to fly. It had been no problem for him. His previous experience only took him so far, but he studied hard and made the excellent grades necessary to get his first choice out of flight training: the F8 Crusader. He had always wanted to fly a pure fighter.

After his normal thorough pre-flight, startup and taxi were normal. The yellow shirts directed him over the shuttle. The bridle was attached to Heater 208, Casper ran up the throttle to 100 percent, turned on his lights, and the cat officer touched the deck with his wand to launch the F8. Immediately, Casper knew he was in trouble. The normal high G-catapult shot did not happen. The plane was meandering down the catapult at maybe sixty miles per hour.

In the Ready Room, SDO Troy Davis watched in horror on the plat TV as the plane slowly headed down the cat, obviously at full power. At the end of the catapult, he saw a bright flash and 208 dropped off the bow of the ship. He thought the flash had been Casper selecting after burner.

Picking up the phone, he dialed the skipper. "Skipper, I think we have lost Dave Casper. He got a cold cat shot and went over the bow in 208."

CDR Prescott thought, *What else could go wrong. Now he had lost one of his best pilots.* He was about to reply when—

"Belay that sir," Troy said. "He ejected. He just landed in his parachute back on the flight deck. It looks like he is OK. The flash I thought was the after burner was the seat firing."

CDR Prescott sighed in relief.

After a few minutes, Casper came in the back of the Ready Room and plopped into his chair still wearing all his flight gear, including his helmet. He sat saying nothing.

"Dave, are you alright? Do you need to go to sick bay?" Troy asked.

"No, I am OK. Thank God for Martin Baker."

The Martin Baker Zero Zero rocket-powered ejection seat, designed to be used with no airspeed and altitude, had just saved him.

Countdown Day 14

Setting up the nightly movie and waiting for Joe Ames to secure from his LSO duty, most of the squadron was in the Ready Room idly watching the last recovery of the night, the KA3 Whale, on the plat TV. The large aircraft appeared for a few seconds, hit the flight deck but did not trap—an apparent bolter. However, it quickly became obvious that it was no ordinary bolter. On hitting the deck, the drag chute played out from its compartment near the tail and prevented the big plane from flying. The plane went off the deck with full power on and essentially landed in the black water, nose up and wings level. Knowing it was the last plane to land, everyone in the Ready Room rushed up the ladder on the starboard side to the flight deck. As other squadron personnel ran up, Ray was relieved to find Frank also looking over the side.

"Frank. I thought that was you. What happened?"

"No Ray, it was LCDR Hart and his crew." Frank Potter answered. "He got a double cycle and had to go to Danang to hot refuel. Of course, they stayed in the aircraft while it was being refueled and had no chance to preflight. The ground crew obviously did not secure the drag chute properly before he took off."

The big plane deployed a large parachute upon landing on a short runway to assist in stopping. Spotlights from the ship played on the still floating plane. It was only floating because, at landing weight, its tanks were almost empty. The helo, which had been hovering off the port stern, rushed to the site just as One, then Two, and then LCDR Hart all got out on the port wing. All three crewmen inflated their life preservers and jumped off the wing as their aircraft sank. The helo swimmer jumped into the water and one by one hooked the crewmembers up to the helo winch, Charlie insisting that he went last.

"Hey Frank. How did that whale float?"

"I never thought it would. We don't even have a ditching procedure in Natops. Guess Charlie was able to keep the wings level and as a result he made a water landing with nose up. I am sure he had no idea what had gone wrong."

The helo landed on the stern and Charlie and his crew jumped down. Dripping wet, but all right.

Frank ran over and hugged his boss. Charlie asked, "What happened?"

"Your drag chute came out on the bolter. If you hadn't kept your wings level and nose up—"

"Hell, all I was doing was trying to fly." He interrupted him. "Did not know why I had no power. Guess we are down to one plane for the Det. Glad we have that spare in Danang. Someone in the shore det is in for a real ass chewing. They need to work more and drink less beer."

Still shaking from the ditching, he asked, "Frank, can you go over to Danang and pick up the spare first hop tomorrow? I will ask if the COD can take you over."

"Sure Boss. Whatever you need."

Countdown Day 10

At 1730 hours, Ray, holding a F8 Natops Manual, stood at the railing in PriFly just outside the air boss's space that served as the tower. Located high above the flight deck on the port side of the island, he was standing the PriFly watch as the F8 representative. The air boss sat in a high swivel chair inside the tower. All sides of the tower had windows in order to see aircraft on the flight deck as well as those in the pattern, launching from the catapults or entering break on a VFR recovery. For every launch and recovery, the air boss—a full commander who

NIGHT CAT NIGHT TRAP

oversaw all air ops on the ship—required a pilot from the F8 squadrons and the A4 squadrons to be in PriFly where he could ask technical questions regarding their aircraft in case of an emergency. Thus, each pilot carried a Natops Manual, which detailed emergency procedures for the aircraft, with them. The junior pilots never tired of that watch. It was a pleasure to watch the actions on the flight deck from above.

Ray watched as Heater 203 taxied up and over the shuttle, preparing for the catapult shot. Looking down, he marveled at how big and pretty the F8 was. When he sat in the cockpit at the front of the plane, he never felt it was as big as it was, especially in comparison to the diminutive A4s. He knew Poet, John Phillips, was in 203 and his wingman was Casper in 207 with Ski in the spare, 212. Phillips and Casper had taken this flight rather than giving it to one of the nuggets. The weather was getting worse, and this was the same type of launch that CDR Huggins had hit the ramp on: Day Cat and Night Trap with bad weather.

As the engine on 203 spooled up to full power, he heard Poet shout over the radio loudspeaker, which hung just above the air boss's stuffed swivel chair, "Suspend the Cat. Suspend the starboard Cat. Smoke in the cockpit."

"Roger that 203. This is the Air Boss. Just reach over and turn that AC knob down and that mist should clear up."

In the F8 the air-conditioning did not work until the engine was up to over 90 percent of thrust. It was common to get a thick mist in the cockpit if the AC was in the full cold position when the throttle was advanced. F8 pilots quickly learned to check the AC on pre-start.

"Boss, 203. Suspend the cat or I will have to blow the canopy on launch." Maintaining full power on the aircraft was the procedure if asking to suspend the cat in the event the launch was inadvertently made. John Phillips wanted to be certain the plane would fly off the cat, smoke or not.

"Boss, LT Rhodes. I am the F8 rep. That is LT John Phillips in 203. He is an experienced two cruise pilot." Ray shouted to the air boss.

"Roger. Now I know who it is. Suspend the cat." The air boss ordered as he pushed the button to suspend. At the catapult, the cat and arresting gear officer on the deck next to the cat also suspended by shutting off his valve. He then moved in front of the wing of the plane to assure the pilot that the catapult would not fire.

"Two-O-Three. The cat is suspended. You can shut down."

Immediately, John shut the engine down, opened the canopy, and as thick, black smoke poured out, clambered quickly out of the cockpit. On the deck, he stopped the firemen rushing to the plane with extinguishers, knowing that the chemicals would make the plane indefinitely down. Once the engine wound down, the smoke started dissipating. As John Phillips suspected, the AC was the culprit, but it was the AC bearing burning out, not mist. Once the bearing had no power, the smoke stopped. Instead of returning to the Ready Room, John made his way across the flight deck to 212 and motioned for Ski to get out and let him have the plane. Ski gladly climbed out and thanked John, knowing that the approach down from Marshal to the CCA and night trap would be brutal in these conditions.

Countdown Day 5, 1600 hours, flying the noon-to-midnight shift.

"What happened?" Troy asked into the phone while sitting in the SDO chair. He was trying to find out from Air Intelligence why Aggie had not returned from his road recce flight escorting an A4.

"What did they say, Troy?" Ski asked.

"They still do not have an answer."

"The Scooter pilot is back. We need to ask him."

In the front of the Ready Room, just finishing his brief for a Barcap, the Skipper said, "I am going to Air Ops myself to sort this out. He probably had to bingo to Danang or something." With that, he stood up and walked out through the rear hatch to the passageway leading forward to air operations.

Soon the Ready Room filled with all the pilots, warrant officers, and some of the chiefs as they heard Aggie was missing.

"That was a nothing hop!" Ski exclaimed, shaking the back of the seat in front of him "A nothing road recce South of Vinh where we go all the time. A wasted nothing hop! Looking for fucking trucks!"

"Before you get all wound up, understand this is the breaks of Naval Air. Something we all signed up for including LT Twain." CDR Scampi said from his Ready Room chair in the front of the room without turning his head.

"Fuck that sir!" Troy shouted from the SDO desk, which he was still manning with the neck brace. "Is that what happened to me too? Breaks of Naval Air? Bullshit! This was crappy intelligence and a crappy meaningless mission." The squadron pilots had little respect for CDR. Scampi. It was well known that the Skipper was not pleased with him.

Returning from air ops, with the Squadron's Air Intelligence officer, LTJG Miller trailing behind, the skipper said, "I am devastated by the news. We have lost Aggie." A gasp filled with grief echoed in the room. "As you know, he was flying escort on an A4 flying in Route Pak 2 South of Vinh. According to the A4 pilot, they were cruising along at about 400 knots, jinking back and forth at about 11000 feet. They were staying out of the range of the 37mm and 57mm triple-A looking for trucks or a truck park. Targets of opportunity. The scooter pilot said that he rolled toward Aggie jinking and saw Aggie's plane, 205, explode. He turned away just in time to avoid another shell bursting where he had been. Fragments actually hit part of his aircraft. He then climbed and turned back in time to see the remains of 207 burning and dropping out of the sky. There was no chute. He called Aggie on the radio but there was no response." His throat closed up with grief. "They apparently flew into a new radar guided anti-aircraft battery, firing either 85mm or 100 mm shells. We used to call them 88s as that was what the Germans had, but they really are Soviet 85s most likely. A direct hit from one of those and Aggie would have died instantly." Dan Prescott was visibly upset, delivering this message. He felt that the heart had just been ripped out of his squadron.

"Fucking Air Intelligence. No SAMs South of Vinh, no Migs South of Vinh, no radar guided guns South of Vinh. What do you ever get right Miller? Safe to fly at 10000 feet because the triple-A can't reach that high." Ski shouted in anguish, pounding his chair with his fists.

"Yeah, junior spy. What do you say about that? We lost Aggie and a plane and what do you guys do, mark it on the map?" Joe Ames joined in.

"Hey guys, it is not Miller's fault or Air Intelligence in general. So ease up. They can only give us what they see and hear." CDR Prescott added. "If anything, it is my fault. Something I should have done before. I am making a new rule of engagement: assume that there are SAMs, Migs, and Radar guns everywhere in North Vietnam and, if we go there, Laos and the trail. No matter what Intel they give you in the brief. Do you all understand? We are now going to fly as if the NVA have SAM sites, Migs, and radar guns everywhere. If they shoot at you, you are free to shoot back, no matter what. I know it is harder to see what is on the ground, but no flights under 20000 feet, even when looking for trucks or SAM sites. It is not worth it. We will have a memorial service for LT Twain tomorrow at 1100 on the flight deck before ops start. Keep your heads up. Dismissed."

As the meeting broke up, Ski went to the coffee mess at the back of the Ready Room and picked up Aggie's coffee mug with the gold wings and Aggie written on one side and the squadron logo of black wasps on the other. As he looked at it, his eyes teared up. Catching CDR Prescott as he started out the door, Ski asked, "Sir, could I see you for a moment?"

"Sure, Ski."

Still holding Aggie's mug he asked, "Could I fly the missing man for Aggie when we fly off into Cubi?"

"All right. You will fly right wing on me in the diamond."

"Also, could I do a tuck under break for him?"

After considering it, the skipper answered, "Only if you do not break below five hundred feet. I will have Ghost schedule us for a day Barcap in the next couple of days. I will teach you how to do a tuck under without killing yourself."

"Yessir."

"I know you were really tight with Aggie. Know that we all loved him. It is a really tough thing to take, and it seems so senseless. But you have to keep concentrating on your flying."

A knot in his throat, all he could do was nod to acknowledge he had heard what the skipper said.

Returning to his stateroom, CDR Prescott sat down at this desk to write Aggie's parents.

Dear Mr. and Mrs. Twain:

I deeply regret to inform you that LT Mike "Aggie" Twain was killed in action today during a combat mission over North Vietnam. Aggie was the heart and soul of our squadron. He will be greatly missed. He added so much to our squadron. My deepest sympathy. If there is anything that I can do for you, please do not hesitate to ask.

Yours truly,
Dan Prescott, CO VF 188

As he pondered the words, he knew that the squadron morale had taken a huge hit. After losing Skipper Huggins, Troy being shot down,

Casper's cold cat, and the negativity that Scampi brought, it would be hard for the squadron to recover. Liberty in Hong Kong could not have come at a better time.

Countdown, Day 3

"Ski, we are doing the standard Barcap. Contact Red Crown, tank, circle, respond to anyone who needs as or any threats. However, we will fly at 10000 feet instead of 20. You will have a better feel for the tuck under at that altitude. I don't know if they teach it now in acrobatics in the training command, but anytime you do an aileron roll you first need to pop the nose up twenty degrees and then roll. That keeps you from losing altitude due to the loss of lift in the roll. We did tuck-unders all the time as solos in the Blues. It is actually easier in the F8 due to our high rate of roll. If you pop the nose twenty degrees and immediately roll, no one will see the nose come up. When we get up on station, I want you to move in to about 100 feet from me and we will simulate coming into the break at ten thousand feet. First, watch me then you do it while I watch. Once you get it down, we will go down to about 500 above Red Crown and give them a show."

Countdown, Day 2

As scheduled, John Phillips (Poet) joined other airwing personnel and rode in the ship's COD, Carrier on board delivery prop plane, to Hong Kong to set up the squadron's admin rooms in the Hong Kong Hilton. While most ship and airwing personnel eagerly awaited the Hong Kong liberty, Aggie's death had shattered the morale of all the VF 188 pilots and staff. John thought that, as sad as it was, the time in Hong Kong was just what they needed to get over that death. Breaks of naval air, they always said. There had been too many of those. This break had been totally avoidable.

Countdown Day, 1

A diamond formation led by CDR Prescott screamed into the break at NAS Cubi at 100 feet above the ground. A trail formation led by LCDR Knowles followed. About one mile out, CDR Prescott signaled to LT Kowalski to break away. Ski then pulled up out of the formation, leaving the gap in honor of the missing man, Aggie. Circling up to 5000 feet he dove back down just below supersonic speed to enter the break at 500 feet as he had promised the skipper. Popping the nose up twenty degrees, he rolled to his right, away from the runway but continued rolling until he had gone just beyond two hundred seventy degrees of roll, then pulled hard to bleed off his airspeed in order to land. It was a truly spectacular break. As soon as Ski taxied in, he shut down the aircraft, climbed out of the cockpit, and walked slowly over to the flight line where Lynn was waiting, dreading the moment.

"Where's Aggie? Did he have the duty?" she looked around, searching for him. "I thought he would make the fly in."

"Lynn," Ski's voice caught. "We lost Aggie."

"Lost him where? Is he riding the ship in?" she frowned.

Shit. "No, he was shot down."

"Oh no! Was he OK? Was he picked up?"

"No Lynn." A heavy sigh ushered in the words he never wanted to vocalize. "He is gone. He was killed."

"Not Aggie." Lynn hinted at a smile, almost as if she thought this was a bad joke. Seeing that Ski's expression didn't change from deep sorrow to gotcha-moment, the brutal reality hit her all at once. "It can't be. No, no. Not Aggie!" she cried.

Ski just hugged her tightly. There was nothing more to be said.

Chapter Nineteen

Hong Kong
30 August 1967 Clark Air Force Base

Excited at the prospect of seeing Astrud but still mourning the loss of Aggie, it was with mixed emotions that Ray Rhodes took the shuttle from Subic to Clark AFB to catch a flight back to the states.

"LT Rhodes, I understand that your travel orders are priority. However, the only flight we have going out to Travis the next twenty-four hours is a C141 coffin flight. It has six jump seats available in the cargo bay, but it will be full of coffins from Vietnam." the air operations sergeant advised.

"I understand. That will be alright. I have to get there as soon as possible."

"Roger that. It will be landing from Danang in about twenty minutes. It will refuel and take off within the hour, so please stick around ops. So far there will be one additional passenger, a marine gunnery sergeant on emergency leave."

As Ray walked up the ramp of the giant transport aircraft, he looked in awe at the coffins stacked from the deck to the top of the aircraft. It was completely full of coffins. They were stacked five high and totally filled the cargo compartment. He wondered who was in the coffins—how many actually had bodies in them.

In the Rag, one of the replacement pilots had flown into the water on a tactics hop. One of his friends had been tasked with escorting the casket back to his parents in his hometown although everyone knew nothing was in the casket as they had not found any remains.

He found one of the six jump seats on the port side near the front, below the cockpit level. The marine gunnery sergeant was already seated but jumped up at his arrival and saluted smartly.

Returning the salute, he noted the rows of ribbons on the dress uniform and said, "At ease gunny. Think we will have a long ride together."

After setting up the admin in the Hilton, while awaiting the ship, John Phillips walked around Hong Kong, took the Star ferry to Kowloon, had a drink at the Peninsula Hotel, and did some shopping at the British China Fleet store. There he purchased the Nikon single lens reflex camera he had wanted on the last cruise, immediately taking it back to his room at the Hilton to avoid walking around Hong Kong like a typical tourist with a camera around his neck. He mainly avoided the other airwing officers. He simply wanted some alone time to try and digest all that had happened so far on cruise. Especially the loss of CDR Huggins and LT Aggie Twain, wondering if their loss had made any difference. He wondered about whether anything they did made a difference. He did not really know what he felt, how to mourn Aggie. With CDR Huggins his feeling was that it would not have happened to him. That he, John, could have made that approach and landed without a problem. Indeed, he had done it many times. With the death of Aggie, it seemed that the life and spirit had been ripped out of the squadron. He was funny and had a big personality. Despite the difference in rank, he did not hesitate to tease everyone, including the skipper. Everyone also knew that despite his joking, he was a very good pilot. Being a good pilot had not been enough. One also needed to be lucky. It seemed that no matter how well, he, John flew, he would not have been able to avoid the same fate as Aggie. It was somewhat depressing to him. He had always thought, when others had been killed in training or combat, that he could have avoided whatever it was because he was a better pilot. In the F8 Rag they had been told over and over again that they were the best fighter pilots in the US Navy which made them the best fighter pilots in the world. And they had believed it. Now there was doubt. Aggie had been slammed out of the sky through no fault of his own. No matter how good the pilot was, the result would have been the same. Not like fighting Migs or even evading a SAM where skill was important. It was simply a matter of very bad luck for Aggie and for the squadron.

One day out from Hong Kong, Chief McDaniel had a meeting with Petty Officer First Class Pearson and the line division. "Men, Hong Kong is one of the best liberty ports you will ever visit. Things are pretty cheap. There are about 10 Hong Kong dollars to one US dollar. You can get good shirts, shoes, etc. Beer is better here and cheap. However, it is also one of the trickiest liberty ports. There are a lot of scammers. There are beautiful Chinese, White Russian, and other mix hookers in the bars. They will not hesitate to rob you or scam you. There are two parts of Hong Kong: Hong Kong itself and Kowloon. You can get to Kowloon from Hong Kong on the ferry. For me, I like Kowloon better. It is not as fancy, but prices are better, but you go where you want. On the Hong Kong side, Wan Chi street is full of bars with good looking hookers. And cheap. If you go, make damn sure to use a condom. There are some bad diseases out there. You don't want to get the Hong Kong Dong. Make sure you go everywhere with a buddy. Don't flash any money around. Before you blow it all, buy yourself a nice Seiko watch or something for a girl back home. Have fun but be safe. Do not even think of breaking any laws. The Brits are really strict and will come down hard on any of us. Also know that the commie Chinese are always watching and listening to you here. Everyone but the duty section has liberty every day. Enjoy but do not get into trouble."

Mears looked at Walker and asked, "Do you want to go together? This is why I joined the navy, to see the world!'

"Sure, me too. I want to see it all, but I am not that interested in sleazy bars. Had enough of that."

With the arrival of the ship, the bar in the admin room that John had set up filled up with the remaining pilots, warrant officers, and a mustang—former enlisted—maintenance officer. The skipper and XO had separate rooms. Phillips and Casper shared a room off the admin suite while Troy and Ski roomed together in another room. Joe Ames paid for a room by himself as did Preacher. The British Navy threw a welcome party for the ship and airwing officers at the China Fleet Club. Not only did they invite the naval officers, they also invited many of the expat women working in various businesses in Hong Kong. Troy and Ski went together. While Ski sat down on an empty bar stool at one of the many bars in the huge ball room, Troy, without the neck brace, roamed the room until he found what he was looking for. A beautiful blonde, at least his age or a little older, sitting by herself in a little lounge area. Experienced in the naval academy tradition of "Tea" fights, he knew it was essential to be quick before the rest of the airwing struck.

"Hi. I am Troy Davis. May I sit?" he asked politely.

"Troy, I am Jeanette Stanley. Please do. I assume you are a Yank from the ships."

"I am. I do not want to be disrespectful; you have a great accent but it doesn't seem to be exactly British."

"No, I am Australian. You have a good ear."

At that moment, an A4 pilot Troy knew from flight training came over and said, "Hey Troy. How are you doing? I was really glad to hear that you got picked up."

"Thanks Gary. This is Jeanette. We were just getting ready to go to dinner."

"Got it. Nice meeting you." Gary said, understanding the rules of the game, walked away.

"I take it you have just invited me to a lovely dinner. I accept once you tell me about your getting picked up. What ship are you on and what is it that you do on the ship?"

"I am in a squadron on the Aircraft Carrier Adams currently at the dock here."

"And what do you do in the squadron?"

"I fly and have a job in admin."

"What do you fly? What did Gary mean when he said that he was glad to hear that you had been picked up?"

"I fly the F8 Crusader."

"And? Are you always this reticent to talk about your exploits? I thought fighter pilots were full of stories."

"It is kind of embarrassing," he glanced at his feet for a moment. "I got shot down by a North Vietnamese missile and had to be rescued by the helo."

"Doesn't sound embarrassing to me, sounds heroic."

Troy, standing, offered his hand to Jeanette and said, "Let's find someplace quiet with great food. Are you hungry?"

"I am starved."

The remainder of the in-port period, other members of the squadron saw little of Troy who was totally enthralled by the beautiful blonde Aussie. He occasionally brought her by the admin, but carefully avoided the rest of the airwing.

Ski mainly hung around the admin and drank, staying moderately high the entire time in port. Preacher and LCDR Robinson shopped for their wives in the duty-free Hong Kong stores. They had lists of items the wives knew were good deals in Hong Kong. On the third day there, CDR Prescott asked every pilot and Warrant Arancio to join him in a trip to Kowloon to the boot maker, Kim Lee, where they all purchased brown ankle top zipper boots to wear with their khaki uniforms. From there, they went to Nita fashions to get fitted for custom shirts. The cost was $12 each and would be ready in twenty-four hours. After a stop at the Peninsula hotel for drinks, the fighter sweep of Kowloon ended with steaks at Jimmy's kitchen. It was a successful day. Although morale was still down, the atmosphere in the admin was a bit more positive. Joe Ames, as he had promised, withdrew all his pay on the last payday before Hong Kong. Up to then, he had only taken out ten or twenty dollars each pay period. With his money in a stack, he proceeded to the China Fleet Club and purchased a brand-new Rolex GMT, the preferred watch of pilots. He and Ski went out that evening to one of the bar/night clubs within walking distance of the Hilton in the Wan Chai district.

As he was admiring his new watch while drinking a beer, one of the bar girls came over, tapped the watch, and said, "Fighter pilot. Big watch, small dick." causing Ski to break out in laughter for the first time since Aggie's death.

The C141, although pressurized, was very cold in the cargo compartment. When the plane stopped in Japan to refuel, Ray convinced the pilot to let the Sergeant and himself ride on jump seats in the back of the large cockpit where it was warmer.

Shooting the bull with the gunnery sergeant, as bored warriors want to do, Ray learned that the gunny was on his third tour in Vietnam, currently based in the valley near Danang, which he affectionately called the All-Shit valley. He had fought at Khe Sanh and most of the other battles in which the Corp had been involved. Just a little older than Ray, he was battle weary.

Arriving at Travis, Ray and the gunny jumped into the available base transportation to San Francisco International Airport to catch their ongoing flights, Ray down to San Diego and the gunny to St. Louis where his mother was gravely ill.

Astrud met him at the airport in the Jeep. After a long embrace, tears streaked down Astrud's face as she said, "I am so glad you are here. So happy that you will marry me."

Still holding her in his arms, Ray said, "When I didn't hear from you on cruise, I thought that you had moved on. I was so unhappy. Now I am happy. I love you and I owe a big debt to Poet."

"So do I," Astrud added. "And I have never stopped loving you. I have been so worried about you."

Ray checked in on his TAD orders with the F8 RAG and dutifully attended briefings on what the Israelis taught them regarding fighting Mig 21s. To Ray it appeared that the Israeli pilots, while undoubtedly good, were fighting very poor or untrained pilots on the Arab side. While at the F8 RAG, Ray was able to recruit two of his friends from the training command who were still there, as well as one of his favorite instructors and a new F8 pilot named Wilson to form the standard arch with swords at the wedding.

LTJG Wilson told him that he had orders to VF 188 as a replacement pilot once he finished carrier qualifications in the next month. He asked Ray, "How is the squadron?"

"I have to be honest with you," Ray said, looking straight into his eyes. "I thought we were the best F8 squadron in the navy which made us the best Fighter Squadron in the world when we did our work ups to go on this cruise. Now, our morale has taken a hit. First, we lost our Skipper just when we got to Yankee Station. Troy Davis, one of my roomies, got shot down. He got picked up but was injured. Should be OK now. And just last week my roomie and the spirit of our squadron was ripped out when Aggie, LT Mike Twain, was killed over the North." The pain in his voice betrayed his calm exterior. "Aggie did absolutely nothing wrong and it was like a giant hand came up and smashed him down. However, glad you are coming. We need you. We will set it up so you room with us and not in the JO Bunkroom."

Ray and Astrud spent the nights in his old apartment making up for lost time. They settled into a very comfortable pace of love making that left both of them exhausted.

"Maybe we should save something for the honeymoon," Astrud said, pulling the sheet up over stomach where a small bump was visible.

"No, who knows what tomorrow will bring." Ray responded and immediately regretted it, reaching out and holding her tight.

While Ray was busy at the RAG in Miramar, Sandy was organizing the wedding with Astrud. First, she had obtained the assistance of the head legal officer at Miramar to cut through the red tape to get the marriage license while Ray was still on his way. All he had to do on arrival was sign the application. Next, she arranged for the use of the chapel at the Coronado Naval Station for the service. The resident navy chaplain would do the honors and conduct the wedding. Ray's father was to be his best man and Astrud's sister had flown in from Brazil to be her maid of honor. Ray's mother provided old family engagement and wedding rings for the service. A small reception was held at the Hotel Del Coronado, paid for by Ray's father. He also picked up the tab for the honeymoon suite for the couple.

The wedding went off as planned. The new couple only had one night in the honeymoon suite before Ray had to fly back. Although their pre-wedding love making had been all consuming, they still managed one last passionate night in that beautiful suite.

Astrud dropped Ray off at Miramar the morning after the wedding. A teary Astrud hugged Ray and said, "I love you so much. Promise me to be safe and get back to me soon. Love you."

"I really love you, Astrud."

A friend of his at VF 126, the instrument RAG at Miramar, flew Ray directly to Travis in the back seat of a TA4. At Travis Air Force Base, he was fortunate enough, with his priority orders, to catch a civilian charter plane taking troops to Vietnam via Clark Air Force Base. When the Adams returned to Cubi from Hong Kong, Ray Rhodes was standing on the dock, his new wedding ring on his left hand, waiting to come aboard.

Chapter Twenty

Monsoon

11 September 1967 Enroute Yankee Station

Over the One MC intercom the Bosun call came, "FIRE, FIRE, FIRE. Starboard side midships. All hands to fire stations. This is not a drill. I repeat FIRE, FIRE, FIRE! This is not a drill."

After a few minutes, a new call: "Now general quarters! General quarters! All hands to general quarters stations."

John Phillips had been sitting in the gun tub on the port side, midships, as the Adams steamed on its way back to Yankee Station from Cubi. When the ship had been updated with the angle deck, steam catapults, and new mirror landing system, the guns had been stripped out. The round gun tubs, just one deck down from the flight deck, remained. Of no use in a modern battle, John had found them on the last cruise. It was the one haven of solitude on the crowded huge ship. One of the few graduates of an Ivy League School in Naval Aviation, John had graduated from Yale with a degree in English literature. On the NROTC scholarship, he had been required to take physics and math classes along with his other studies. A good student, he had done well in the ROTC program. Although he had no flying experience, he had excelled in flight training. Natural hand eye coordination and good spatial awareness, his grades both in the navy classroom and flying were excellent, leading to his selection of F8s. Casper had the head start, but John Phillips had quickly caught up to be one of the best pilots in a very good squadron. After his experience with the short-lived marriage to the hippy girl, he was reluctant to get into another relationship. However, he, too, had met an attractive Australian girl with whom he had ended up enjoying his liberty. Deep in his thoughts, he had ignored the noise of the flight deck. Two of the A4 squadrons had poor boarding rates during the last line period. CAG had asked the captain of the Adams to let them "run the deck" while sailing back to Yankee Station to get some extra landing practice in.

Hearing the bosun call of Fire and General quarters he knew that *Something has obviously gone wrong on the flight deck*, John thought as he hurried back to the Ready Room, which was the squadrons assigned station for general quarters.

On the flight deck, the normal organized chaos was even more chaotic. An A4 was in the refueling pit up near the bow on the starboard side on fire. The pilot, who had gone into the pit to hot refuel, half jumped, and half climbed out of the aircraft and ran from the fire. The aviation bosun mate refueling the aircraft screamed as he was engulfed in the flames, running out on fire where an alert airman put out the flames with a fire extinguisher. In the pit, the third-class petty officer handling the refueling valves, Petty Officer Tom Rogers, while personally engulfed in the flames, quickly turned off the main valves to the fuel. Within a few minutes, the MB5 crash truck located just aft of the island, rushed to the scene. Spraying foam, the fire was out within minutes. After a quick discussion with the A4 Squadron CO, the decision was made to push the A4 off the deck into the ocean. Severely damaged by the fire, it was beyond repair and any parts taken off it would most likely have been heat damaged.

 Ray had been in the line shack meeting with Petty Officer Pearson and the entire crew when the alarm had sounded. With the A4s running the deck his plane captains had stayed off the flight deck and out of the way since no squadron aircraft were involved. At the sound of the alarm, the crew all rushed to their firefighting stations on the flight deck. After a few minutes, Petty Officer Pearson came back into the shack.

"What happened?" Ray asked.

"They were hot refueling a Scooter up on the forward bow. Looks like the hose slipped or was broke. Fuel got on the hot section and the fire started there but spread right away," Pearson said.

"You know that fuel system is supposed to have an automatic shut off but somehow fuel kept spilling out. That bosun had fuel on him and was set on fire. He ran out of it but fell down and they sprayed him down with an extinguisher. He is burnt bad. The petty officer third class manning the main fuel valves had flames all around and on him, but he stayed there until he got the valves shut off. He was burnt real bad. The MB5 crash truck run up the deck real fast and put out the rest of the fire with foam. But if that valve hadn't been shut off the whole ship mighta gone up."

Knowing Ray had been in the line shack when the fire started, he was besieged with questions when he entered the Ready Room after the call to general quarters.

As he started to answer, CDR Prescott said loudly, "Quiet. Ray come up to the front of the Ready Room and give us a briefing on the Fire."

"Yessir," Ray answered. "First of all, the fire is out. It appears that it started when JP (Jet Fuel) spilled on the hot section of an A4 that was hot refueling while the Scooters were running the deck. The pilot got out and away before the fire got to him. The aviation bosun mate fueling the A4 was not so lucky. He was severely burned but after running out of the fire, but it looks like he will survive. For reasons unknown, the automatic shutoff valve did not work, and JP kept flowing after the fuel nozzle was dropped. Fortunately, although engulfed in flames, the petty officer third class operating the refueling station stayed at this post until he was able to get the master valve shut off. He was so badly burned that it looks like he will not survive. The MB5 crash truck arrived in a matter of minutes and put the fire out with foam. It looks like the A4 will probably be struck and pushed off the deck to get it out of the way."

"Hope you all understand what that means." CDR Prescott added. "If that petty officer had not followed his training and had run instead of shutting off that valve, the entire JP tank could have gone up and set the whole ship on fire. We owe a lot to that petty officer."

A vinyl headrest with each pilot's name on it identified the assigned Ready Room seats. Since the loss of Aggie, Ski had insisted on sitting in the chair marked LT Mike Twain.

No one objected. Now he said, "that petty officer should get the Medal of Honor."

At that moment, on the plat TV they all watched an A4 trapping aboard.

"Flight ops have to continue." CDR Prescott said, "Aircraft are airborne that need to land. I am sure they will secure flight ops once any planes still in the pattern have trapped aboard. Also, I want to take the opportunity, while we are still at general quarters, to go over a few items. First, a lesson from today's accident. The rule of the navy: you can delegate authority, but you cannot delegate responsibility. That means, in this case, that the officer in charge, probably the aircraft handling officer, will be found responsible for the fire. What does that mean for us? Well, we all, and me especially, are responsible for what those under us do. It comes from the days of the British Navy when the captain would go down with his ship. As captain, you have full and ultimate authority. But you also have full responsibility. You can pass authority on to those under you, but you will still be responsible. It seems a bit harsh, but it is a good rule. As officers, we can't weasel out of things by blaming others. Now as soon as general quarters end, I have a meeting with CAG to hash out how we are going to operate in this monsoon weather. All officers meeting (AOM) before the film."

In spite of the fire, the ship continued steaming toward Yankee Station in Tonkin Gulf. The monsoon season was now in full force. Gray clouds hung low from the sky. Rain showers pelting the aircraft and men on the flight deck. In air ops, the COs of all the squadrons as well as the whale and photo detachment bosses were gathered for a meeting with CAG Wilkins. The front blackboard was covered by a photo of what appeared to be all North Vietnam from very high altitude. The photo showed thick clouds covering most of the territory. Through a few holes in the clouds known landmarks could be seen. The other walls of air ops were covered with detailed maps of North Vietnam with locations or known or suspected SAM sites, radar sites, and heavy anti-aircraft sites. There were photos of targets on the target list, a description and picture of a SAM airborne, and photos of the two types of Migs.

"Greetings gents," CAG said standing at the podium in the front of the room. Dressed in the tropical khaki long uniform, he said, "From what I saw, looks like everyone had a good time in Hong Kong. Now we have to get to work. An update, Petty Officer Third Class Sanders, who stayed at his station and turned off the master fuel valve, has passed away from his burns. He almost singlehandedly saved the ship. Prayers to his family. Do not know what the ship will do, but he certainly deserves the highest medal one can get. Unfortunately, it did not happen in the combat zone—had it been on Yankee Station, Petty Officer Sanders would have posthumously received the Medal of Honor or at least the Navy Cross."—pointing to the photo on the front board where the weather map was displayed "Returning to the line, we can expect this weather to continue or even get worse over the entire line period. I have had conversations with the Admiral, and we are trying to come up with a reasonable tactical plan to meet our objectives, the first of which is the railway depot in Vinh. The Admiral is under pressure from Cincpac to continue the bombing campaign per the rules of engagement set out by the Department of Defense."

"Shit CAG, how are we supposed to do that with ceilings of 10 grand or less?" CDR Jeffries of VA 14 asked.

"We are trying to work that out. Obviously the Barcap can keep going at a lower altitude as long as we have good enough weather to operate. Chuck, your whale will have to operate. We will probably need tanking more than ever, but since you only have one plane left, you will need to do it from Danang. We can't risk you not being able to get back aboard."

"Yessir. We will get that done."

With only one plane and four pilots in the det, they would rotate to always have the tanker in the air during flight ops. In many ways it was a good deal to now be based on the "beach" in Danang. Aside from the occasional rocket attacks, the officers would work out of the detachment shack on the line. After flight ops they would be able to get a beer in the club the marine officers had set up in a hooch.

"CAG, under DOD rules of engagement, we must visually identify the target before dropping, right? But under our tactical rules we are supposed to be pulling off to not go below 6000 feet to stay out of the 37s and 57s, right?" asked CDR Johnson of VF 123.

"That is right, Greg. Especially you guys doing flak suppression have to see the target and get out. That is what we are trying to get with the Admiral and come up with a reasonable solution. For now, we are going to take our target assignments, plan the strike as usual, and cancel if the weather is too bad. We are going to need to run the photo F8s over the targets as a weather recce to decide to go or not a cycle before the strike."

"Hey Greg. Do you have a minute?" CDR Prescott called the CO of VF 123.I

"Sure. Where do you want to meet?" CDR Johnson replied.

"It is confidential. How about your stateroom or mine."

"I am in mine. Why don't you come over?"

"Roger. Be there in five."

CDR Prescott knocked on the stateroom door. "Come in Scott."

The stateroom was identical to Scott's, and just as neat. Greg sat in his desk chair turned to face a guest chair where he motioned Scott to sit. "What's up?"

"I think I have a tactical plan that will enable us to hit the Vinh Railway yard on our target list with a minimal chance of losses. I wanted to go over it with you before I took it to CAG". Looking directly at CDR. Johnson, he continued, "I propose we take six of our F8s, three from 123 and three from 188, and load them each with two, two thousand pounders. Launch before the rest of the strike group and rendezvous below 500 feet. Have the strike group rendezvous and talk on the radios as a normal Alpha Strike would. However, they would only be decoys. CAG would lead it as normal, give the normal calls and head in toward Haiphong. We would take our two flights down to below 100 feet and fly straight into a point at the beach at Vinh going buster, as fast as we can, leaving ten minutes before the strike group. We would stay below the gook's search radar."

"How would we navigate to that point?" Greg asked. "Nothing to see at 100 feet flying fast over the ocean."

"We would get the airborne E1 radar plane to give us headings to fly in. We would use a simple code like calling our headings thirty degrees north of actual, which should coincide with the strike group. Once we hit the beach we would pull up in a rolling wingover into the clouds, go inverted, pull down through the clouds and, breaking out at about 8000 feet, have 2000 feet to find your target and drop."

"If we do that, won't we be exposed on the pull out? Dropping at 6000 feet we will bottom out below 4000," Greg said.

"I am counting on those twelve, two-thousand pounders and the surprise attack keeping the 37s and 57s quiet. I will lead our section, and I am going to have two of our best sticks flying wings. Men who can fly low and fast and good form in the goo."

"I like it." Cdr. Johnson said, nodding his head. "I will lead our section. Let's take it to CAG I am sure he will want to change a few things."

CAG Wilkins had a few changes, but overall approved the plan. He added a photo F8 to the Vinh attack group to get real-time bomb damage assessment. He also added a F8 Mig Cap and F8 Flak suppressors to the strike group feint. No one in the strike group was to know that they were not actually going in, not even his air intelligence officer. The strike briefing was conducted in a normal fashion, with brief of target, anti-aircraft, suspected SAM sites, etc. CDR Prescott selected Dick Knowles and Ray Rhodes as his wingmen who were briefed and cautioned not to let anyone know.

"Flying outbound, Ray you stay on my Starboard side and Dick you stay to port. I will take us down to fifty feet. Just stick tight on my wing and you will be fine, got it?"

"Yessir," both answered.

Knowing his own limitations, the photo det. officer in charge, Charlie Hicks assigned the second-year tour pilot who he knew could fly the low level over the Tonkin Gulf, Bob Ramsey, who was commonly called Ramjet. "Bob, you will fly in trail on us. You have to keep it down to 50 feet so the radar doesn't pick us up. Try to stay back at least 1000 feet. Once we hit the beach we will pitch up into the goo. You should just ease up to just under the cloud layer with the camera on. We will be back down in our target run in a matter of seconds after pitching up. You should fly your route heading about 180 just behind us. If we catch them by surprise, there shouldn't be much flak."

The six F8s manned first and were first launched. They rendezvoused just South of the ship at 500 feet, effectively showing on radar as planes in the pattern. Once together, they descended to 100 feet above the water. Then, Cdr. Prescott requested a strike heading from the airborne E1.

"Roger 201. Fly heading 242 to feet dry." With a code of 30 degrees, CDR Prescott turned to 212.

No other radio transmission was made except for a later correction to heading 239.

Chapter Twenty-One

Bean Counters
13 September 1967 Vinh, People's Republic of Vietnam

The six F8s launched first and quickly rendezvoused in two flights of three off the starboard stern, hoping the clutter of the activity around the carrier would block any long-range radar signal. The photo followed and trailed both flights. Launching with the heavy bomb load, all six fighters had to tank. Normally this was done between 10000 feet and 20000 feet. On this mission it was done at 500 feet of altitude to minimize the possibility of radar picking them up. The KA3 had been tasked with this since it was able to quickly tank the planes. After all, had tanked, they immediately descended to 50 feet in their sections. CDR Prescott, after seeing the Russian Trawler in the distance to the south of the ship, briefed all the pilots before takeoff that they would be flying lower, at 50 feet above the ocean to reduce the chance of detection. The flight, led by CDR Johnson, flew about 1000 feet to the right of the VF 188 flight. On reaching the railway yard, their targets were in the more northwestern quadrant. As briefed, once the sections were in place, they flew off in an initial heading of 232.

On the strike radio frequency, CDR Prescott made a brief transmission, "strike up."

The E1 radar plane, which was in the second hour of a six-hour flight above the ship, responded with a simple "Roger." Keeping transmissions to a minimum. However, as briefed, the call meant that they had radar contact with the section and would be giving headings to steer to Vinh.

Ten minutes later, the decoy strike group began to form with CAG Wilkins in the lead. Using the normal amount of radio checks with the call, which the Russian Trawler monitored, it appeared to be a large Alpha Strike forming. Once formed, the strike group headed in the general direction of Haiphong.

"Trombone flight, check master switches on. Do not arm your bombs yet. Wait until we go feet dry." CAG called.

Silently, the F8 pilots all checked their switches hot and armed their bombs as briefed.

At that point the E1 radioed, "Trombone flight come left to a heading of 261."

Screaming over the ocean at 50 feet and five hundred knots, CDR Prescott adjusted the heading to 231. Ray, in tight formation was relieved that no noise of radars detected came out of his ALQ gear. They were succeeding in avoiding the North Vietnamese radar.

Minutes later, the E1 radioed, "Trombone flight come further left to 259."

First Lieutenant Tran Chien of the North Vietnam People's Army sat on the metal seat used by the gunners in his command to direct their 57mm Russian anti-aircraft gun. Under his command were the two northern batteries protecting the railway yard at Vinh. When he first came on duty that morning, he had made certain that the guns were properly sighted to fire at the point he knew any dive bombers had to cross. He had also conducted the daily drills of loading and dry firing the weapons, ensuring that all the proximity fuses on the six-pound rounds were set for 1800 meters. That was the altitude just above where the bombs were normally released. After receiving word from the battalion commander that a large raid had been seen on radar heading for the Haiphong area, but nothing was seen in their area, he had relaxed some, but remained attentive, watching the gray sky and listening from where he sat. His men, eight for each gun, were spread out around the battery. Several were playing cards. One was reading a newspaper and one, Dao An, a loader, was returning from the squat toilet.

Tran first heard the jets as they screamed down at him. They had crossed the beach and traveled 5.8 miles to the railway yard at almost supersonic speed, in less than thirty seconds. As he looked to the sky, Tran saw first one then two and three jets pointed directly toward the rail yard and the batteries. He screamed to his men to man the guns, but it was too late. The plane directed at his battery had already released its lethal load of two-thousand-pound bombs, each with a blast radius of a quarter of a mile. Anyone in the blast radius was almost vaporized.

As Ray came down through the clouds on the skipper's wing, he broke to the right as briefed with his nose pointed to the ground. He immediately saw his target, the 57mm gun site, adjusted the heading to line up his gun sight on the target and dropped both bombs. In a matter of seconds, he was pulling off. In a turning climb, before he entered the cloud layer again, he was able to see the mass destruction the raid had caused. Fires were burning, ammunition was going off, but no anti-aircraft fire was visible. What was left of a locomotive was on its side and burning. Warehouses had been leveled. Tracks had been unearthed and bent. Just as he was entering the clouds he saw the photo F8 crossing the area. Once over the ocean, feet wet, he saw the skipper's and Dick's planes. As he joined them, the photo F8 also appeared over the clouds and joined in a loose cruise formation as did the three F8s from VF 123. Looking each other over for battle damage, no one appeared to have been hit. The raid had been a total surprise.

"Trombone lead, this is Heater One."

"Go ahead, One." CAG answered.

"We hit a home run. I say again, Home Run!"

"Roger that. Trombone flight switches off. We are bingo to Sand Box."

The pilots in the decoy flight had begun to suspect something was up when they had headed into the Haiphong area at full speed with switches on but had turned before crossing the beach and gone into an orbit offshore. All planes returned to the Adams for a normal recovery. After recovery, the pilots of the F8s and Ramsey, the photo F8 pilot, met with CAG in air ops for a debrief.

"CAG I think we completely surprised them. As far as I could see, there was no flak. Think the rail yard was completely destroyed as well as their air defenses."

"What did you see in your viewfinder, Bob?"

"I think the film will show a 100 percent success. First time I have been over the beach where no one shot at me. As far as I could see, the entire railway complex was destroyed."

CDR Dawkins, the head of air intelligence was also there, obviously upset at not being read into the raid, said, "CAG, if you had let me in on the planning I could have helped with the strike."

"No offense meant, Fred. You and your guys do a great job, but I just wanted to limit the number of people knowing about the raid. Did not think of you as a security risk. I thought we knew that target well enough without any help. Please have your photo interpreters jump on that film as soon as possible. I want to get a copy to the Admiral asap. He needs a success to fend off Cincpac and the DOD bean counters. Now CDR Prescott, tell me what worked and what didn't. Critique your own raid if you will. Also, Greg, Dick, Tom, Ray, and Juan, great job, but what could we do better?"

Dan Prescott began, "I thought this worked well but I am afraid it is a one-time shot. Those gooks—er, North Vietnamese soldiers—learn fast. This time they took the decoy hook line and sinker. I don't think they will next time. Without the decoy of you leading an Alpha Strike into Haiphong, they would have been sitting at their guns ready to open up as soon as they heard us. You can bet that in the future they will always be ready."

"How did the headings given by the E1 work out?" CAG Wilkins asked.

"They put us exactly where we needed to be. We hit the point almost supersonic, immediately climbed into the clouds turning toward the rail yard. I don't think it took us over thirty seconds from hitting the beach to dropping on them. This would not work for an inland target. They would hear us coming and we would be eating small arms fire the entire way like the A6s are having to deal with."

CAG then spoke to Ray, "Lt. Rhodes I think you are the youngest here. How was it for you?"

"Frankly sir, it was almost a piece of cake. All I had to do was fly form on the Skipper. When we burst through the clouds I was almost exactly lined up with my target. I just adjusted, dropped, and got out of Dodge. I don't think I was over the beach more than a couple of minutes."

Captain Wilkins said, "Again, an outstanding job. I will let you know how the film comes out for the bomb damage assessment (BDA)." Captain Wilkins ordered CDR Dawkins to contact him when the BDA film was ready.

The film showed the extent of the destruction in vivid black-and-white detail. The rail yard and its defenses had been obliterated. One of the ninety-four targets authorized by the White House had been taken out.

"Admiral Johnston, Captain Wilkins on the secure line for you."

"Go ahead, Captain." Admiral Johnston, in charge of Task Force 77 on Yankee Station, said.

"Sir, I sent the photos of a raid we made this morning on the Vinh rail yard. It was a complete and total destruction."

"I saw your photos. Unfortunately, Cincpac also sent me photos from the *Washington Post* showing pictures of dead children, a burning school, and assorted other atrocities. The North Vietnamese government is calling this their Pearl Harbor. An attack without warning. It is total propaganda fiction. I know your photos are accurate, but they are so good at twisting things. One of McNamara's bean counters, the Assistant Secretary of Defense for blah, blah, blah, is being sent out here to see why we aren't flying normal Alpha Strikes and to chastise us for the sneak attack. You and your pilots did an outstanding job. If we were in World War Two everyone would get medals. Now we will be lucky if we don't get a letter of reprimand."

Chapter Twenty-Two

15 September
TF 77 Spaces, USS America

Assistant Secretary of Defense Krupp, formerly VP of Finance for Ford Motor Company, was speaking while seated at the conference table in the flag spaces on the America. "Admiral, these are all weather aircraft. I do not understand why you are not bombing the targets we have selected."

Under Secretary Krupp, after graduating from the Wharton School of Business, had spent World War Two as a civilian employee of the War Department. He had encouraged Ford into converting their assembly lines into the production of all manner of war materials from tanks and trucks to bombers and fighters. After the war, Ford had offered him a position in their finance department. He rose to become the senior vice president of finance. When Robert McNamara had left Ford to become secretary of defense, he had brought Krupp with him—part of McNamara's Whiz Kids.

Reaching into his inner jacket pocket, he pulled out a pack of Lucky Strikes and proceeded to light one.

The admiral's aide, Commander Wilson said, "Mr. Krupp. There is no smoking in here. The smoking lamp is out. Too many sensitive materials here."

Reluctantly, Mr. Krupp put out the cigarette in a bowl that CDR Wilson held out.

Admiral Jim Johnston, in charge of TF 77, did not suffer fools lightly. He had fled post-depression Oklahoma to attend the Naval Academy, graduating and receiving his commission in 1941. He had orders to Pensacola and naval aviation training. Initially he spent most of his time in "pools" waiting to enter training. Pearl Harbor changed that. In early 1942, a push in training was made to get pilots out Admiral Johnston was a good student, by midyear he was targeted to get fighters, either the Corsair or the new Hellcat. Due to the problems the Corsairs had in operating off the carriers, they were sent to the marine corps to operate off land bases while the navy took the Hellcats. As a result, Admiral Johnston was sent to Hellcats. He finished training in time to join a Hellcat squadron for the Marianas Turkey Shoot. As a new LTJG, he became an ace in that battle, eventually shooting down twelve Japanese zeros during the war. In Korea he flew, as an experienced, senior lieutenant, the F9F Panther, where he again served with distinction. His decorations after World War Two and Korea included the Silver Star, Two Distinguished Flying Crosses, and a Navy Cross. Toward the end of the 1950s, he was promoted to commander and was selected for command of one of the new A4 squadrons. From there he rapidly progressed, serving as captain of the carrier Ticonderoga. He made admiral in 1964 and was appointed to lead TF 77 in late 1966.

"Begging your pardon, sir. We can fly in almost any weather. However, if our pilots cannot see the targets we cannot bomb. Also, they need to see the SAMs to evade them. In bad weather, overcast below 10000 feet, they cannot stay above the triple-A targeting us. Per the DOD rules of engagement, we must see our targets before we drop. The only aircraft we have that can fly at night in weather and navigate to a target is the A6 Intruder. However, when they fly in low every farmer or peasant has a weapon to fire at them. Our loss rates were unacceptable, so we had to stop those raids. And right now, the airwing on the America is the only one with A6s. Only the A4s and F8s can fly off the old 27C World War Two carriers. Those airwings are doing a great job with what they have, but they cannot fly IFR to the targets. None of us can." Admiral Johnston explained.

"Why was the strike on the Vinh rail yard so successful? Why can't you duplicate that on other targets?"

"The airwing commander on the Adams was able to plan a strike in secrecy and execute it. They caught the enemy completely by surprise, but the North Vietnamese learn quickly. They will not be caught again"

"I have seen the pictures your photo aircraft took but did you see the pictures the Vietnamese provided to the *Washington Post* and the *New York Times*? The *Times* headline was Pearl Harbor in Vinh."

"I did see that" The Admiral answered. "The media is against us. They don't publish anything about the mistreatment of POWs or the slaughter of civilians in the South by the VC, but we can't do shit without being blamed for targeting children and civilians. Our pilots do everything possible to hit legitimate targets and take a lot of real flak for doing so."

"No matter what, we are ordering you to launch Alpha strikes per our targeting list by each one of your airwings within the next two or three days regardless of the weather."

At this, Admiral Johnston stood up and walked to the front of the room, clearly furious. While the admiral was of average height, he had a certain presence that caused his aides to quickly obey any order. He waited to answer but then said, "Mr. Krupp, you are a civilian. I am the tactical commander here. You cannot order me to do anything. It is only out of courtesy that we are listening to you."

"Admiral Johnston, I fully understand my role and the secretary's role. While I cannot order you, Cincpac can—and I am sure he will—order those strikes. They are to be carried out at the time specified. We must notify the Russians of the strikes to ensure that none of their advisors are injured." Mr. Krupp stood up, towering over Admiral Johnston as if mockingly challenging him to a physical confrontation.

CDR Wilson broke the tension by asking incredulously, "You, in Washington, are advising the Russians of our strikes? The Russians who have a trawler following us all over the gulf. The Russians who broadcast our strikes. The NVA do not need to spy. They have Mr. Krupp here and the secretary spying for them. How many of our pilots have you been responsible for killing, Mr. Krupp?"

Krupp, visibly angry, said, "Nothing more to be accomplished here. You will hear from Cincpac I am sure. I am going to my quarters." With that he walked out of the conference room.

The next day, over the secure teletype orders came in from Cincpac to plan and attack three targets from the target list within 48 hours. CTF 77 was to notify Cincpac of the planned attacks, what targets and when they would be attacked

Chapter Twenty-Three

Rolls Downhill
15 September 1967 Yankee Station

All the airwing commanders had been summoned to the America to meet with the Admiral regarding new orders from Cincpac. Deputy Secretary of Defense Krupp was in attendance as well as the admiral's staff and the captain of the America. They met in the conference room in the flag officer spaces on the America.

"Gents, I summoned you here to discuss how to deal with some very difficult or almost impossible orders we have received from Cincpac. The Bean Counters at DOD have no real concept of what happens when we send our squadrons on strikes. I am hoping Mr. Krupp here will leave enlightened. Commander Wilson, please pass out the target packets." CDR. Wilson walked around the room, handing thick packets to each officer.

"We have been ordered to plan and execute strikes at these targets on our target list within the next forty-eight hours. You each have received information on your assigned target in the packet. That is as much info as we have on them."

"Admiral, we cannot control the weather," Tom Kennedy, airwing CAG on the Jefferson said.

"Tom, I am well aware of that. I have tried to convince Mr. Krupp here of that fact. But Cincpac has ordered us to do this regardless of the weather. I have tried to speak to Cincpac, but he has not been available. I doubt if he will be available until after this is over."

"Assuming this weather holds, does anyone have any bright ideas how we can do this, follow DOD rules of engagement, and not have our airwings decimated?"

"I did not think so. Mr. Krupp not only told us we would need to do this following the rules of engagement, but that Washington needed to know the location and timing of the strike since they were required to notify the Russians in order for the Russians to get their people out of the way of the strikes." He said angrily, thoroughly disgusted with what he was ordered to do.

Cutting them all off before they spoke, he said, "One more thing. You are all grounded. No CAGs will fly in these strikes. That is an order from me."

"Good luck. Forward your tactical plans to me as soon as possible."

In air ops on the Adams the mood was tense. All squadron COs, detachment Oincs, air intelligence officers, and the weatherman had been called to a meeting with CAG immediately upon his return from the America.

"Gentlemen, I have extremely bad news. We have been ordered by Cincpac to attack the bridge at Dong Phong Thuong within the next forty-eight hours. Actually, now it is the next forty-six hours. Not only do we have to attack, but Washington will also tell the Russians that we will be attacking."

The room exploded with shouts of "What? What idiot thinks this up? This is a load of shit" and worse expletives. Senior officers were shaking their heads in disbelief, looking first at CAG and then around the room at each other.

"Men, I totally understand. That was exactly my reaction as well as Admiral Johnston's reaction. However, we do have orders no matter how stupid they are. So, let's see if there is some way to comply with a minimum of damage to our squadrons."

"Spook, show where Dong Phong Thuong is on the map." CDR Johnson shouted to CDR Dawkins.

Dawkins looked at the map and located a red pin that his intel clerk had placed at the bridge. He pointed to the spot, some twenty-five miles south of Hanoi and about seventy miles inland. "It is 105.47E and 19.58N. It is about 20 miles southeast of Hanoi. The bridge is both a railway bridge and highway. From this photo supplied by the air force, you can see that it is a relatively long and thin bridge, only about 24 feet wide. Trucks use the same bridge as the trains. Just here"—pointing to an area in the upper right corner of the photo— "is what is believed to be a warehouse holding arms, anti-aircraft shells and some SAM parts. From the photo, you can see that there are two main anti-aircraft batteries on either side of the bridge. These are believed to be 57mm sites."

"That is a long way to go over Indian Country in bad weather," CDR Jeffries of VA 18 said.

"What is the weather supposed to be in the next forty-eight?"

CDR Dawkins answered, "About the same as now. A broken layer down about at 5000 feet and a solid overcast at 8000 feet."

Reconciled to the fact that they were going to do this, CDR Prescott said, "We either go in the goo at 20000 feet and the SAMs eat us up, or 8000 and deal with the triple-A. For my boys and the flak suppression, I think we must go in at 8000. We won't be able to see the targets otherwise. Hell, we don't even have a bombsight, much less inertial nav." Referring to the new navigation system used by the A6's on the big carriers.

"I want this strike to be as minimal as we can and still have a chance of knocking down that bridge. Can we just send in four flak suppressor F8s and twelve A4s?" CAG asked.

"CAG, if anybody gets through, we are going to need more than four flak suppressors. They will have triple-A up the ass. They will know we are coming. Flying in at 8000 feet there is a good chance the flak suppressors will get hit before they get to the target."

"Agreed. We will need to go with eight flak suppressors. Four from each squadron and four A4s from each of the three squadrons."

"Know Washington is going to tell the Ruskis. That sucks. But can we fudge the time a little. Tell them 1000 hours and hit at dawn?" asked CDR Jeffries.

"I think that is the least we can do. Striking at the crack of dawn. Maybe we could get a little bit of surprise."

"Bill, the Admiral has grounded me. Can I count on you to lead the strike since the F8s will hit first?" CAG asked CDR Jeffries of VA 14.

"Yessir."

Shuffling papers until everyone else had left, CDR Prescott said, "CAG, can I have a minute?"

"Sure Dan."

"I have a bad feeling about this and need a favor from you."

"I'll try Dan."

"If I don't make it back, don't turn the squadron over to Scampi. He's no good. Give Dick a temporary promotion to Commander and have him run the squadron. I am not letting him go on the strike. I should have sent Scampi home when I had the chance."

CAG turned to Dan Prescott and place both hands on his shoulders and said, "I have no doubt that you will make it, but if you don't I promise you that I honor your wishes."

CDR. Prescott was relieved. Catching CDR. Jeffries in the corridor before the returned to his ready room, he asked, "Bill, can we get our guys together and brainstorm how we can get this done and keep our losses minimal?"

"Sure. Let's get the COs, XOs, and OP officers of all the squadrons in a group meeting in our Ready 4. Let's make it around 1230 hours, just after the last recovery. I will have our spook pull up the maps and photos."

Still on the midnight-to-noon flight schedule, CDR Prescott called another AOM at 1200 hours after the last Barcap had landed. Because of the bad weather no other planes were flying.

"Men, we have been given a very important but dangerous task. In two days, we are going to strike the bridge at Dong Phong Thuong. It is located about seventy miles inland and twenty miles south of Hanoi. It is an important bridge for the flow of material to the VC fighting our guys down South."

"What about the weather?" Joe Ames asked.

"The airwing is going no matter what the weather is. We will take four of our planes and 123 will send four of theirs as flak suppressors. There should be no need for Mig Cap as they do not normally fly in this weather."

"Yeah, they aren't stupid," Ames said.

"We will attack at dawn. We will hit the triple-A around the bridge while the scooters knock it down. This will be a tough mission, and I am asking for two volunteers."

"Two?" Dick Knowles said, "I thought you said we would have four planes."

"That is correct. Sorry Ray, but I volunteered you to fly with me."

"Yessir. I am in," Ray said without hesitation.

Preacher spoke up and said, "I will lead the second section."

His roommate LCDR Robinson said, "I will fly on your wing, Preach."

Dick Knowles spoke up, "I will go. Let me go instead of you, Skipper."

"No. I need you to stay here and hold down things."

Ames, Phillips, Casper, Kowalski, and Davis also volunteered, but the skipper said he was going with the experience of the LCDRs.

At 1230 hours, CDR Prescott and Dick Knowles went down to Ready Four to plan the strike with VA 14 and the other squadrons.

Commander Jeffries opened the meeting and said, "Gents I am going to ask you to agree to keep all our conversation in this room. I am going to say some things and we will probably have some suggestions that certainly DOD wouldn't approve and might get CAG and the Admiral on a hot seat. I do not want to go on a suicide mission and refuse to ask my pilots to risk their lives unless we come up with a plan that has at least a fifty-fifty chance of survival. Otherwise, I will just suggest we form up, head for the beach, drop our ordinance in the Gulf, and come back."

"Bill, I totally agree with you. But let's think about what we can do. We know a normal Alpha Strike in this weather would end up with massive losses to either SAMs in the clouds or the triple-A below the clouds," CDR Johnson said.

"How did your strike on the Vinh Rail yard work so well?" LDR Charles, Op O of VA 18 asked.

"We caught them with their pants down. It was only about thirty seconds from the beach. We went in supersonic and dropped before they knew we were there. No way we will fly seventy some miles inland and surprise anybody." CDR. Johnson replied.

"No, but maybe we can change up our tactics some." LCDR Rames of VF 123 said.

"How so?"

"Well, they all know that we come in first with flak suppressors and then the dive bombers. Why do both?"

"What do you mean?"

"Well, dropping our two thousand pounders anywhere near the flak sites shuts them up. With those big bombs we don't have to be very accurate. With a blast radius of a quarter mile and force to go through a foot of reinforced concrete, if we have enough bombs, we should be able to take out the flak sites and the bridge."

"Then what would we do?" CDR Jeffries asked.

"In a normal Alpha strike, the F8s go first followed by the A4s. What if, in all the clouds etc., you got slightly off course and in the weather accidentally hit that warehouse area just north of the bridge. Fog of war and all that."

0430 17 September 1967

They pre-flighted their aircraft in the dark and rain. It started raining steadily at midnight. The ceiling had dropped to around 6000 feet, but there was some indication that it might improve at dawn. When Ray went out to the flight deck to man his plane, Heater 207, he tossed his helmet as usual to Mears. Wet, it slipped through Mears' hands and dropped gently to the ground. He quickly scooped it up, but in his mind the damage was done.

The F8s, with their heavy bomb load, launched first and then immediately flew to an A3 tanker off the port bow and tanked. Once the final A4 launched, the strike group formed with the F8s leading as the sun began to come up. They had briefed to fly at 450 knots, as fast as the A4s could cruise with a bomb load. Navigating by a combination of dead reckoning, navigation points on the ground such as rivers, roads, and hills the strike group sped across North Vietnam. Occasionally, someone would open up with a machine gun or small anti-aircraft. The weather had improved, and they were able to fly at about 9000 feet. The time to target from feet dry was about nine minutes. As they flew along with only minor triple-A shooting at them, Dan Prescott became more optimistic that they would achieve some sort of surprise. When they reached the target and rolled in, that thought was quickly dispelled. More triple-A than he had ever seen opened on them. Obviously, a warning had gone out from units or radar they had overflown on the way to the target. In section, CDR Prescott took the left side of the bridge with Ray Rhodes.

CDR Johnson took the right side with his wingman. The eight, two-thousand-pound bombs hit the targets within seconds of each other. Approaches to the bridge on both sides of the river were wiped out. The triple-A was greatly reduced but still firing. Because of the low clouds, they had to drop and pull out at lower altitudes putting them not only in range of the 57s, but also of the 37s. As soon as Heater 201 pulled off target it was hit in the tail area and caught on fire. Dan Prescott fought for control and turned to try to fly to feet wet. Ray pulled off, saw 201 on fire and raced to help his lead.

As the fire progressed 201 became uncontrollable. When the fire reached the cockpit, Ray said, "Two-O-One, eject, eject, eject." In response, he saw the ejection and was relieved to see a good chute. His own plane, 209, was shaking and responding sluggishly to the controls. Knowing he could not help the skipper, seeing, as he flew over, a group of villagers and what appeared to be NVA army waiting below the parachute., he struggled to keep his aircraft flying, trying his best to make it at least to the gulf.

On the PRC radio Dan Prescott had pulled from his survival vest he said, "Heater 201 on Guard. Descending in my parachute I see villagers and a NVA unit waiting to take me in. There is no chance for rescue. Two go feet wet."

Preacher in Heater 205 was also hit on the pull off target. Flying as fast as he could with a failing hydraulic control system, he was just able to make it feet wet and ejected near the Rescap helicopter waiting offshore.

LCDR Robinson's plane, apparently hit just as he dropped, exploded in midair with no chance for ejection; he was instantly killed in the explosion.

The VF123 F8s fared no better. Dollar 101, flow by CDR Greg Johnson, blew up before dropping. His wingman was hit and made it part way back out before ejecting after a dual PC failure. He was captured. LCDR Rames was hit but made it back feet wet before ejecting. His wingman was hit and presumed dead since no one saw an ejection or heard a beeper.

As the flight of A4s neared the bridge, CDR Jeffries veered slightly to the north of the bridge. Immediately, he lined up on the warehouse complex and dropped. At first, there was little resistance, but as the remainder of the A4s attacked, leaving the warehouse complex burning, the two triple-A sites protecting the warehouse complex opened up. One of the sites, using the 57mm guns, was largely ineffective since their rounds were set to explode just at the base of the clouds around 9000 feet. As briefed the A4s began their runs at 8000 feet. While avoiding most of the flak from the larger guns, they were in range of the 37s on the pull out. Still, they fared better than the F8s. Leaving the warehouse leveled with secondary explosions continuing to go off, seven of the twelve A4s on the strike made it back to the ship. Two others made it feet wet before ejecting from battle damage. The three that did not make it were either captured or dead.

In total, out of twenty planes on the strike, eleven were lost. Out of twenty pilots, two were known captured, eight made it back to the ship, four were picked up by helos in the Gulf, and six were missing in action.

Struggling to fly the ball and trap aboard with his damaged aircraft, Ray was relieved to make it back but extremely upset. After trapping aboard and taxiing forward, he climbed down from the aircraft and sat on the flight deck next to the nose wheel. Emotionally exhausted, Mears helped him up. Together they looked over the plane to find the battle damage.

Half the rudder was missing which explained why Ray's radio was out: the antennae was shot off. The wings were riddled with holes as were the ailerons, leading to the sluggish controls. It seemed incredible that he had been able to fly the plane back aboard the ship. If repairable, Heater 207 would be down for a long time.

In total, two squadron skippers had been captured. Two were dead. The airwing was decimated. Out of the pilots who returned, no one knew or cared if the bridge had been hit.

After taking off his G-suit, survival vest, and torso harness, hanging them on the appropriate pegs, Ray made his way to air ops to debrief. The first one there, CAG asked, "Did Dan make it?"

"He was hit pulling off and on fire. I followed him for about a mile, but I had no radio. When I got back, I saw that my antennae had been shot off. Skipper had to punch out. He got a good chute. I circled for a little bit, but he dropped right down into a crowd of villagers and NVA. I have never seen such thick flak. They had to know we were coming. Guess we can't fly over seventy miles of territory without somebody hearing us and calling it in."

"Did you see anybody else?"

"No. I heard that Preacher punched out feet wet. Hope he is OK. I didn't see what happened to LCDR Robinson."

The seven surviving A4 pilots made their way to air ops a few minutes later. As they reported what they had seen, the depth of the losses only increased. All the surviving pilots seemed to be in shock. The most senior pilots, commanding officers, ops officers, and senior lieutenant commanders had been lost. Captain Wilkins realized that he no longer had a functioning airwing. As it was, he sent the damage report to CTF 77, Admiral Johnston. He also sent a message that the losses had been so great the airwing would have difficulty manning Barcap and could not mount another strike. The only capability the A4s might have would be road recce's south of Vinh.

Remembering his promise to Dan Prescott, Captain Wilkins told Ray to come with him back to Ready Two. When they walked in, Commander Scampi was conducting an AOM, explaining to the remaining pilots, including Dick Knowles, that he was now the skipper and things were going to be different.

Having overheard Scampi, Captain Wilkins, CAG, took over and said, "things will definitely be different without Dan Prescott. He was one of the best fighter pilots and Skippers I have ever seen. The only good news is the report that the NVA has confirmed that he was captured." Turning to Scampi, he said, "Sit down, Commander. Dick Knowles, come up here." Once Dick had come up to the front of the Ready Room, CAG said, "Dick, I am promoting you to Commander. This is a temporary promotion, but I am also making you the new Skipper of VF 188 for the rest of the cruise."

"You can't do that. I outrank him," Scampi said.

"I can and I did. Do you want me to bust you down to LCDR?"

The airwing on the America and the Jefferson had similar results on their strikes. Many pilots, radar intercept officers, and bombardier navigators lost. More than half the strike aircraft lost in their strike on the assigned target. Planes that did make it back had such severe damage that it was doubtful they could be flown again. They would become hangar queens useful only for parts.

Seeing the results, Krupp said, "Well those are just numbers. We will send out replacements."

"No, you asshole. Those are people. Our people. They have wives and children. They had friends and lives. That is all you bean counters see. Numbers. Fuck you Krupp. You and the Secretary and your target selection. You and the politicians make tactical decisions that get our people killed and leave our forces shattered."

"You can't talk to me like that, Admiral. I will have your star."

"I can talk to you any way I want. I am putting in my papers to retire. You are a fucking asshole. You better get your ass off this ship before somebody ties you to an anchor and throws you overboard."

Chapter Twenty-Four

Gray Days
18 September 1967

Dick Knowles stood in the front of Ready Room Two and spoke to the pilots and officers gathered there for the all-officer's meeting. The mood was somber. They never expected that the skipper would be shot down. They knew he was brave, but he seemed invincible. LCDR Robinson was also well liked and a good stick. Rumors had gone around the ship that the assistant secretary for McNamara had insisted on the strike. Also, it was heard that he had described the losses as just numbers. The morale of the entire airwing was destroyed.

"Men, I need your help. As you know, we lost all four of our aircraft from the strike on the Dong Phong Bridge. So far, out of twelve aircraft we came on cruise with, we have lost seven planes. Two-O-Seven will eventually be repaired but it is hard down for some time. That leaves five planes. We have 203 in Check in Cubi. Hopefully it will be ready when we pull in there. Preach, either you or Ray do a maintenance check flight as soon as it is up."

Preacher, back on the ship after spending a night on the destroyer that the helo had dropped him on after his ejection, said, "Ray, can you do that. My back is still a little sore."

"Sure boss," Ray answered.

"Back to my count, we have one plane, 208, that is an unofficial Hangar queen. We have been waiting on parts to repair the PC system for more than three months. That leaves us with three operational aircraft. Four if we get the check aircraft. That means that we can barely support one Barcap flight every two launches. We will not have aircraft for photo escorts, road recees, and certainly not for Mig Cap or Alpha strikes. I am going to CAG and explain the problem. Hopefully he can get the Admiral or Cincpac to come up with more planes for us. But I think we all know that F8s are in short supply."

"We will be heading back to Cubi in the next couple of days. With only three planes, we will have to do a double missing man coming into the break. Sorry for your people, Preach, but maintenance is going to have to work extra hard during the in-port period to try to get 208 up and make sure the plane coming out of check is ready. Overall, our morale has taken a huge hit. It affects me as much or more than you, but we all still must keep pushing to finish this cruise. We won't have much flying due to the shortage of planes. Keep your chins up. We are still the best fighter pilots in the world in the best fighter squadron."

"CAG, this is Dick Knowles. Could I come see you for a minute?"

"Meet me in air ops now Dick."

"Yessir."

It only took Dick a few minutes to reach his destination.

"Hello Dick. How are they accepting you?" CAG asked as Dick Knowles entered air ops.

"I have no problem with any of my people but, morale of the squadron is as low as it can be. Have you heard the rumor going around that the Admiral did not authorize the strike, but it was called by that DOD guy? Also, that he called the losses, just numbers."

CAG, who had been overheard talking to his ops officer, telling him exactly that, said, "I heard about that. Unfortunately, I cannot deny it. Admiral Johnstone resigned and turned in his retirement papers over the strikes. However, lucky for us, Cincpac did not accept his resignation. That's a good thing. We need him here to fight for us. The result of all this is that there will be no strikes unless the weather permits. That comes from Cincpac. What do you need, Dick? I still owe you for saving my butt and I have not forgotten."

"CAG, I was glad to help, but I hope you know I would have done it for any of our pilots." Dick said, "I need your help now. We have a big problem with aircraft. In addition to the Skipper and Wild Bill, we lost all our aircraft from the strike. Ray brought his back, but it is hard down and will be for some time. It is full of holes and the top of the rudder was shot off. We do not have enough aircraft to handle our Barcap responsibility and I don't think 123 does either."

"I know. We are trying to think of alternatives. The Admiral is aware of our problem. We cannot leave the fleet with no protection. The Migs have never come out, but knowing our problem they might try."

"What would you think about our sending up an A4 with one of our guys or 123 on Barcap? The radar signature would show two aircraft. Just in case, we could load a couple of sidewinders on them. The A4 guys are trained in dog fighting and could fight if they had to." Dick asked.

"I don't think we will need to do that now. We only are supposed to have two more days on the line, but I think the Admiral is going to have us leave today." CAG replied.

"I do think it is not a bad idea to have the A4s help with Barcap, but they need to train some. They do some dogfighting in their squadrons. If we are going to stick them out on Barcap with your guys, then they need to be trained." Captain Wilkins continued.

"I think it would be good for morale if we did some flying in Cubi. Pair an A4 pilot with an F8 and fight two A4s who would simulate the Migs. What do you think, Dick?"

"I think that is an outstanding idea. Sure, would help with our morale and I imagine it will be good for the Scooter guys." Dick replied.

When Dick returned to Ready Two most of the pilots were still hanging around the Ready Room, not knowing what to do with themselves without a flight schedule. LT Ames and Kowalski were playing the Navy version of Backgammon, Acey Ducey, in one corner of the room.

"Now listen up." They all turned to listen to Dick. "I just got back from seeing CAG. First, the ship is heading back to Cubi today. So, fly off tomorrow. Me, Ray, and Ski. Sorry, but the rest of you guys must ride the ship in. Ghost, in port we will have a flight schedule. We will do two hops a day, with one of our birds per hop. So, plan on writing a schedule on your way into port. The SDO will stand watch out of the BOQ and base ops while we are flying. CAG knew we had a problem with aircraft, and he already asked the Admiral for help. Cincpac got involved but the best they could do was four aircraft. Two for us and two for 123. They are coming out of the Rag and that replacement pilot you met Dusty, Wilson, will be flying one of the planes out on a trans Pac. Still, we will be short of aircraft for the next line period. CAG has the idea of pairing an A4 with one of us for Barcap. Since there is now an absolute block on strikes until the weather improves, the Scooters don't have much to do. However, we need to practice tactics with an A4 partner if we are going to use them on Barcap. They can carry sidewinders and do have guns. They turn well but cannot zoom up and down like we do in our tactics. I want each of you to pair up with an A4 pilot for the next line period. Find someone you like or know today. Give the name to Casper and he will schedule you. That will be your partner for the next line period. Poet, sorry to have you riding the boat in. Please get with a senior LT in an A4 squadron who you know and figure out the best tactics we can use to fight together." Dick instructed.

"Aye, Aye, Skipper."

"Ghost, write the schedule, starting the day after tomorrow, as soon as the ship docks, two on twos in ACM hops. For example, Ski and a partner against Poet and a partner. Make sure that everyone gets at least one hop while we are in port. In these practice tactics, the losing team buys drinks and dinner at the O'Club."

All three F8s of VF 188 were up to fly into Cubi. Dick briefed a two-man missing man. He would fly lead, Ray would fly on his left wing, and Ski on the right. As he did the preflight inspection on 211, Ray could not help but feel a combination of sadness and guilt. In some ways, he thought he should have been shot down, not the skipper who had done so much for him and Astrud.

The flight deck was silent initially, then gradually the noise increased to the normal roar as Huffer starting units began to turn up the jet engines. Yellow shirts started directing the aircraft up to the cats. It was noticeable that the flight deck was not as crowded as usual. Many planes were missing. The gray overcast, missing aircraft seemed to cause everyone to move slower. The normal, frantic pace of a launch was gone for now.

On top of the clouds, at 41000 feet, the flight to Cubi had gone well. Dick led them down on an IFR approach until they broke out of the clouds at 8000 feet. Descending to 500 feet for the break at almost supersonic speed, when they approached the tower, Dick signaled them to break away. Ray flew up and left to 5000 feet while Ski flew up and right to the same altitude. As they returned to the runway, Ski slightly ahead with Ray in trail, the effect was like a two-leaf clover. Ski screaming down the runway, did his now familiar tuck under break. Ray followed with a very low fan break in a spectacular fashion.

After landing, Ray changed and immediately went to the officer's club and called Sandy.

"Sandy, I am so sorry about the Skipper. He did get a good chute, and I saw him almost down on the ground, but they were waiting for him. I am so sorry."

"Ray, Dusty, thank you for the call. I know the hell he is going through but at least he is alive. Greg Johnson was killed, wasn't he?"

"Yes ma'am. It was an awful mission. We tried our best. Bill Robinson was killed also, and many other guys were captured. We should be home soon. Rumor is that they will cut the cruise short since we lost so many pilots and planes."

John Phillips spoke to the rest of the squadron as the ship steamed to Cubi. "We are going to cover Barcap with one of our birds and an A4. That way the radar signature will show two aircraft. The Scooters will carry sidewinders and can fight if they have to, but each of you will be the lead. In your brief, discuss how you would fight the Migs in that configuration. I think we will still use combat spread and loose Deuce, but the Scooter can turn inside us and keep up with the Migs. They cannot go vertical like we can. But I think this will be a lethal combination if we can keep the mutual support of loose deuce. Please give the names of the A4 pilots you are going to partner with to Ghost so he can write the schedule. The A4 squadrons will get copies of our schedule so we should all be on the same page."

After the AOM, Troy found his way down to Ready 4. Pilots were lounging around the Ready Room much like in Ready Two, not knowing what to do with themselves without a flight schedule and almost moping around due to the disaster of the Dong Phong strike. He located Phil Patch, a friend of his from the training command. From VT1 through Meridian and Kingsville, they had been in the same training squadrons.

"Hey Phil, did you hear about the combination of us and you guys flying Barcaps next line period? Want to fly with me?"

"Definitely. I don't know if you remember, but you and I flew that ACM flight two on one against that instructor in Kingsville. I thought we beat him, but he denied it. Still gave us good grades. I love dogfighting. Beats the shit out of dropping bombs on a combat sky spot where you don't know what you will hit."

"Got to tell you Phil, we don't call Barcap Bore cap for nothing. Normally it is just boring holes in the sky, but you never know. Anyway, we are going to do practice hops from the beach once we get in. Think you and I will be first up against one of our best, John Phillips, Poet, and one of your guys."

Together they discussed in detail how they would handle the first dogfight from the beach. Troy explained the F8 tactics of high and low yo-yos. Phil came up with the idea of doing modified high and low yo-yos. He would go up and down like Troy, but to a lesser degree and use the superior turning of the A4 to stay in sync with Troy. In the first of the two on two dogfights, F8 and A4 against F8 and A4, Troy and Phil went up against John Phillips and his A4 partner, Jim Kinney, a senior lieutenant from another A4 squadron. They flew to a draw in each of three separate engagements. Once they landed, the arguments started.

"I had a good tone and winder shot right after we passed on that first engagement." Troy claimed.

"Bullshit. If you had had the shot, you would have called fox one."

Since there was no clear winner, all bets were off.

In the line shack, while writing up the report on the maintenance check ride on Heater 203, Ray Rhodes was approached by Mears.

"Mr. Rhodes, how are you doing? I was sad to hear about the Skipper and LCDR Robinson. Really glad you made it back."

"I am just OK. How are you?"

"I am OK. But sir, do you remember that girl I told you about from Bagio, Emma?"

"Sure, I do."

"Sir, she is sweet. Do you think that maybe I could get some leave next time in port and go with her up to Bagio to meet her family?"

"Do not plan on marrying her, Mears. Why do you want to meet the family?"

"It's not that. I haven't even kissed her. I just think they need some help, and I thought maybe I could take them up some stuff from the commissary. They don't have much to eat, she says. That is why she has to work."

"We'll see Mears. But that sounds to me like the story all those girls tell. If I let you go, you must guarantee me that you will come back on time and that you will not do anything crazy like marrying her without permission."

"I would guarantee that sir."

Refreshed after the long in-port period, morale had improved. The daily flying had helped as well as the passage of time. A Rag instructor and LTJG Wilson had arrived with two planes for them from the Replacement Air Group. The aircraft in check had passed the test flight and was now aboard. Maintenance, working feverishly with Warrant Arancio, who used his cumshaw miracles to obtain parts, had managed to get 208 up. The last day in port, Preacher and Dusty arranged a barbeque for the whole maintenance division at one of the athletic fields on Cubi. Copious quantities of San Miguel Beer, "a headache in every bottle," were consumed. As a result of the hard work of the maintenance crew, VF 188 now had enough aircraft to handle Barcap. Still, the ability to pair up with the A4s in a tactical situation other than flak support had been good for the entire airwing.

After ten days, on 28 September 1967, the Adams left Cubi to make its way back to the line. Flying in the dreary weather became routine. The landings after night Barcaps were even more stressful than usual due to the reduced visibility, but the squadron had returned to normalcy, with flying Barcap and a movie after the last hop. Of all people, Dick Knowles had a bolter on a night flight, having to go around in the pattern and land again. He swore it was a hook skip bolter, but Ames denied it, giving him a "fair, high in close" bolter. He did follow up with an OK 3.

After seven days of dreary, rainy monsoon weather the forecast improved. Admiral Johnstone, now firmly back in tactical command, sent a list of potential targets for the airwing to attack weather permitting. Captain Wilkins called a meeting of all the squadron commanders in air ops to consider one or more mini-Alpha strikes involving not more than four A4s and two F8 Flak suppressors. On the board behind the lectern in the center of the briefing room were photos of several locations, which were identified as potential targets.

"CAG, just looking superficially at these targets I like the one just inland from Haiphong the best." CDR Hanson, as executive officer of VA 18 he had taken over as skipper with the loss of CDR Jeffries at the Dong Phong strike. "It doesn't look as well defended as some of these other sites. It is a warehouse facility which is a lot easier for us to hit and it is close to the beach in case of a Rescap."

After considering many alternatives, the warehouse complex just outside of Haiphong was selected as the strike target. The planners decided on using two F8 Flak suppressors and four A4 bombers to hit the warehouses.

Like the Vinh railway strike, the F8s would streak in nearly supersonic. The plan was to fly in toward Haiphong with the entire strike group below 100 feet above the sea. Hopefully the North Vietnamese search radar would not pick them up until they popped up at the harbor.

John Philips and Dave Casper volunteered for the hop. As close as brothers, they flew together as often as possible. Knowing they were among the best, Dick Knowles agreed to have them take the strike.

The day of the attack, the weather was good, a ceiling above 18000 feet. Hopefully, the North Vietnamese would think that attacks would follow the normal pattern of approaching at relatively high altitude, sending the flak suppressors in first followed by the bombers.

Flying in at nearly 600 knots, Casper and Phillips, the Ghost and the Poet, were flying in a loose deuce formation. As they reached the shoreline, they pitched up and flew up in a high-speed wingover to the roll in point. As briefed, they each targeted one of the two 57 mm gun sites and dropped. The A4s behind them also pitched up and then proceeded to bomb the warehouses, causing several secondary explosions. Anti-aircraft fire was relatively light after the F8 Flak suppression.

Pulling off target, John Phillips' ALQ 100 electronic warfare console began to sound the *deedle deedle* of a Fan Song SAM radar. Casper also heard that radar. However, when it went to a high pitch, only John Phillips heard it. The surface-to-air missile had locked on to his aircraft.

After zooming up after the attack, John turned to head to the beach and feet wet. Looking for the SAM by following the strobe of the ALQ 100 electronic gear he saw it barreling toward him. Waiting until the last second, he rolled up and over it in a high G-barrel roll, pulling down toward the ground.

The SAM passed by him exploding well out of range, but he was now in a dive toward the triple-A of Haiphong harbor. He pulled hard to stop his descent, rolling to his left to head more toward the opening in the harbor. While the plane was in the turn, a shell from one of the 57mm guns exploded just outside the cockpit, shattering the plexiglass and hitting John Phillips in his left shoulder and side with shrapnel.

With Casper tight on his wing, he struggled to control the aircraft. Damage to the left side ailerons meant that he had to hold almost full right stick to keep the plane from rolling hard. The engine began to make noise, and all his warning lights were on.

Casper called, "Eject, eject, eject!"

Holding the stick with his right hand, he reached down and pulled the ejection D handle between his legs with his left. Immediately he shot out of the plane, already at a low altitude, the parachute swung twice, and he landed in the mouth of Haiphong Harbor. Struggling, he was able to use his right hand to open the Koch fittings holding the parachute on and release it. His life raft had inflated as advertised on ejection as had his life vest. He pulled the raft over and hid behind it as bullets from shore landed nearby.

Casper immediately radioed on the prearranged Rescap frequency for the strike, "Superheat 208 is down. Need Rescap to Haiphong harbor."

Immediately the helo answered, "Big Mother 7 on my way. Be there in ten."

As the North Vietnamese boats in the harbor began moving to pick up Poet, Casper started flying low and fast, almost touching the water. With his 20mm guns he split a junk that was moving out in two.

On seeing the Junk sink, a Russian cargo ship that had been lowering their boat, pulled it back up.

As Casper kept flying in the racetrack pattern low over the water, he was joined by Ray Rhodes. Dick had instructed CDR Scampi and Ray to fly their Barcap just off Haiphong as potential Rescap just in case something happened. As soon as Casper had radioed for Rescap, Ray had not waited for CDR Scampi to react. He had simply radioed, "Heater 212 responding."

Both F8s were flying so low that the anti-aircraft guns could not depress low enough to hit them. Out of shells, Casper dropped his tail hook, intending on hitting the mast of the junks. Most of the boats turned around and returned to the docks. Ray lit his afterburner just as he passed over one of the junks and blew it over. Shortly after that, a golden BB shot from one of the small boats with an AK 47, hit the afterburner section of the plane. Spilling fuel on the hot section, the F8 was soon on fire.

The helo arrived and spotted the bright yellow life raft. Looking closely, they saw John Phillips hiding behind the raft. The gunner on the helo opened up his machine guns on any small boat that made it past the two F8s. Navy Swimmer Petty Officer Second Class Thorsen jumped into the water and helped the injured John Phillips into the sling for the helo. Just as he motioned for the helo to hoist him up, one of the other F8s, trailing flames, crashed near the abandoned life raft.

The pilot, Ray Rhodes, ejected at the last second. Too late the rocket powered ejection seat fired pointing at a ninety-degree angle and skipped across the water with the pilot still in it. After skipping across the waves about three times, the automatic seat man separation activated. The seat immediately sank leaving the pilot floating, supported by the life vest on his torso harness, which had automatically inflated. The parachute trailed out over the water connected to the pilot by the Koch fittings in the torso harness.

The pilot lay motionless in the water face down, only supported by the life vest.

Chapter Twenty-Five

Do or Die
9 October 1967

Petty Officer Thorsen, after connecting the D-ring of the hoist to LT Phillips, motioned to the hoist operator to lift the injured pilot up to the helo. He waited for the sling to be lowered back to him where he was floating near the first life raft. When the sling was lowered, using the intercom, he asked the pilot, LT Sullivan, to fly him over to the second pilot, in the sling.

"Thorsen. Just get in the sling. We're getting out of here. The second guy is dead. He is floating face down. We need to go now. That's an order!" LT Sullivan called on the intercom connected to Thorsen's helmet.

"Sir, I don't care, and we cannot leave any of our people behind. Dead or alive!"

Reluctantly, LT Sullivan dragged Thorsen the two hundred or so yards in the sling to where the other pilot was floating. Flipping Ray over to undo the Koch fittings attached to the parachute, he found a mess. In the violent ejection and its aftermath, Ray's visor had been shattered on the left side. The oxygen mask was still connected, but the face was a bloody mess up to the left eye. Thorsen worked feverishly to connect the sling to the small V-fitting on Ray's torso harness. The small fitting was difficult to connect.

He transmitted, "He is bleeding. That means he is alive, but unconscious."

"Hurry. We are taking more fire."

To accentuate the need for speed, the machine gun in the helo opened up on boats trying to get to them. At that moment, CDR Scampi finally joined the battle and began strafing any boats nearby. Casper had continued to fly low and fast over any approaching boats, but he obviously was out of ammunition. CDR Scampi started strafing and the boats began retreating.

Finally snapping the D-ring into the V-fitting, Thorsen snapped his own fitting on the hoist line and motioned for them to pick him up. LT Sullivan immediately turned toward the open sea and flew as fast as he could out of the harbor with the swimmer and the injured pilot hanging down. Once out to a safe distance, he hovered to allow them to be hoisted up.

A navy corpsman, as part of the rescue team, Petty Officer 1st Class Golden known simply as Doc, had placed John Phillips on a stretcher and was treating what appeared to be a severe shrapnel wound to his shoulder, placing a compress on it to slow the bleeding.

When LT Rhodes was pulled into the flat bay of the helicopter and placed on a stretcher, Doc Golden moved to him. First, he cleaned out the oozing wound on his face, then he checked vitals. The breathing was shallow, and the blood pressure was low. He started a Saline drip, thinking that there was probably internal bleeding from the vicious blows his body had taken skipping across the water. His oxygen mask had saved him along with the life vest. In the seat pan was a small oxygen bottle designed to provide oxygen in the event of a high-altitude ejection. Even though Ray was lying face down in the water, the tight seal of the mask kept the water out while supplying oxygen. Petty Officer Golden gently removed the mask and, after checking the mouth and throat for obstructions, replaced it with an oxygen mask from the helo.

In Ready Two, they all gathered around the SDO desk and the radio, listening to the rescue.

LT Sullivan, in the helo, radioed: "Sand Box, Sand Box, Ripline 1 inbound with two. Both wounded, one unconscious. Request Charlie on Clear Deck on arrival."

"Roger Ripline, cleared to land on arrival."

"Heater Base to Heater 207, Come in 207."

"Roger base, this is 207", Casper responded.

"What happened?" An anxious Ski asked.

"Base, unable at this time. Tanking." Casper responded. In the heat of the battle, he did not exactly know what had happened. He knew Poet had evaded the SAM but then had been hit by triple-A. He had no idea what had happened to Ray. He had been surprised but pleased to see CDR Scampi help with the Rescap, but he was confused about where he had come from.

Casper and Scampi had escorted the helo out of the harbor, then immediately climbed up to the KA3 Tanker that had been orbiting just offshore at 20000 feet and tanked. Casper, at a low fuel state, took two thousand pounds quickly and pulled out. He had enough to enter the break and trap aboard. After CDR Scampi had finished his tanking, Casper joined on him, and they headed for the ship.

"Sand Box, Sand Box, this is Heater 202. Request Charlie for two."

"Roger 202. Hold at angels 12 directly overhead. We have a Rescap helo enroute for landing. Will advise ready deck."

"202 Roger."

As soon as the helo touched down on the flight deck, LT Ray Rhodes was carried out on the stretcher. Mears and other members of the line crew rushed out to help carry him and LT Phillips down to sick bay. In sick bay the chief medical officer, Captain Watson was standing by. Captain Watson was no rookie. He had seen a lot of combat wounds during two tours with the marines. He was bored with the lack of activity on the carrier. In a brief triage, he directed the crews to place Ray in one operating room and John in another. Although John Phillps' shoulder was in tatters, it was determined that he was in no danger of dying. One of the junior doctors was standing by and rushed to John Phillips' side.

On the other hand, Ray was unconscious and barely breathing on his own. He obviously had internal injuries, and it was suspected that he had internal bleeding. Other than the shredding of the skin on one side of his face above the oxygen mask, he was not obviously bleeding. Doctor Watson did not suspect a brain injury since Ray was still wearing his helmet when they carried him into sick bay. He ordered X-Rays over the entire body. With the suspicion of internal bleeding, he thought that the spleen had most likely ruptured. Noting the shallow, labored breathing, the chest had probably been damaged, and ribs broken. Carefully removing the helmet, he visually inspected the head and also ran his hands all over to see if he felt any wounds. Concerned that a spinal cord injury was likely, he asked the corpsman to remove the flight boots in order for him to test the Babinski reflex. With a tongue depressor he aggressively stroked the bottom of the foot from the heel to the big toe. A positive sign, the foot and toe made some movement down. He was confident that the spinal cord had not been severed. X-Rays of the neck and back did not show any definite breaks, but as a precaution he ordered a hard collar to be placed on the neck to prevent excess movement. Since it appeared that there was fluid buildup in the chest and abdomen, using a large needle, he drew fluid out of the left lung. X-Rays showed that a rib fracture had penetrated the lung into the chest cavity. Inserting a small chest tube hooked up to a water seal helped with the shallow breathing. After extracting more fluid from the abdomen, Dr. Watson was able to confirm internal bleeding. His main concern was to stabilize LT Rhodes in order to medevac him back to Balboa Naval Hospital in San Diego. He ordered a rapid infusion of saline to stabilize the blood pressure.

Having done all he could for LT Rhodes, he turned his attention to LT Phillips. He ordered dressings to be applied to the shattered left shoulder, gave him injections of morphine, and put him on oxygen to help with his breathing. LT Phillips was barely conscious but not in any immediate danger. By now all the pilots in the squadron plus CAG had gathered in the small outer office of sick bay.

Dr. Watson spoke to all of them, "Both LT Phillips and LT Rhodes have suffered tremendous trauma. We are working to stabilize them. LT Phillips is in better shape but will have a long and difficult recovery. LT Rhodes is still unconscious." Both relief and concern flashed across their faces. "There is a limit to what we can do here on the ship. Therefore, I am going to send them to Danang to Medevac back to Balboa Naval Hospital for treatment and rehabilitation over the long term. And no. You may not see them."

In addition to the two F8s that were lost on the raid, one of the A4s that made it back to the ship was struck due to battle damage. With his airwing in tatters, Captain Wilkins, CAG, called the admiral.

"Admiral Johnstone, you have Captain Wilkins on the secure line."

"Sir, did you see the damage report from the last raid?"

"I did. Seems to me that you barely have an airwing left. For the rest of this line period, do not plan on anything other than Barcaps and the A4s bombing down in the South below the DMZ in support of the Marines at Khe Sanh. After clearing it with Cincpac, I am going to send you, the airwing and ship home after this line period. Do not lose any more planes or pilots. That is an order. Amazing rescue in Haiphong. Your guys did well there. How are the two pilots?"

"Both are in bad shape. One worse than the other but the Doc has decided to Medevac them ASAP to Balboa."

In Ready Two, the remaining pilots were surprised that the ship and airwing were returning to San Diego. In shock from the most recent losses, they were happy to go home and relieved to know that there would be no more missions over North Vietnam. The squadron slowly began to return to a somewhat normal routine of Barcap, standing the alert 5 watch, and watching a movie after securing from flight ops. The only news they had received regarding Ray and John was that they had arrived at Balboa Naval Hospital after a Medevac of almost twenty-four hours with stops at Clark AFB, Travis AFB, North Island Navy Base, and an ambulance to Balboa. The cruise had been costly. Counting CDR Huggins, the squadron had lost six of their best pilots. Losing two more aircraft in the strike on Haiphong, the squadron had lost ten of their aircraft. For a proud squadron it was a sad result.

Pearson shouted on the flight deck, "Mears, come over here."

"Yeah Pearson, what do you want?"

"Go down to the maintenance office. LCDR Johnson wants to see you."

"What for?"

"I don't know. Just get your ass down there."

Mears went down the ladder from the flight deck to the maintenance spaces where Preacher had his office. Knocking on the bulkhead, as ordered: "Airman Mears. You wanted to see me sir?"

Preacher looked up from the desk where he had been writing evaluations and said, "Take a seat, Mears. As you know, your division officer is now in Balboa Hospital. A few days before his last mission he came to me, asking me to handle this in case he could not. I understand you asked for leave to go to Bagio to meet the family of a girl you met in a bar in Olongapo. Correct?"

"Yessir. But it is not what you think. I am not asking her to marry me or anything like that. I haven't slept with her. I just like her and want to help her family."

"Well, LT Rhodes has granted you that leave. However, you only have three days. The ship will only be in port for five days. I want you to get off the ship immediately when we get in. One day to Bagio. One day there. And one day back. Understood?"

"Yessir."

"Additionally, you are ordered to take Walker with you."

"Thank you, sir. Thank You."

"You need to thank LT Rhodes when we get back. Another thing, he told me to remind you to take the Third-Class exam. He is recommending you for promotion."

Chapter Twenty-Six

28 October 1967

There was no fly off of any aircraft to Cubi. Everything was to be loaded on board including the one aircraft VF188 still had in check. As the ship pulled into the dock at Cubi Point, Ski, Troy, Ames, and Wilson the FNG waited in their civilian clothes for Liberty Call.

Casper sat at the SDO desk dressed in the tropical khaki Uniform of the Day. Since John Phillips' evacuation to the Balboa Hospital, Casper had taken over the job of Senior Watch Officer. As such, he had given himself the duty for the first day the ship was in.

"Ghost, go ahead and go on liberty with the other J.Os. I have stuff to do here on the ship. I'll handle the SDO." Preacher, LCDR Johnson, said.

"Thanks, Preach, you've got it."

They went directly to the O'Club and once again commandeered their "normal" round table overlooking the dance floor. "It just doesn't seem right to be here without Aggie, and Poet and Ray. What a shitty cruise." Ski said. "Do you have orders, Ghost?"

"Yeah. I am going back to the F8 rag. Miramar, good flying and the beach. I got lucky."

"How about you Joe?" Troy asked.

"I asked to transfer to a squadron relieving us, but they turned me down."

"You wanted to stay here? After all that happened?" Wilson asked.

"Yeah, I got nothing to go back to. Sam, the Cag LSO, knew I wanted to stay and hooked me up with orders to be a Cag LSO for an airwing scheduled to come back out in eighteen months. I'll get most of that time, except for workups, as shore duty. I was afraid of getting detailed to aircraft handling officer or the basic training command"

"I thought you hated Sam Franks after the skipper's ramp strike" Troy added.

"I went back and reviewed the plat tapes and calls and realized it wasn't his fault. He and I have been good all cruise. Ski where are you going?"

"I guess Troy and I will be the senior Lieutenants in the squadron. I want to stay on in maintenance as a division officer like Ray was. Airframes and Ordnance sounds good to me. Imagine we will be on the beach for a while until we get new pilots and new airplanes."

"Wilson, you are going to have the shortest tenure of any FNG. You weren't even here long here long enough for Aimless to give you a call sign, but it was good that you had one line period. Got some Barcaps and night traps under your belt. Learned your way around the ship. It will serve you well next cruise." Ski added, nodding at him. "You can come to maintenance with me. Put in for line officer."

"Actually, I think I want to try to be an LSO." Wilson answered, turning his head to look directly at Ames. "Hope I can be half as good as Joe."

"What are you going to do Troy?" Wilson asked.

"Right now, I am taking leave and going to Australia while you suckers ride this tub home."

"Ok. But what job do you want in the squadron?"

"I am hoping to replace Ghost in schedules."

Ski picked up Lynn in a base taxi which drove them to the Subic O'Club for dinner. As they sat down at a table overlooking the harbor, Lynn began to tear up. "Ski, I can't help but think about Aggie.

Every time I hear or see an F8 in the pattern I think that maybe he will come back. That it was all a mistake. Or that he will show up captured. He was so full of life. We didn't have much time together but what we had was intense," she put her head down, wiping her eyes with a tissue.

"Lynn, he was the best friend I ever had, bar none. He was the absolute spirit of our squadron. Morale and everything else went to shit after he was shot down. We lost the skipper and LCDR. Robinson. Preacher was shot down and rescued. Poet and Ray were shot down. We lost most of our aircraft. It turned into a real shitty cruise." Big, tough Ski, also looked down with a tear in his eye.

"Will I see you here when we come back on our next cruise?" he asked.

"I don't think so. I am going back to the states when my contract is up. I can't take it here anymore."

When the ship pulled in, Dick Knowles went to the phones in the O'club and called Sandy to see if she had any news about the skipper and to get an update on how Poet and Ray were doing.

"I still have heard nothing officially regarding Dan's capture, but he is listed as a POW by the International Red Cross. So, I am hopeful." He sensed the hint of hope in her voice. "John Phillips is looking at a long and hard rehab of his shoulder. The doctors say that he will probably not regain full use of it. Ray is still unconscious. Astrud goes and sits by his bed as often as she can. His spleen was ruptured, and he had various other injuries, but just bruising of the spinal cord. The doctors are optimistic that he will recover, but it is not a certainty."

Not wanting to prolong the conversation, Dick said, "Thanks Sandy. That sounds like mostly good news. We will be back in a couple of weeks. See you then."

Monotony. Riding the ship back from Cubi Point in the Philippines to San Diego, some eighteen days of sailing, after the frenzy of the combat line periods, boredom was the dominant feeling. The old Carrier, seemingly comfortable in the frantic role of a combat ship became a boring, monotonous large transport.

Officer meals were now only served in the wardroom as the "dirty shirt" mess was closed to the air wing. Disregarding wardroom etiquette, Ski, Casper, Ames, and Wilson ate together in three settings on the large table where their squadron mates' places were still set with silverware and napkins. Despite the move, the wardroom was especially depressing as large gaps were evident of the losses the ship and airwing had suffered.

With no flight schedule and after the all-consuming combat flying, the pilots lounged around the ready room, not sure what to do with themselves. Throughout the ship it was much the same. While the deck crew, as usual, were chipping and painting their way across the Pacific, the yellow shirts, aviation bosun mates, and other ships company personnel who worked on the catapults and arresting gear were left doing routine maintenance that was generally finished after a few days.

Preacher assisted by Ski had finished all the maintenance evaluations. Ski spent more time than he ever had before down in the maintenance spaces as the mechanics worked on the few planes they had left to prepare them for the fly off.

In the ready room, Preacher organized an Acey Ducey tournament in the corner, but after a couple of days they were bored with that. Ames had purchased a dart board and darts at the base exchange in Subic. He hung it on the bulkhead on the starboard side of the ready room. For a few days, they played darts by the rules. However, on the third day

Ski came in from the passageway and said, "Screw this" and proceeded to back up to the wall by the center passageway, throwing the darts as hard as he could. Bored, Ames and Wilson joined him. That game was ended when Dick entered from the starboard hatch and had a dart whiz by his head.

With ten days left until the fly off, Ski found the gun butts that John Phillips had spent time in. He sat out there by the hours going over in his mind the cruise from the start riding to the ship with Ray and Astrud as they departed to all the losses they had suffered.

He could not get the image of Aggie out of his mind. He mostly missed Aggie and knew he would never reconcile how he had been killed. To him Aggie' death would always be totally unnecessary. The mission was unnecessary, and the briefing was just wrong. How the skipper had been captured and LCDR Robinson killed was also a waste. There was nothing in all of North Vietnam worth one of their pilots or one of their planes, yet they kept flying the missions.

15 November 1967 Miramar Naval Air Station, San Diego

Only able to get five planes up for the fly in from cruise, the Black Wasps of VF188, entered the break in a four-plane diamond with Ames in a tight trail as the fifth plane. One by one Ames, Casper, Dick Knowles, Ski, and Preacher broke. After landing they taxied in together, parking on the apron by air ops where a big Welcome Home sign was held by two wives: Sandy and Preacher's wife. Astrud was standing behind Ray who was in a wheelchair. John Phillips stood by them. His shoulder was covered by a massive dressing and his arm was in a sling.

The 1967 Vietnam Cruise of VF 188 was over.

Epilogue

Reno, Nevada 7 November 2023
Harrahs Casino, 2023 Tail Hook Convention

He stood at the mezzanine level overlooking the convention floor filled with young men and women in flight suits and uniforms. Medium height, while he had military bearing, his gray hair was a bit too long and sideburns extended down below his ears, covering small scars on the left side of his face. Physically, he looked fit for his age. Looking down on the young Naval Aviators, he thought back to his first cruise.

His thoughts were interrupted. "Ray. Wishing you were young again?" John Phillips asked from behind him. "Ready to go back on cruise?"

Turning around he almost did not recognize John Phillips. "Poet. I did not know you were coming to the Last Annual Crusader Ball." John Phillips had not aged well. His long hair, spilling over his collar, was pure white. The scars on the left side of his face had become more pronounced with age. His left shoulder drooped and his arm seemed nearly useless.

"I wasn't but some other old fogey insisted. Admiral Ghost is here somewhere." He said, gesturing out to the open convention floor below filled with young Naval Aviators, civilian DOD personnel, and Defense Contractors. Booths with mockups of missiles, electronic systems, book stands, and videos of weapons covered the walls of the floor.

"Ray there is a rumor going around that you are participating in the blood sport of politics. Any truth to that, Congressman?"

Sighing he said, "I literally got roped into it, Poet. Astrud and I had an agreement. I stayed in for my twenty but after my tour of X/O, CO of VF 172 we retired to the ranch in Southwestern Colorado."

"We were happily taking it as easy as you can on a ranch when some of the locals convinced me that I could do a good job as a county commissioner. After that, the party kept pushing me until I finally accepted to run for congress. Surprised that I got it. It is a lot harder than flying an Alpha strike up north."

"Poet, I heard something about you not staying out of trouble in Argentina. What happened there?"

"After rehab I went to Stanford and picked up a PHD. Out of there I got a research grant Fulbright to go to Argentina to study the Gaucho history. Not able to keep out of trouble, I got involved in something they called the Dirty War. It was Dirty. Not nearly as clear cut as Vietnam."

"I lost track of you and the other guys when I went down to Argentina. Just lately Casper looked me up and insisted that I come here. What happened to you in the hospital? I left before you got out."

"I was in rehab for almost a year. Preach got assigned to Air Pac at North Island and came by to see me and Astrud almost every day. I have to say that he was a very positive influence on both of us."

"Astrud had the baby while I was in the hospital. We named him Dan for the Skipper."

"After almost a year, I passed the flight physical. They sent me to VF 126 to get my touch back. Then I joined Casper and Dick at the F8 rag. In 1972 I went with both on one of the last F8 combat cruises. It was a lot easier than our '67 cruise."

"Our old Cag, Captain Wilkins, made Admiral. Think he got Dick set up as C/O of the first F14 squadron. Casper and I both went with him. Both of them ended up making Admiral. I got out after twenty and retired." Shaking his head, he continued, "I partly got out because I did not want to get stuck in the puzzle palace at the Pentagon but look at me now. Think Congress is worse."

"What did you do after Argentina?" Ray asked.

"I ended up teaching in a small college in Texas. I like the calm of the college setting and the small-town atmosphere." John answered. "What happened to everybody else?"

Ray answered, "Like I said, Casper and Dick Knowles both made Admiral, Dick three star. I heard that Ski and Troy went to Southwest Airlines."

"Preach retired in San Diego and went to work for a non-profit helping with Christian ministry in Africa."

"Let's go find the F8 ready room. Maybe Casper or someone else we know will be there." Ray said.

Glossary

AAA: Triple A anti-aircraft guns

APC: Automatic Power Control. Used in landing the F8 on the carrier to maintain proper speed.

BARCAP: Barrier Combat Air Patrol. Flown in a racetrack pattern between Haiphong and Hainan, Island

BIG LOOK: Code name USAF Aircraft monitoring all radar and radio transmissions in North Vietnam

BOSS: The airboss of the carrier. Essentially in charge of the "tower" controlling take offs and landings.

BURNER: The short term for the jet engine after burner that produced extra thrust when in engaged.

CAG: Carrier airwing Commander. Navy captain in charge of the squadrons and planes on the carrier

CAT: Short for Catapult, used to shoot planes off an aircraft carrier

IFR: Instrument Flight Rules

SOP, standard operating procedures

TRAP: Arrested Landing aboard an aircraft carrier

TANKER: Any aircraft capable of aerial refueling.

BOLTER: Unsuccessful attempted landing on an aircraft carrier

WAVE OFF: Command not to land on aircraft carrier

LSO: Landing Signal Officer

CDR: USN Commander

LCDR: USN LT Commander

MIGCAP: Combat Air Patrol flown over a target area to engage any Migs attacking the strike force

REDCROWN: US Navy Destroyer stationed between Haiphong and Hainan Island, Radar control of Barcap

IRONHAND: Code name of mission to fire Shrike Missiles at Surface to Air missile sites during a strike

SAM: Russian Surface to Air Missile

85: 85 Milimeter Antiaircraft battery

57: 57 Milimeter Antiaircraft battery

37: 37 Milimeter Antiaircraft battery

Sidewinder: Missile used by USN pilots to track and shoot down Migs

Two Thousand Pounder: Very large bomb.

Zuni: Large rocket propelled bomb fired from aircraft.

ACKNOWLEDGEMENTS

A particular thanks to two dedicated professional, Brunella Costagliola, the Military Editor, and Andrea Reider. Brunella was a pleasure to work with and very understanding of a war novel, specifically a Vietnam War Novel. Andrea was so patient with my limited computer skills. She never complained about the numerous changes we made in formatting, titles, and general repairs of the manuscript.

She also was responsible for what I think is a stunning book cover which she made from a faded photograph.

My Beta readers, Gene and Laura DeBardelaben, Anthony Savaglio, Jim Kinney, and my son Colin. All offered great ideas and their help was greatly appreciated.

Author's Note

When referring to skippers of other squadrons the last name was added as in Skipper Smith of VA 12. Navy pilots, known properly as aviators to distinguish them from pilots of ships, were all officers. Ranks O1 to O4 were formally addressed as mister in contrast to the other armed forces where officers were addressed as lieutenant, captain, or major. Within the squadron, among themselves, the aviators used first names or nicknames.

Made in the USA
Columbia, SC
07 November 2025